FOR KING OR COMMONWEALTH

Richard Woodman

This first world edition published 2012
in Great Britain and in the USA by
SEVERN HOUSE PUBLISHERS LTD of
9–15 High Street, Sutton, Surrey, England, SM1 1DF.
Trade paperback edition first published
in Great Britain and the USA 2012 by
SEVERN HOUSE PUBLISHERS LTD.

British Library Cataloguing in Publication Data

Woodman, Richard, 1944–
  For King or Commonwealth.
  1. Great Britain – History – Civil War, 1642–1649 –
  Fiction. 2. Historical fiction.
  I. Title
  823.9'14-dc23

ISBN-13: 978-0-7278-8172-4 (cased)
ISBN-13: 978-1-84751-427-1 (trade paper)

All Severn House titles are printed on acid-free paper.

Severn House Publishers support The Forest Stewardship Council [FSC],
the leading international forest certification organisation. All our titles that
are printed on Greenpeace-approved FSC-certified paper carry the FSC logo.

Typeset by Palimpsest Book Production Ltd.,
Falkirk, Stirlingshire, Scotland.
Printed and bound in Great Britain by
MPG Books Ltd., Bodmin, Cornwall.

For Arlo

Prologue

The Hague and Helvoetsluys

January 1649

'They say there is plague in London.'

'There is a Parliament in London, that is plague enough,' the younger man responded off-handedly as he worked over some books and papers. After a moment's silence, he put down his quill-pen with a sigh, rubbed his hands together and blew on them in an attempt to warm his fingers and looked across the room to where Sir Henry Mainwaring sat by the window, smoking his pipe, wrapped in his cloak and staring down at the street below. Even with the wind-rattled casement shut, the noise of the vendor's guttural Dutch could be heard bawling his wares. After a short pause the younger man asked, 'You are not thinking the unthinkable, are you?'

Mainwaring turned shivering from the window. 'God's teeth, but it's cold.' His flesh hung from his once handsome features, the weathered skin fallen with age and anxiety. He removed the pipe from his mouth, blew a plume of fragrant smoke into the room and nodded, his mouth curling in a sad smile. 'I am old, Kit, and likely to die soon. I would make my peace with the world.'

'Are you not at peace here? These solid Dutch folk have tolerated us, I'd have said.'

'Perhaps, but they are not my people . . .' Mainwaring said, his voice thick with sudden emotion, his meaning vague.

Captain Christopher Faulkner sighed and shook his head, returning his attention to his papers. There was a long silence and then Mainwaring spoke again.

'You give too much notice to those damned documents, Kit.'

'If I do not,' the younger man said, his eyes and attention

firmly on the bills and manifests before him, 'no one else will. Good God!' he said, gesturing around the room. 'There is little enough money as it is and few among this remnant court seem minded to pay the matter the attention it is due . . .'

'It is trade, Kit,' Mainwaring said, his tone ironic, his expression full of mock disparagement.

'Nonsense; it is war, even if of a kind the Prince's followers misapprehend. At least these Dutchmen comprehend it, thank Heavens . . .'

'True,' Mainwaring nodded, 'but perhaps you should set it aside, even for a while.'

Faulkner sighed again and pushed aside the heavy ledger before him. 'If I do not attend to these matters, when the time comes, nothing will be ready for His Majesty's service . . .'

'To which Majesty do you refer?'

'What?' Faulkner looked up, faintly exasperated.

'To which Majesty? The King is in the hands of the rebels and unlikely to require either your services or those of your ships.' Having delivered this final summary of the political situation in London, Mainwaring stuck his pipe back in his mouth and surrendered his attention to the street again.

Irritated and diverted from his work, Faulkner remarked, 'I thought the purpose of monarchy was to ensure succession and stability. We have a Prince here in The Hague that would be King if anything ill befell his father.'

'Stability? Hah!' Mainwaring removed his pipe, but did not turn his head. 'King Charles has lost the throne of his father; that is scarcely stability.'

'I would caution you against such talk, Sir Henry. There are those who would call it treason.'

'There are those who would call it common sense too,' Mainwaring said wearily. 'I am an old man and the future has only one thing in store for me, but men like you, men with a wife and family in London —' Faulkner swore. Mainwaring was looking directly at him now and added with a hint of remorselessness — 'and a mistress in The Hague, had best look to their future.'

'You know, Sir Henry,' Faulkner said, his tone as icy as the wind outside, 'as my dearly beloved benefactor and a man whom I esteem above all others, whose skill as a seaman I have stood in awe of for more years than I care to count, I have never had the gall to ask you why, in your youth, you turned pirate.'

Mainwaring smiled. Faulkner, his protégé, possessed all the attributes he could wish for. Even the chill in his voice Mainwaring admired as evidence of the iron soul of the man, and this was indeed a time for iron in the soul. 'We are,' he responded with a matching edge, 'debating your morals, not mine, Captain Faulkner. May I remind you that I am an admiral and deserving of your respect.'

'Which you well know you have, but I divine in your discourse, Admiral Mainwaring, a distinct prejudice against the cause we have spent—'

'Wasted . . .'

Faulkner ignored the interruption. '*Spent* the last several years – what, four or five? – supporting. Even now I am attempting to muster a squadron capable of bearing your illustrious flag, with all honour due to it, in order to cruise against the King's enemies.'

'A squadron,' Mainwaring said, his tone reflective, and ending with a prolonged sigh. 'A squadron of worn-out armed merchantmen . . . Oh, Kit, do you not see the hopelessness of it? With the King in the hands of Parliament our cause will wither. He will be held prisoner, Parliament will rule in his name and our young gadfly, clever though he is, will succumb to women and, in consequence, the pox. If nothing else those Puritan souls in Westminster know the workings of indulgence and excess; they have only to bide their time. England will prosper and find it is possible to live without a king.' Mainwaring paused then went on, 'I thought that all this would happen years ago and if you ask me why I turned pirate it was out of disgust. I thought the wheel would turn in King James's time but it did not. I came home and made my peace and served the King, *and* his catamite Buckingham, *and* his son whose future lies in the hands of his enemies, but what have I got for it, eh? The empty dignity of admiral, unable to fly his flag over an insignificant squadron, which rots in Dutch mud and is, in any case, under the nominal command of Batten . . .'

'Batten! Do not speak of that treacherous villain William Batten! Why, he is the self-same man that harried His Highness off the coast of Cornwall and I hear he has been made knight for abandoning the Parliament and burying his head in Prince Charles's under-breeches, God rot him!'

'Forget Batten, Kit. His Highness has replaced him with his kinsman Rupert and he is likely to set me aside in Rupert's favour . . .'

'Rupert,' scoffed Faulkner. 'A courtier general of cavalry with scant understanding of the usage of the sea . . .'

'But a doughty name, a tenacity of purpose and the high birth that this world requires of those to whom it bows the knee.'

'Huh! That is not what is happening in England,' Faulkner remarked. 'There matters are increasingly governed differently.'

'Precisely,' Mainwaring snapped, but before Faulkner perceived the way the conversation was drifting, he lowered his voice. 'But I am tired, Kit, tired and sick of it all. And, above all, I wish to die in England.'

'You are not going to die,' Faulkner said drily, resuming work at the table. 'And our few ships are not going to rot in Dutch mud, or any other mud, if I have my way. We have nine men-of-war at Helvoetsluys . . .'

'And how many seamen?'

'Enough.'

'Not for a dozen men-of-war.'

'Five good ships. I can make a competent squadron of five ships and command the Strait *and* the Thames . . .'

Mainwaring shook his head. 'You would sting them, Kit, like a bee may sting a horse, but the horse will still stand and gallop while the bee dies. Do you not see the utter hopeless-ness of it all? Besides, the decision will not be yours. Prince Rupert—'

'Suppose they kill the King?' Faulkner said abruptly, interrupting.

'*What*? They would not *dare*!' Mainwaring was outraged.

'Suppose that they did dare. You said yourself his future lay in the hands of his enemies; they have his body and may take his head. I'm damned if I know what there is to stop them.'

Mainwaring expelled his breath in a long, wheezy sigh at Faulkner's proposition. 'It would alter the case,' he said solemnly.

'It would indeed.'

'But surely . . .?' Mainwaring hesitated and gave Faulkner a shrewd look. 'You have heard something?'

Faulkner nodded. 'I have. Nothing but a rumour, but a rumour of such portent that I cannot think it a fabrication. We had it from a fishing boat off the Haak Sand. He had come from Yarmouth market where the talk was of an arraignment of the King on charges of treason.'

'Treason? Treason! For God's sake! How is that possible? How can a King be charged with treason? Why, 'tis like accusing the Pope of being holy! Pah! Preposterous!'

'But Sir Henry, if the court can persuade itself that a king can be charged with treason it can persuade itself of his guilt and, having assumed a legitimacy on behalf of the people, or Parliament, or whatever else these Puritans call upon – God Almighty, I imagine – to justify their actions, then they can condemn him . . .'

'To execution, d'you mean?'

'I think that possible, yes.'

Mainwaring let his breath out in a long, sibilant and despairing hiss, shaking his head and neglecting his pipe. 'I had thought,' he said reflectively, 'that all this talk of Parliament acting on behalf of the kingdom was clear intent that they would mew him up securely and rule in his name.'

'It seems not,' said Faulkner, leaving Mainwaring to his dolorous reflection and then, scooping up his papers and putting them away in a large leather satchel, he rang a bell and called for wine.

'Why did you not tell me of this intelligence directly, Kit?' Mainwaring asked, then added with gentle remonstrance, 'I am, after all, the King's admiral.'

Faulkner nodded, sat back and regarded Mainwaring. 'You are indeed, Sir Henry, and it was my purpose, before telling you, to ascertain the power of the ships we could assemble in the river's mouth to demonstrate in His Majesty's favour.'

He made a gesture of impotence. 'But now we have Rupert and Batten . . .' Faulkner sighed. 'You should have known shortly.'

'I understand,' Mainwaring said and then they were interrupted by the arrival of the wine. Faulkner rose, poured two glasses and carried them across the room, offering one to Mainwaring.

'And when the King is dead, will you still wish to return to England?'

Mainwaring took a deep draught of the wine then looked at Faulkner. 'Kit, you are younger and wiser than me; what do you see of the future?'

'Exile.'

'That is cold comfort.'

'Indeed. Moreover, this wine is expensive. We should drink either Hollands or beer if we are to become Dutchmen.'

'I have no intention of becoming a Dutchman; besides I cannot stand the taste of their Genever and beer is a drink for workmen, draymen and other villains . . .'

'Not admirals,' Kit remarked with a rueful smile.

'No, not even ragged-arsed admirals with no fleet to speak of . . .'

'Come, come, Sir Henry, we do have some ships of quality.'

'Perhaps, but few to match your own *Phoenix* and she—'

'Is eating money, Sir Henry, as are the others mewed up in these damned meres by forming ice. They need employment, active employment; if not a cargo then a cruise against our enemies . . .'

'Our countrymen, Kit,' Mainwaring interjected, though Faulkner took no notice.

'. . . For these burghers are crafty at their business and once they know of our penury will turn against us quicker than our Lord and Master learned to tack the *Proud Black Eagle*.'

'I don't know,' Mainwaring said uncertainly.

'Sir Henry,' Faulkner said sharply, accompanying this with a slap of his hand on the leather satchel lying on the table before him, 'the matter must be resolved today or tomorrow. If not we shall be obliged to sell at least half of the ships to keep us in firewood, let alone beer.'

'How is Kate?'

'What?' Faulkner frowned. 'She is well . . . why, you saw her but yesterday. Come, you cannot divert me from my purpose.'

'I heard . . .'

'What did you hear?' Faulkner's tone was full of exasperation and he stared at Mainwaring through narrowed eyes. 'That she miscarried? Well, 'tis true but she is blithe enough. God knows we cannot afford another mouth to feed, still less do I wish to risk her life in childbirth.'

Mainwaring hesitated before speaking and a man less preoccupied might have divined a change of mind, but all Faulkner heard was the old man's commiserations. 'I am sorry to hear the news, Kit. I had thought she looked overly pale.'

'Yes, well, 'tis bad enough to be a King's man in these troubled times, but to be a woman must be nigh intolerable.'

'Aye. The ships then, what of them?'

Faulkner counted them off on the fingers of his right hand. 'The *Constant Reformation*, *Swallow* and *Convertive* are ill fitted and least able. *Crescent* and *Satisfaction* are in poor condition, and there are others to number of seventeen, I believe. Of them, *Antelope*, *Roebuck*, *Hind*, *Pelican* and *Phoenix* will do well enough to keep the sea when the season suits.'

'And their companies?'

'Near enough mutinous but how can one blame them with no pay, the winter upon them and the greater part of their families in penury in England reduced to beggary by lack of income and the hostility of those against them – which, if rumour is to be believed, is most of London and much of the country who want only a return to peaceful living. They are besides upset by the taunts of Warwick's men when and where the Dutch let them land, who guy them mercilessly, telling them of proper victuals and steady money in the Parliament's ships. Of them all, the *Antelope*'s people are the most disaffected.'

'And the *Phoenix*?'

Faulkner looked up, a spark in his eye. 'Thanks to all this –' he gestured at the ledgers and papers – 'I have managed to keep my own men loyal – at least, until the spring.'

'The spring.' Mainwaring's tone was ruminative. 'Perhaps too late, if what you say proves true.'

'Exactly.'

'You think a demonstration off the Knock . . .'

'Off The Nore . . .'

'The Nore? God's teeth, Kit, that is bold!'

'Put the stopper in the bottle, Sir Henry, with the first east wind that allows the ships out of the Haringvliet.'

'I took a Moor off The Nore in sixteen,' Mainwaring mused before recollecting the immediate problem. 'But what of the ice?'

'Already forming but we might contrive to move them,' Faulkner said resolutely.

Mainwaring shook his head. 'No, the fair east wind you seek will freeze the Haringvliet. Then the men will not muster and will gripe unless they have some liberty. Christmas was bad enough. No Dutchman will move on our behalf for the money we could offer before Christmas, let alone afterwards.'

'Must we have Dutchmen? I'd rather my English dogs.'

'Aye, for a certainty, but needs must when the devil drives and methinks there are too few proper jacks who, with a few square-heads . . .'

'I could take the *Phoenix*,' Faulkner said with such a sudden conviction that Mainwaring stared at him.

'Alone?'

'Aye, alone but with such teeth as will bite the Puritan in the trade, where it hurts him most.'

Mainwaring smiled. 'Ah, me, Kit, you remind me of the man Henry Mainwaring once was.'

'I was taught well, Sir Henry,' Faulkner responded, raising his glass in an ironic salute to his senior.

'D'you recall we called you Mr Rat when we found you on the quay in Bristol?'

'Only too well; and a damned hungry rat.'

The two men smiled at each other and a silence fell between them. Warmed by the wine Faulkner restrained himself from pressing Mainwaring on the subject of moving the ship. Instead he fell into a study, thinking of the most pressing tasks to bring the squadron to a state of readiness. Perhaps one ship was insufficient but if he could get three, say the *Antelope* and the *Roebuck* commissioned quickly, he might achieve something. He might save the *Antelope* for Prince Charles's service if he could get her to sea and take a prize or two.

'Where is Katherine?' Mainwaring suddenly asked.

'Eh?' Faulkner was recalled to the present with a start. It was growing dark rapidly as the sky clouded over the low sun of the late winter's afternoon and the chill made him shiver. 'Katherine? She is without . . .'

'Waiting on His Royal Highness?'

Faulkner frowned. 'Perhaps; I don't know . . .' He looked at Mainwaring and knew the expression he wore. 'Why? What is troubling you, Sir Henry?'

'Apprehension, Kit, apprehension. His Royal Highness is no more to be trusted than any other man and perhaps less than most.'

Faulkner frowned. 'What exactly are you insinuating?'

'I think you can guess. There is talk.'

'There is always talk around the Prince,' Faulkner said tossing off his wine, but his face wore an expression of such agony as he put the empty glass down on the table before him that Mainwaring was minded to change the subject and sought to mitigate the damage he had done.

'That is very true,' he said hurriedly.

Faulkner was of like mind. 'What of you, Sir Henry? Are you still intent upon returning to England despite the chance to command at sea against the King's enemies?'

'Kit, Kit,' said Mainwaring shaking his head and smiling ruefully, 'despite her most excellent qualities the *Phoenix* is not the *Prince Royal* . . .'

'Would to God that she was,' said Faulkner sharply, recalling the puissant man-of-war which Mainwaring had once commanded and in which he himself had served as a lieutenant. He helped himself to another glass of wine from the flagon. 'I should take all the shipping in the London River with her had I the men to man her and the powder and shot to do proper execution.'

But both men heard the voices below and fell silent as the

familiar footfall on the stairs preceded the opening of the door. Both men rose as Katherine Villiers entered the room. She was flushed, a high colour in her cheeks as she moved quickly to the fire, rubbing her hands.

'Gentlemen,' she said, acknowledging their bows. 'God's death, but 'tis cold without! I pray you be seated.'

'A glass of wine, Kate?' Faulkner said moving to the door and calling for a glass.

'If you please, thank you.'

'How is His Highness today?' Mainwaring asked.

'Very well . . .' Katherine broke off, perceiving too late, as he shot Faulkner a look, the trap that Mainwaring had laid for her. Recovering quickly she added, 'And he particularly wished to commend himself to you both. "They are my most devoted followers, Mistress Villiers", he was pleased to say, "upon whom I rely for my flag's maintenance upon the Narrow Seas".'

'How very grand,' Mainwaring said as the red-faced maid-servant brought in a fresh glass and a second flagon of wine.

Katherine broke the inevitable silence that this necessary intrusion caused, not warming to Mainwaring's tone. 'Well, gentlemen, why look you so glum? Have you instead been plotting treason? This is passable tipple.' This last a distraction for she was wary of too open a discourse and Mainwaring was too old a bird to wish to linger. At best a tiff was imminent and these were, after all, Faulkner's lodgings; his own rooms were next door in this rented floor of a Dutch house and the walls thin enough to learn if matters between these younger people, whom he regarded in his straightened circumstances as his family, took a turn for the worst. Tossing off his wine he rose.

'I shall take leave of you. We may discuss the plans for the, er, squadron, tomorrow, Kit. I shall give the matter thought overnight and we will draft a paper to place before Prince Rupert. Saw you the Prince, Mistress Villiers?'

Katherine shook her head. 'No, he was said to be at Helvoetsluys with the ships, but was expected back in a day or two.'

'Very well, then I bid you goodnight, Mistress Villiers.'

Sweeping up his worn and shiny hat with its bedraggled ostrich feather, Mainwaring made his courtly bow and left the room, leaving Katherine staring after him and her lover staring at his boots. In the wake of Mainwaring's departure a deathly silence fell, broken at last by Katherine, who asked in a low voice, 'What is the matter, sweetheart?'

The endearment brought Faulkner's head up with a jerk. His eyes were bright and he said, in a strangled voice, 'I beg you, do not call me that.'

'Why I—'

He stood up suddenly, so that she drew back in surprise. 'You spend,' he said with difficulty, 'too long in his company.'

'Whose company?'

'Do not fool with me, Kate. You know who I mean.'

'He is a Prince, Kit, and commands me.'

'Commands you to *what*, for Almighty God's sake?'

'Why,' she said in a tone so reasonable that it left him speechless with a disarming mixture of anger, confusion and humiliation, 'to attend him, of course.'

'Attend him? *Attend him?*' He could not bring himself to make the accusation whose confirmation he did not wish to hear.

'He holds court, he is a Royal Prince,' she repeated, as if repetition would allow the import of Prince Charles's status to sink in.

Sensing the argument was diverging from the truth towards which he felt irresistibly drawn he asked the question that had – he now realized – been forming in his mind for weeks. The decision once made restored his manhood and he felt an icy calm fill him, casting out the demon of weak and pitiful supplication. 'And does attending him require you to lie with him?'

The colour draining from her face she stepped backwards as though struck. For a moment he thought that he had it all wrong and a spark of hope threatened to tip him into a doting, slobbering apologist for entertaining the very suspicion.

Shaking her head, she said, 'Not lie, Kit. Not as a man does with a woman.' She hesitated. 'That I have denied him but he likes a little frivolous diversion.'

'A play, you mean?'

'Aye, nothing more . . . and . . .'

'A Prince shall have his way,' Faulkner finished the sentence for her in a snarl.

'It means nothing, Kit . . .' Perceiving the hurt the honest confession was inflicting she sought, inadequately, to find reasonable ground between them. She made a circular movement of her hand, embracing them both. 'We . . . we are not married. We cannot be married . . .'

The reference to Faulkner's wife Judith caught him for a second but he had long ago reconciled himself to his own betrayal. That he would burn for it he had no doubt, but that he had found in Katherine a love worth risking damnation seemed – at least in the heat of their passion – a price worth paying. Now he was seeing that hell was not beyond this life, but of it and that other people were the devil's agents.

'Not perhaps in the eyes of the church,' he remarked coldly, 'but I had thought that I meant something unique to you. I see that pride fooled me.'

'No!' she cried. 'You are my own true love.'

'But you would handle the royal prick . . .'

'Stop it!' She put her hands over her ears and sank to the floor. He refilled his glass, the effects of the wine stirring him as he regarded her with distaste.

'You have all the vileness of the Villiers blood,' he said, half to himself and referring to her distant kinsman George Villiers, the late Duke of Buckingham and Lord High Admiral of England. He, it was said, had risen to greatness for acting as King James's catamite. Himself a voluptuary, Buckingham had been a contradictory character: a competent administrator and a corrupt courtier and politician.

'I never experienced anything but kindness from your great relation,' he said to Katherine who was looking up at him, her hands still pressed to the sides of her head, 'but I heard enough stories about him to know why the assassin Fenton dispatched him that day at Portsmouth! God, now I know why . . . you are all poisoned and stink of putrefaction!'

'He is a Prince, Kit, and it is his right to command. Why, you do his bidding . . .'

'Indeed, when he orders me as his lawful commander my life is pledged to his service but he knows you are my mistress and . . .'

'He takes other men's *wives*, for God's sake,' she retorted, gathering up her skirts and scrambling to her feet, 'and most do not complain but rise from it.'

'They are men halfway up, who acquired their wives as they do their horses, by barter and trafficking. Besides, would you have me Sir Kit Cuckold?' He made her an ironic half bow. 'If so,' he added half to himself, 'I would rather I had languished Mr Rat and caught the pox from some quayside whore than from the woman I esteemed and loved above all others, even my own sons. God rot you, Katherine, for he surely will.'

She had sunk into a chair and her shoulders heaved with her sobs. For a moment the sight affected him and he was moved to crouch by her side and take her in his arms; but then pride touched him and he drained the glass of its wine.

'I have it from London that the King is to be tried,' he said off-handedly.

She looked up frowning. 'On what charge?' she asked, glad that the conversation had taken another turn and willing to be diverted from this unpleasantness. She was, besides, courtier enough to be intrigued, for no one to her knowledge had yet breathed a word of any such suspicion in the Prince's presence. She had, however, noticed those furtive glances among those who surrounded him that bespoke state secrets and matters not to be spoken of before the women.

'Oh, treason I expect,' Faulkner said, aware that in some way he might wound her by threatening her royal lover.

'How can that be? He is the King. It is only his subjects that can be traitors.'

'I imagine the lawyers' brief will be treason against his oaths, tyranny against his people. Of one thing you can be certain,' he added ironically and enjoying the intellectual superiority he realized he had over her, for she did not understand what was happening in England, 'God will be at the bottom of it.'

'*God*?' Her face was scornful. 'Why, God put Charles on the throne, he is God's anointed.'

'Indeed. That is what he believes, but the argument so skil-fully deployed is that Charles has betrayed God's sacred charge – hence he has committed treason against his people.'

'But treason is punished by . . .' She hesitated, as though to utter the word was a kind of blasphemy.

'Execution,' he said with helpful casualness.

'They would not *dare!*'

Faulkner laughed. 'Sir Henry said the self-same thing. And why should they not dare? King Charles is in their hands and is a man. His head may be struck from his shoulders as readily as yours or mine.'

'And who will rule England?' she asked as though the ques-tion put the King's life beyond peradventure.

He laughed again. 'Why, that which is presently ruling it: Parliament. What is so difficult for you to understand? These people think the King has misruled them and that his father was not much better. Oh, you think the son will be a paragon of kingship, do you? Well, if his present desires indicate char-acter he will at least be different. King Charles was no forni-cating adulterer! Indeed, one might charge him with taking too much notice of his French and Catholic wife.'

Katherine was silent and Faulkner went on, a pent-up anger now replacing his calm resolution. 'Your Royal Prince could make you a queen now! Had you not better run to him and snuggle properly into the royal bed and make certain none other is there before you?'

But she came back fighting, disbelieving him and snarling with a measure of contempt. 'Where did you hear all this? You have not been to England – or have you? You know a great deal about it and seem to espouse these *Parliamentary* views with relish.' She laced the word with heavy, sarcastic and accusatory emphasis.

He smiled at her. 'Of course you would think that. You not only have a woman's brain, you have a Villiers' brain.' He put one foot on the chair and leaned forward, his right elbow on his knee, his right index finger wagging in her pale yet lovely face. 'I learned it from some fishermen from Yarmouth . . .'

'Fishermen,' she snarled dismissively. 'Fishermen? What do fishermen know of these things?'

'They knew the Word of God when it called to them from the Galilean shore,' Faulkner said sententiously, but she was the measure of him.

'God walked on Galilee, not Yarmouth beach,' she said with a flick of her head that Faulkner did not like in the circumstances, though the evidence of spirit would have melted his loins a day ago. 'If I have paid a Christian Prince too much attention, you have been reading Puritan tracts.'

'Those fishermen were informed folk,' he said slowly, with measured emphasis. 'You, and your like, mistake the common man if you consider he lacks intelligence. He might lack education, breeding, manners, money, land, titles, horses, silks, satins, slashed sleeves, gloves of morocco and boots of kid, but he breeds no more idiots than your Villiers clan and may possess the cleverness—'

'Of a Faulkner, no doubt,' she interrupted.

'I was not about to say that,' he rejoined coldly. 'But there are men of intelligence in Parliament –' he gave the word the same inflection as she had done, mocking her – 'whose claim on wisdom outshines the King – and hence they have His Majesty arraigned before them on a perfectly reasoned charge, in their eyes, of treason.'

She remained silent, her breast heaving; her world was falling about her ears and he thought her very beautiful in her distress. They had not eaten well these last months and her figure was slimmed by hunger, her face drawn with indigence and yet she seemed to shine in adversity. He could not blame the Prince for . . .

He did not wish to think more of it. His anger was quelled. He must think instead of what was to be done. As if reading his thoughts and sensing her own irresistible seductiveness she said quietly, 'He was very charming, sweetheart . . .'

'You were weak, then,' he said quietly, at which she nodded.

'As you were when you left your wife having set eyes upon me.'

'Is that what happened?' he asked, half to himself.

'So you told me.'

'I have forgotten.'

'We all forget things we should remember.'

'Aye, but my forgetfulness has time to justify it; yours has only passion.'

'*Only* passion; which do you think the stronger?'

'Oh, passion, to be sure, but whatever the cause, betrayal is betrayal.'

'And you are betrayed?'

'You have to ask me that?'

'To be sure, just as you had to ask me whether I had lain with the Prince . . . which I have not. You could,' she said tentatively, repeating herself, 'you could . . . forgive me.'

'What? For you to succumb to the Prince's charm again. And if you can so relent when I am here, in The Hague, what might you not do – what might you not have been doing – when I am at sea proving myself His Highness' most loyal servant at risk and peril of my life? Huh?' He dashed his hand on his knee, upset the chair and stood straight, shaking his head. 'I realize now he has been laughing at me for months. Those jests that I took for intimacies, for manifestations of trust and confidence, those little asides about Kit and Kat . . . God he has made a fool of me many times over. No wonder you think fishermen fools; sea officers, it would seem, are little better. Men to be gulled! Why, he might have tweaked my nose and I would have gone off to die for him. No wonder the English have come to their senses.'

Katherine was suddenly on her feet. His rant had gone too far and she stood triumphant. 'Treason! *That* is treason!'

'So you would run to your paramour and tell him he is mistaken in Kit Faulkner's loyalty, would you? You damnable bitch!' The blood roared in his ears as he reached out for her and she dodged away, putting the table between them. 'God's blood, Katherine Villiers, but if you think I have exposed myself, so too have you. I would not have you back in my bed were you to crawl naked on your knees with the crown of England in your pox-rotten mouth!' He thrust the table with such violence that she was jerked off her feet and fell forward over it. He had her by the hair and twisted her face up towards his.

'I loved you to distraction.'

She spat in his face, whereupon he banged her head down

on to the table then thrust her from him. He wiped away her spittle with a gesture of disgust. Gathering up his satchel, his hat, cloak, baldric and sword he made for the door. Standing in the open doorway he looked round. She had picked herself up and was rubbing her bruised cheek, her face aflame with fury.

'Be so kind as to inform Sir Henry that I shall be aboard the *Phoenix* by tomorrow,' he said coldly. 'And you may say the same to His Highness and tell him that Kit Faulkner shall serve him as he deserves and as he judges of my loyalty. As for you, you had best set your cap at the crown, though whether you will ever wear it in London is a matter for others to arrange. Goodbye, Katherine.'

She stared at the door as she heard his steps fade on the stairs. She could sense the presence of Mainwaring, holding his breath beyond the closed door across the landing. Gradually her thundering heart subsided. She knew, had known for months, that this moment would come in due time. She could not resist the Prince; indeed, was powerless to do so, though she knew this was incomprehensible to Faulkner to whom she was, paradoxically, devoted. The peculiarity of their circumstances, his as much as hers, made such strange and illogical consequences as inevitable as the surge of the tides.

She did not blame Faulkner for acting as he had, but she resented the fact that while she understood his reactions, he could not understand her own plight. Were they the soulmates he had fondly supposed he might have acted with more sympathy. Were he the sophisticate he thought he was, he might have deployed more worldliness but, as she – and Mainwaring – knew, the peculiarities of his impoverished background and the singular nature of Mainwaring's upbringing of his protégé had ensured that Kit Faulkner, though bright, was lopsided in his character.

As for her, she was no stranger to living on her wits. Swallowing some wine she crossed the landing and knocked upon Mainwaring's door.

Mainwaring caught up with Faulkner at Helvoetsluys the following afternoon after a hard ride. He was stiff, resented the costs of the hire of the horse and regarded Faulkner with a certain irritation. The younger man sat behind his table in the great cabin of the *Phoenix*. It was a modest space, lit by the late-afternoon sunshine flooding in through stern windows, neatly fitted out in polished wood, the home of a modestly successful master mariner. Mainwaring noted the papers, chiefly a Dutch chart of the Thames Estuary over which Faulkner was bent. He did not look up as Mainwaring eased himself down into a creaking chair and sat back, regarding his younger friend.

Faulkner was in middle life, though still short of his fortieth year, and a fine-looking man who, although he had removed his wig and wore an old and threadbare grey coat, bore himself with a confidence that Mainwaring flattered he had recognized many years earlier. But Faulkner's origins had ill prepared him for the station to which sheer ability, along with a little assistance from Mainwaring himself, had elevated him.

For some moments a palpable silence hung between them. Then Faulkner picked up his dividers, splayed them and marched them with practised ease across the chart and laid them off against the scale of latitude that ran, from north to south, up the side of the chart. Still preoccupied, with his eyes downcast, Faulkner said in a low voice, 'If you have come as her ambassador, I shall pay you no attention.'

'I come as your admiral,' Mainwaring responded, watching Faulkner as he finally looked up. His eyes looked tired, not those of a man who had wept, but of one who had not slept well – if at all.

'You have orders for me?' Faulkner said, his voice tight, controlled.

'I had hoped you would ease an old man's burden and have suggestions for me.'

'Indeed, Sir Henry.' Faulkner paused. 'Well, if you want my opinion and as I suggested yesterday, we might make a demonstration off The Nore and snap up a prize or two.'

'And when could you sail?'

'Whenever you give the word, the wind serves and the ice permits.'

'You are eager to be gone?'

'Oh, for God's sake, I beg you not to toy with me.'

'I would not do that,' Mainwaring said sufficiently sharply to remind Faulkner that whatever their private relationship, he was, in name at least, Faulkner's superior in rank.

'Of course, Sir Henry,' Faulkner said, his voice again level. 'Forgive me.'

Mainwaring raised his hand in a deprecatory gesture, as if there was nothing to forgive. There was indeed iron in the younger man, he noted again, a product of those early years of abject penury which, allied as it was with a quick intelligence, produced a character of singular distinction. In different times, Mainwaring thought, Faulkner might have risen far by his own abilities and with a woman of Katherine's beauty . . .

'How is she?' Faulkner asked casually, bending over the chart again.

'Distraught. She came to me last night and begged me to come to you.'

'Not as an admiral.'

'No, as a . . .'

'Go-between.'

'Perhaps.'

'Perhaps, Sir Henry,' Faulker said, interrupting and sitting back in his own chair, 'you are grown blind but what I wear instead of my wig is a pair of horns: she has cuckolded me, sir. And since she has done so with His Highness, I am unmanned, humiliated and made to feel my own insignificance. It is not, I assure you, a feeling that I much like. Were our royal wastrel here in person I should be tempted to run him through and thereby perhaps do us all, and England most of all, a great favour. No doubt they could find a royal bastard to fill the breach, but I think the pretensions of the House of Stuart would not translate into England again. Indeed, I am not certain there is the slightest chance of His Highness succeeding in this regard which makes me incline to your own plan.'

Mainwaring leaned forward. 'You are of like mind?' he asked.

Faulkner sighed and nodded. 'Who is going to stay loyal to a prince who cuckolds his most devoted servants? The son is no better than the father; true the method is different, but the infirmity of morality is identical.'

'Aye.'

Faulkner looked at the older man. 'You are weakening in your resolve?'

Mainwaring shook his head. 'No, though I admit the contemplation of the effort necessary exhausts me. They will suspect us, Kit.'

'Of course. Tell me, what did she ask you to say to me?'

'Mmm? Oh, to point out that she admitted the betrayal, but it was no worse than your betrayal of your wife and, in point of detail, a good deal less.'

Faulkner rose, went to a sideboard and lifted a decanter and two glasses from the fiddles. He filled them and passed one to Mainwaring. 'She admits to playing with his prick and no doubt he toyed with her cunny. 'Tis a technicality . . .'

'If it is true, though, your abandonment will drive her the more to his bed.'

'If she has not been there already.'

'But . . .'

Faulkner held up his hand. 'Lay it aside, Sir Henry. I can no longer trust her. As for my wife, it is nothing like, and she knows it. I was fond of Judith but knew not a great passion for her such as Katherine aroused in me. Do you know of what I speak, Sir Henry?'

Mainwaring shrugged. 'I have not been a man greatly favoured by women,' he said. 'My career, such as it was, was too volatile.'

Faulkner smiled. 'But you are not unknown to women, Sir Henry, I know that. You are not a man like our late King, for example.'

'God, no!' Mainwaring broke off to take wine, after which he stared for a few moments into the middle distance, leaving Faulkner to contemplate a career that had led Mainwaring from Oxford University by way of military service to piracy and from piracy to the office of Gentleman of the King's Bedchamber and confidant of the Duke of Buckingham. He had then become first a captain and then an admiral in the King's Royal Navy, besides holding the Mastership of the seafaring Fraternity of the Brethren of Trinity House.

'I took my pleasure when I required it,' Mainwaring resumed, his tone gently reminiscent, 'for which there are women willing enough, but as to wilting love, no, it never troubled me.'

'I,' put in Faulkner, 'had not the disposition to engage with whores.'

Mainwaring laughed. 'Oh, they need not be whores, at least not always, though a seaman must resort to any port in a storm.'

'Sometimes the port has its own attractions,' Faulkner responded, 'and the voyage ill fits one for a wanton.'

'No, you did well by Judith,' Mainwaring said, stirring himself. 'And you doubtless will again if we throw ourselves upon the mercy of the Parliament.'

'I doubt that, if I know the lady's character,' Faulkner said. 'As for our future . . .'

There was a knock at the cabin door and the two men fell silent as a gentleman entered. 'Captain Faulkner?'

'Yes?'

The man was elegantly dressed under his cloak and he withdrew a sealed letter from his gauntlet. 'His Highness Prince Rupert heard of your return to Helveotsluys and desires that you wait upon him at your earliest convenience.'

Faulkner looked at Mainwaring and the unspoken thought flashed between them. 'I am obliged, sir,' said Faulkner with a heavy emphasis that placed the matter of his discussion with Mainwaring beyond recall.

'You may take my horse, Kit,' offered Mainwaring, indicating his understanding.

'If you are Sir Henry Mainwaring,' the stranger said, 'I am charged to request that you also attend His Highness.'

Part One
The Exile

1649

The Council of War

January 1649

'God's wounds, but this wind chills to the very marrow of my bones and these casements give it free and unhindered passage!'

Shaking his head, Mainwaring removed his hand from the window and stared at it, as though the keen gale, blowing in from the North Sea through the interstice, would leave some visible mark upon his skin. Neither Faulkner nor Katherine Villiers responded to Mainwaring's unnecessary remark. The former stared half-heartedly at a chart spread out before him, a Dutch Waggoner lying open beside it; the latter bent over the threadbare stockings of Sir Henry's that she was darning.

A week after the two men had answered Prince Rupert's summons, and attended his council of war aboard his flagship, the *Constant Reformation*, they were back in their rooms at The Hague. Faulkner and Katherine had patched up their quarrel after a fashion, but the mood of both had been subdued. Their spirits had been further depressed by the news that had come from London a few days later: the King had been put on trial in his own palace. Faulkner recalled the white splendour of Whitehall Palace beneath the walls of which he had reacquainted himself with the lovely Katherine Villiers in happier times, times that seemed in retrospect to be so full of promise.

He shot a glance at her, bending solicitously over Mainwaring's laddered hose. Half his mind filled with venom, half with a tender pity that forced him to suppress a sob and turn it instead into a cough. He lowered his eyes swiftly as Katherine looked up. She must not divine his distress, whatever her own agony.

His eyes wandered unseeing over the chart dedicated to 'The Master, Wardens and Assistants of the Honourable Corporation of Trinity House'. It depicted the entire estuary of the Thames, extending to the so-called Weilings, the archipelago that choked the estuary of the River Schelde, and ran on to include the deep tidal inlets that ran between the islands. One such was the Haringvliet, or Herring-fleet, as the English mariners called it, upon which lay the port of Helvoetsluys, the base of the exiled Royalist fleet of the former King Charles I.

But Faulkner saw none of this; his head was too full of Kate and her *affaire* with Charles, Prince of Wales, who, if the King's trial came to the fatal term predicted by its advocates, would soon be King in the eyes of his supporters. Instead of the shoals and channels scrupulously laid out before him after assiduous survey, his mind's eye could see only Katherine's face, pale and pleading as she knelt before him after Mainwaring had dragged him back from Helvoetsluys.

What, he had repeatedly asked himself, was he to make of her protestations?

'But Kit, it was nothing . . . nothing. A mere amusement . . . a playing between us, affectionate yes, but not . . .' Her voice had choked with the humiliation of it. 'Not a carnal *knowing* such as you and I have known each other. Why, he esteems you, relies upon you for your loyalty.'

'Am I to be content with such an assurance?' Faulkner had asked, pricked by conscience following his discussion with Mainwaring. 'What more might he not do when I am at sea, which I shall surely be as soon as the ice breaks up? Will he want more than thy hand about his member? Besides, what did he want of you?' He was himself choking now and she had reached up and placed her hand across his twisted mouth. The other had fluttered about her bosom, indicating the focus of the royal attention.

'Only a little unlacing,' she had admitted, her own eyes filling with tears. He had felt bile burning his throat, the more so since he had fancied fortune had raised him and the realization that he was so subordinate cut like a sharp blade into his soul. He had closed his eyes and, unseeing, gathered her into his arms; and so they had embraced with what passed for forgiveness.

But he could not drive the image of them from his head and doubted the lolling voluptuary had restrained himself as Kate claimed. Furthermore, what added to his torture was his liking for the Prince – a liking which would be complicated should he assume the title of King. How should he stand with regard to the young rake in that capacity? He himself had taught him how to handle a boat and flattered himself that His Highness had some regard for him. A tear dropped on to the chart before him and he hurriedly brushed it away before it distorted the paper. *This* was what he must think on, this cunningly delineated plan of . . . of what? Christ! Did not the very debouchement of the Schelde look like some pox-rotten prick aimed at the vast cloaca of the Thames?

He shook his head to clear it of such a foul thought, squeezing his eyes as though to dry them of incipient, weak and unmanly tears. He was, for God's sake, a sea officer, not a wailing, unrequited swain. With an almost savage gesture he thrust his index finger near the chart's western margin, obscuring the sandbank and its attendant legend The Nore.

'*Here!*' He breathed through clenched teeth so that Katherine looked up and Mainwaring roused himself. Seeing him thus preoccupied, for so they thought, they exchanged glances and Mainwaring smiled away Katherine's distress. 'He will be himself again,' his kindly expression seemed to say. 'He is not like us and is, for all his years, experience and responsibility, still something of an innocent.'

Court bred, she understood him perfectly and responded with a shy, hesitant smile of her own.

With a mighty effort of will Faulkner had driven his mind from one painful reminiscence to another scarcely less so, coming as the event he recalled did so hard upon the heels of the other and prefaced, as it was, by discussions of defection. The council of war aboard the *Constant Reformation* had been an odd affair, stiff, when you thought about it, with men of dubious loyalty. Both he and Mainwaring had not an hour since been questioning the Royalist cause; two others, Batten and Jordan, had both come over to the Prince after troubles with the Parliament and the fleet. Neither was held to be entirely trustworthy. Even Prince Rupert, the shining star of Cavalier chivalry, had found himself spoken against by those close to the King and estranged from his uncle in the last year of his freedom. And now, here they were, with the captains of some eight or nine half-provisioned men-of-war whose crews were unpaid and mutinous, mewed up in a Dutch ditch while Warwick's fleet, if it lay not now in the outer waters of the Schelde, was not far away – only the width of the chart upon which Faulkner's now blazing eyes gazed: Here! At The Nore!

The Prince had served them honey in that ill-lit cabin. The red sun of an early setting ensanguined every artefact capable of reflecting its bloody redness as it sank over the flat and frozen landscape. Rupert's goblet, the rings upon his soft-gloved hand, the sword pommel and its buckled baldric that lay upon the table before him, Batten's pretentious half-armour, Jordan's gold necklace, even Mainwaring's soiled lace, picked up the ominous, scarlet splendour of the wintry sunset.

'There are now sufficient funds at our disposal,' Rupert had said without further explanation and in his perfect but accented English, 'to enable us to commission several of the ships, all, in fact, whose commanders are here present, with the exception of the *Antelope*. She I intend to sell, having first disposed of her artillery, some among your ships, some to a buyer eager to get his hands on heavy English iron guns.'

He had looked about, confident, but making certain they were all attentive. 'Now, as for our dispositions for the coming campaign, I intend to carry my flag to Ireland where my lord, the Marquess of Ormonde, maintains the struggle. You will all accompany me with the exception of Sir Henry Mainwaring and Captain Faulkner. You, Sir Henry, having employed your well-known talents in preparing my squadron, will remain here in charge of our interests and acting on behalf of Captain Faulkner who is, I know, like unto your son. He shall be charged with taking his own ship under warrant of the Prince of Wales. My commission unto you, Captain Faulkner, is to cruise in the mouth of the River of Thames, to annoy our enemy and to seize as many prizes as you may be able and disposing thereof among these greedy Hollanders, thereby engorging our war chest.' Rupert paused again, staring directly at Faulkner until he nodded assent. 'If you are able to take such vessels that may be persuaded to join us, and seem proper to you and Sir Henry in both their company and their soundness, particularly in the manner of their bearing arms, then you shall direct them to join my flag either in Ireland or at

Lisbon, where I have friends, and where they shall find orders from me. Captain Allen –' Rupert had indicated the officer who had boarded the *Phoenix* to summon them to attend His Highness and who seemed to execute the office of a flag captain – 'Captain Allen will give you written orders to this effect. He will also provide the remainder of you with such instructions as I shall deem necessary for the orders of sailing and battle.'

The council broke up over wine and sweetmeats, and a desultory conversation from which Faulkner felt isolated. He gleaned that Rupert had sold all his jewellery – or much of his mother's, depending upon the narrator – to raise money for the Royalist cause and that his brother, Prince Maurice, would be joining them. Shortly before Captain Allen gathered them all up and swept them from the great cabin and out into the icy wind, the Prince himself came and spoke to Faulkner as he stared gloomily out through the stern-windows at the desolation on the far side of the Haringvliet that was the island of Over Flakke and the ship that lay moored in mid-stream.

'I hope, sir, that you will be of more cheerful countenance when next we meet.'

Faulkner started. 'Forgive me, Your Highness, these days are gloomy and dispiriting.'

'Indeed; and it behoves us to set our shoulders to the wheel and turn events to our purpose.'

'I assure Your Highness . . .' Faulkner began, flushing at the imputation, only to be cut short by the lightest touch of Rupert's gloved hand upon his arm.

'I perfectly understand, my dear Captain Faulkner, but we have to hope for happier times, and your charge is a most important one.'

'I am sensible of the fact, Your Highness,' Faulkner replied with a bow, his spirit rising to the Prince's well-intentioned condescension. 'I would recommission *her*,' he ventured, indicating the ship moored in the Haringvliet, 'had Your Highness not found it necessary to strip her and sell her.'

'Ah. The *Antelope* has to be sacrificed for the welfare of the fleet. Her crew is a disgrace and there are besides insufficient loyal men to man the remainder properly.'

'Therein lies my own anxieties for your service, Your Highness,' Faulkner said boldly, for there was little point in dissimulation at such a juncture. 'The opportunity and the wherewithal to execute your commission is a burden I shall bear with the requisite fortitude, but one of which the outcome is not at all to be relied upon.'

'You will do it, sir, I know it for a certainty. Tell Allen of what you are most in need. Ah, and here *is* the good Captain Allen with your papers. I wish you Godspeed.' And he was gone. Faulkner took the packet of papers from a silent Allen and sought out Mainwaring. He found him in earnest discourse with Batten. The two exiled Elder Brethren of Trinity House might have been gossiping at Deptford itself after a Trinitytide dinner for all the apparent seriousness of their present situation. Faulkner was not deceived; he had seen Sir Henry fishing for information before and sensed Batten and Jordan had been a little free with the decanters before the council had been called.

'He does not trust either Batten or Jordan,' Mainwaring had remarked later, referring to Rupert as they walked back in the evening's darkness along the frozen quays and out, beyond the few guttering lights of Helvoetsluys, along the dyke towards the distant *Phoenix*. 'While I should have liked to kick the frozen dog turds of this accursed place from my feet, His Highness has favoured us both with a particular charge, Kit.'

'Then you are no longer minded to die in England,' Faulkner had riposted drily.

Mainwaring sighed, his air of resignation exhaled in the mist of his condensed breath. 'The habit of obedience,' he had said quietly, leaving the sentence as incomplete as his explanation of having changed his mind. 'Without it nothing can ever be accomplished.'

'And besides,' Faulkner had added in a low voice which indicated his own sentiments were, at least for the time being, in accord with the old admiral's, 'it is an old comfort among a sea of uncertain shallows.'

It was then that Mainwaring had determined to drag him back to Katherine in The Hague. 'Always the lure of the *status ante bellum*,' he had remarked softly to himself as he followed

Faulkner up the gangplank on to the *Phoenix*'s deck. 'And so infinitely preferable to the present moment.'

It was now almost dark in the room. Katherine set her darning aside and poked the dying fire. 'I shall get some wood, if any is to be had,' she said, rising stiffly.

'No, my dear, allow me,' said Mainwaring, turning from the window with the energy of a gallant half his age and shuffling from the room, muttering about fair recompense for Kate's attention to his stockings. She stood uncertain for a moment before cautiously approaching Faulkner. He had by now seated himself and was scribbling in a small notebook, breaking off intermittently to bestride the chart with extended dividers, or lay a brass and ivory rule alongside one of the several compass-roses that bedecked it.

For several moments she stood motionless beside him, watching him as his strong and competent fingers manipulated the instruments and then set the dividers down to take up his quill. She knew he was aware of her proximity and was content to let him finish, to burn out the passion of their unhappiness in his professional preparations. He would, she knew, come to her when he was ready.

Finally he laid down the pen and closed the notebook. Sitting back in the rickety chair he remained staring ahead but he put out his right hand, feeling for her hand. It was thin and chilled, and he raised it to his lips. Still without turning his head he said, 'These are terrible times to live . . .'

And she bent and kissed the crown of his head, smoothing her other hand over his long hair.

The Affair at The Nore

January — April 1649

Thanks to the commercial energies of the Dutch that maintained an ice-free navigable channel in the lower Haringvliet, Prince Rupert's main squadron left Helvoetsluys on 21 January, as soon after the council of war as Mainwaring's strenuous efforts had fitted his ships for their long cruise to the coast of Ireland.

'His Highness has only eight vessels,' Mainwaring had said. 'The *Charles*, the *Thomas*, the *Mary*, a ketch, and the hoy *Elizabeth*. His only vessels of force are the *Swallow*, *Convertive* and *Constant Reformation*, and constant reformation of His Highness' squadron is just about all I can achieve for His Highness' power.'

'You have wrought mightily, Sir Henry, and have no reason to reproach yourself. It was Rupert's decision to abandon the *Antelope* after her crew mutinied.' They both recalled the Prince's suppression of the mutiny during which he had picked up one of the rebellious seamen and held him over the *Antelope*'s side. 'He carried his point,' Faulkner added, 'though I should like to have known his thoughts at the men's disloyalty.'

'Oh, that he carried off with his customary aplomb,' Mainwaring reported, having attended the Prince shortly after the incident. '"I would rather fight and die with twenty loyal men", he said, "than triumph with two hundred turncoats." That sort of nonsense.' Mainwaring paused, catching Faulkner's eye. Both men thought of their own intention to turn their own coats. 'Admirable, of course, but scarcely practical,' he added with a finality that curtailed the uncomfortable recollection.

'Indeed not,' Faulkner had said.

The departure of Faulkner's *Phoenix* was both more complicated and yet simpler than that of the Prince's squadron.

Complicated because she lay further upstream, in an ice-bound creek free of the heavier tolls attracted by Rupert's ships. On the other hand, she was in better shape than many of the Prince's men-of-war and Faulkner had, thanks to considerable skill, managed to feed and more or less keep his seamen in paid employment. This was in part owing to her having a smaller crew and in part to the close loyalty that Faulkner's leadership had engendered. Though few felt passionately about the predicament of King Charles, as seamen they appreciated Faulkner's concern for them. As poor men, most of whom had neither family nor home, he was their lifeline to survival, not least because he knew what it was to go hungry, for Faulkner's origins were, though never advertised by himself, not such that they could be kept entirely secret.

Besides her commander, the *Phoenix* carried two officers: her long-time chief lieutenant, named White, and another of Faulkner's former mates, Mr Lazenby, who had turned up in Helvoetsluys a few days after the exiles in Holland learned that on January 30th King Charles had been executed, his head struck from his body on a block surmounting a scaffold erected outside a window of the splendid Banqueting Hall of Whitehall Palace in which the King had been tried for High Treason.

The news shook all those who adhered to the Stuart cause and the assumption of the empty title of King by Prince Charles, though it spoke of continuity, only rang hollow. The new King was a callow youth whose only talents seemed to promise a life of dissipation and excess, eroding the remnant loyalty of cuckolded husbands. Nevertheless, in the wake of the execution of the King a few men for whom the regicide made England intolerable began arriving in Helvoetsluys. Among these was Lazenby, and it was with him that Faulkner was walking the deck a week or so later as the *Phoenix*, under a press of canvas, chased a small but heavily sparred cutter to the northwards.

'What d'you make of her?' Faulkner had asked when he had come on deck in response to Lazenby's summons.

'She's a packet, sir,' Lazenby had remarked confidently, handing his glass to Faulkner. 'Mark the spars . . .'

'Indeed, and the extent of her sails,' Faulkner said, lowering the telescope and returning it to its owner. 'She may outrun us.'

'Aye and let every vessel on the coasts know of us.'

Faulkner chuckled with some satisfaction. 'I doubt not that we are already well known to the under-writers and on "Change".' In ten days they had taken three prizes, two off the Texel fresh from being nipped in the Baltic ice and full of Russian hemp and flax, Swedish iron and timber from Dantzig. Shifting his cruising ground, Faulkner had next crossed to Orfordness and, finding a large vessel anchored in Hollesley Bay, had swooped upon her flying the new cross-and-harp ensign of the English Commonwealth. Ranging up alongside with his guns run out, Faulkner was gratified in seeing half her company escape towards Harwich in the ship's longboat.

'God's blood, Mr White!' he had called to his lieutenant commanding his small broadside in the waist. 'They fear we are about to press them!'

Faulkner could scarce believe his luck, though it cost him a quarter of his own company to send her home to Mainwaring's care as Prince Rupert's prize-agent. Worthily named the *Hope*, in due course he was to learn that she had been commissioned as the *King's Falconer* in his honour. Drawing offshore to cover the *Hope*'s passage to Helvoetsluys, the *Phoenix* recovered her prize crew without putting in to the Haringvliet, Rupert using their return to send two of his ships out to watch for the Earl of Warwick's squadron that was expected daily, intent on blockading the Royalist fleet in the Haringvliet.

Faulkner crossed to the vicinity of the Smith's Knoll, picking up intelligence from the fishermen drifting for herring. Among the news that he gleaned was that Warwick, his loyalty to the Parliamentary cause in doubt, had been replaced by Vice-Admiral Robert Moulton. As to the fishermen, he was scrupulous in making no move against them, except to ask if any wished to serve the King. He picked up three young men anxious to avoid service in the army, but, more importantly, his investment in Genever gin yielded the latest news of the King's trial which both he and Mainwaring were anxious to learn.

'We must keep abreast of events, Kit,' the old man had

insisted, casting a significant glance at Katherine by the fire. 'Do not trouble yourself about her,' Mainwaring had added, squeezing Faulkner's arm. 'She too has a future as dear to me as mine own life.'

It was after the recruitment of the three young fishermen that they had sighted the packet and given chase and now Faulkner, with Lazenby pacing beside him, made up his mind. Looking at the distance of their quarry, Faulkner turned his attention to the sky and ceased walking. Beside him Lazenby paused and, seeing Faulkner's attention had focused on the sky, followed his gaze.

'No. But you are correct, Mr Lazenby. We shall have a change in the weather by tomorrow. Do you maintain the chase until darkness and then we shall haul our wind and stand to the southward. I have a mind to pursue a favourite scheme and now is the time.'

'May I ask where you intend to strike, sir?'

'The Nore, Lazenby, The Nore.'

It felt as though spring had deserted the mouth of the great river as, two days later, the Phoenix ghosted up the Swin in a light and freezing north-easterly breeze. She seemed like a phantom to the two Leigh bawleys fishing on the edge of the Barrow Sand, the sea-smoke rising about her and almost entirely concealing her so that they were afterwards unable to tell the two grim-visaged and pot-helmeted cavalrymen sent to enquire what ship had created such havoc through the Warps, the Oaze and The Nore itself.

Faulkner, of course, knew nothing of this, nor that questions were asked in Parliament itself as to why 'a Malignant pirate' could, 'in defiance of the might and majesty of the State's Naval force in the Medway, cause such harm to our trade?'

The truth was, it had been a simple matter, for the *Phoenix* had had not only a fair wind but a favourable spring tide and had passed through the outer anchorage while the seamen in the anchored merchant ships awaiting convoy had been breaking their fasts. Bringing out only one small bilander, Faulkner had determined not to take any prizes. Prince Rupert's faith in supposing they could recruit sufficient seamen to man captures

and turn them into Royalist men-of-war was hopelessly opti-
mistic and he considered he might do more damage by pure
destruction.

He made his preparations with care, briefing his officers and
men with that tone of confidence and conviction that swiftly
won their enthusiastic support, giving to individuals especially
crucial parts to play and to which occasion they could only
rise with enthusiasm.

Having made his plan, which obliged John Matthews, a
former seaman promoted to gunner, to spend some hours of
meticulous preparation in the magazine and drew from Mr
White the coarse observation that he hoped Matthews could
properly charge a shell carcass since 'he could not shit a sailor's
turd', Faulkner took the con. The masts and spars of the large
convoy, which, he had learned from the fishermen, lay awaiting
its naval escort, showed clear above the low fog that rose like
the smoke that gave it its name. From the anchored ships and
vessels he hoped the *Phoenix*, herself similarly shrouded, would
look like a late arrival, delayed by the contrary wind that had
blown itself out two days ago. Closer-to he hoped to convince
them she was one of the very escort for which they waited
and, to this end, she wore again the new ensign of the
Commonwealth. Only at the last moment would he break out
the red flag at the fore masthead and substitute the King's for
the Commons' colours.

As the *Phoenix* crept up on the flood tide, her longboat was
hoisted out and, after three men – all volunteers – had climbed
down into her, several packages were carefully passed to them
by those on deck. The boat was then streamed astern on a
long painter and the remaining men were sent to their battle
stations.

'Time, Mr Lazenby, to see what sort of an artilleryman you
might make with that coehorn.'

Acknowledging Faulkner's order, Lazenby bent to his task
over the small mortar which was secured in the larboard waist,
behind the main guns which, ready loaded, lay behind closed
ports. Lazenby had tried several shots on their way along the edge
of the Gunfleet Sand and judged he had the amount of powder
exactly correct for the purpose Faulkner had briefed him.

'I hope you don't foul yourself with these bombs of yours,' the taciturn White remarked as he readied his gunners and sharpshooters, himself hefting a matchlock. 'I should hate you to be hoisted by your own petard!'

To preserve his deception, Faulkner sailed serenely past the first three ships, hailing each through his speaking trumpet and, standing beneath the listlessly flaunting cross-and-harp, affecting the tone of naval command, called out to each, 'Pray tell your master to prepare to weigh; the signal will be a red flag and three guns!' No one aboard any of the three vessels noticed the boat towing far astern of the passing 'frigate' – as they supposed – lost as it was in the sea-smoke.

Faulkner was again imbued with that strange quasi-religious exaltation that he had experienced when conning the *Phoenix* through the reefs west of Guernsey, months earlier. Under its influence his agonizing over Katherine had faded entirely from his mind which, or so it seemed to him through the long hours of that intense forenoon, was serenely calculating, as though elevated beyond the plateau of fearful anticipation that he guessed many of his men were enduring as they held their fire, as instructed. He had first experienced the sensation earlier that morning, when he first realized the extent to which the conditions favoured him. The north-easterly breeze he had foretold without much trouble from the omens in the sky off the Smith's Knoll, but its temperature he could not have guessed, nor the dense sea-smoke that was its consequence.

As he lowered his speaking trumpet after hailing the third merchantman he called softly down to White and Lazenby in the waist, 'Make ready, gentlemen. The next is ours to gull.' And then, walking quickly aft to the taffrail he simply called out to the coxswain in the boat hidden astern in the low sea-smoke, 'What sounding?'

The coxswain responded as he had been coached. 'By the mark five, sir.'

'Cast well to starboard!' Faulkner called, maintaining the fiction of sounding to test the depth of water, but instead of taking a cast with the lead, the man put the boat's tiller to port and the longboat sheered out on the *Phoenix*'s starboard quarter while her crew blew on their slow-matches.

Faulkner nodded to the man at the wheel, and he too did as he was told without an order that might have carried the deceit to their quarry now only yards away, downwind. The *Phoenix* veered in her course, as though sloppily handled and prompting a hail from the merchantman next in line.

'Mind your helm there!' Faulkner roared in the mock admonition that was the signal for the boy to prepare the ensign halliards. Faulkner watched the lad until he was ready, with the King's ensign bent on the same line that held the cross-and-harp aloft. Satisfied, he watched the anchored merchant ship that was suddenly very close as the light breeze and the strong tide swept them past.

'Now, gentlemen, now!'

From the waist rose a rolling concussion as each gun was fired into its hapless victim. The noise was punctuated by the heavier thud of the charge in the coehorn as the smoke of the guns' discharges hung almost motionless above them, partly obscuring Faulkner's view of the merchantman. Only her upper masts and yards rose clear into the bright blue sky and then the shell, lifted by no more than a few pinches of black powder, burst in a vivid, blinding flash. The crash of the detonation was followed by a series of unidentifiable noises as shell fragments indiscriminately struck rope, wood, iron and human flesh, not all of it aboard their quarry. Faulkner himself felt the sharp, searing slash of an iron splinter as it scythed across his cheek so that he felt the heat of it as it gashed him, followed by the warm trickle of blood. Of this he took little notice, eager to see whether their last stratagem had taken effect.

Delayed some seconds after their own passing, as the air was filled with the screams of the wounded and the cries of horror at the outrage being perpetrated against them, the towed long-boat swept alongside the anchored vessel. Into a porthole, opened as Faulkner had anticipated, to air the ship, the long-boat's crew tossed one of their fused packages. Another was lodged on the ship's starboard main chains so that, as they drew past, Faulkner saw the combustibles burst into flame and the fires take hold.

Faulkner had a clear view of the stern now and saw where a man, probably the ship's master engaged in the very act of opening his bowels, thrust a pistol muzzle through the glass of the privy to take a potshot at him. He ducked the ill-aimed ball and waved.

'Damn you!' came the furious response. 'Who the devil are you?'

'The *Phoenix* of the King's navy!'

'We have no King you malignant bastard!'

'Ready, sir!' Lazenby was calling up from the waist where the guns and coehorn had been reloaded. Faulkner abandoned the fulminating ship-master to his fire and his soiled small clothes, turning his attention to the next ship in the anchorage.

Before the sun had gained sufficient heat and altitude to begin to burn off the sea-smoke so that all possibility of subterfuge had vanished, they had struck four more vessels, two of such substantial size that Faulkner thought them Indiamen. The timing, circumstances and ruthlessness of the attack caused confusion and alarm so that Faulkner boldly stood on, ordering an increase in the charge of the coehorn so that it bombarded another four ships at a range of several hundred yards, supplemented by the broadside guns which, if they did little real harm, shot up rigging and swept the waists clear of opposition. Only one of the Indiamen got a gun into action before the *Phoenix* had passed out of range. As he looked astern coils of thick black smoke rose from three of their targets, thinner wisps ascended from two more and in one little ketch so fierce a fire was consuming her that her small crew had already taken to their boat.

By the time they were off The Nore the tide was on the turn and Faulkner ordered the longboat's painter shortened, so that her crew could scramble aboard, and the ship's yards hauled. Hard on the light wind, her yards braced sharp-up, the *Phoenix* stood boldly out to sea, this time following the South Channel. Lazenby went forward to look out for the buoy of the Spile. A mile or two to the north and soon moving astern, a pall of smoke hung over the anchorage off Shoeburyness, while not half a mile away to the south-west a small man-of-war was making sail as she weighed her anchor in hot pursuit.

'He'll not catch us,' White remarked contemptuously as the

outgoing tide, already ebbing steadily in the South Channel, carried the *Phoenix* eastwards.

Faulkner was less confident, but held his peace and in the event White proved correct; by noon the pursuing frigate had hauled up and was returning to The Nore. Faulkner stared through his glass at the retreating man-of-war and then shifted his glass. The ships he had attacked that morning were indistinct under their pall of smoke; the small coehorn, a Dutch invention, had been a wise investment.

'You are wounded, Captain Faulkner,' White remarked and Faulkner put his hand to his cheek and felt the dried crust of blood.

''Tis nothing; a scratch.'

'It'll scar though,' White said in that terse way he had, as though his statements were incontrovertible.

'Hm,' Faulkner grunted. 'What of our own butcher's bill?'

'Three men hurt, one badly from that damned Dutch spitfire of yours,' White reported with evident disapproval. 'But they'll all live.'

'Good. Is that your opinion, Mr White?'

'Yes, but the surgeon shares it.'

Inwardly Faulkner grinned to himself. 'I didn't think you had a very high opinion of our surgeon,' Faulkner remarked.

'His barbering is excellent, Captain,' White replied, his eyes twinkling.

Faulkner hove-to during the hours of darkness and was in the cabin breaking his fast with White when Lazenby, who had the deck-watch, burst through the door.

'Cap'n Faulkner,' he said excitedly, 'there are Commonwealth ships off Goeree!'

'You're certain?'

'Aye, sir. The cross-and-harp at the fore-truck on one and he's standing towards us . . .'

'Warwick!' exclaimed Faulkner, immediately correcting himself. 'No, that will be the new vice-admiral, Moulton. Very well,' he said sharply to Lazenby. 'Hoist Dutch colours.'

'Aye, aye, sir.' Lazenby hesitated, then added, 'There's something else, sir . . .'

'And what might that be?'

'I think I recognized one of our ships in the squadron . . .'

'The Dutch fleet are at sea and Moulton's crop-heads have been suborning our men,' White concluded with his usual conviction. Faulkner, however, had no doubt but that he was right. 'See to those colours, Mr,' he snapped, rising from the table.

Lazenby was gone. White followed his commander to his feet. 'Clear for action,' Faulkner said. 'Hold the men out of sight behind closed ports. I'll try and bluff it out.'

'If they've taken any of our ships we'll certainly be recognized.'

'We'll try, nevertheless.'

'I hope our men won't fail us,' White remarked as they left the cabin.

'Load your pistols, just in case.'

Faulkner approached Lazenby who handed him his glass and indicated the ships. Ahead lay the low coast, grey-green above its golden strand of sand, and spiked with the spires of distant churches and crossed with the slowly turning sails of windmills. But lying on the grey sea between, many with their main topsails to their masts, were some twenty vessels, mostly men-of-war. Faulkner could see the Commonwealth ensigns and, just as Lazenby had reported, the adapted flag that marked a flag officer flying from the nearest, just herself heaving-to in the grain of the approaching *Phoenix*: Moulton.

Faulkner looked aloft at the horizontal stripes of the Dutch ensign, then ordered a slight alteration of course that would cross Moulton's stern. They were closing fast and the Parliamentary admiral, having brought his vessel to a standstill, would now be hoping that Faulkner would not rake him if he opened fire.

'The first round is mine,' Faulkner murmured to himself, though with little confidence in the outcome of the bout.

'Ahoy there! What ship?'

Faulkner ignored the hail. They would see the ship's name soon enough when they read it across the stern but until then . . . He went to the larboard rail and raised his hat as they made to pass across the flagship's stern. Already the men were labouring in the waist, hauling the yards for fear the approaching vessel would open fire into her almost defenceless stern.

'*Goedmorgen, Meneer*,' he shouted. '*Ik ben na een lange zeereis op mijn weg terug van Batavia*,' explaining they had had a long passage from Batavia in the East Indies.

Faulkner's Dutch was crude and rudimentary but good enough to buy him the respite to pass under the flagship's stern and head towards the other ships lying between the *Phoenix* and the shore where the entrance of the Haringvliet lay open to the north of Goeree. Then the shout of recognition as their name was seen was quickly followed by the boom of a gun and the skipping splash of the ricocheting ball passing along their larboard side. But Moulton had left the firing of a broadside too late. Already his ship's yards were swinging her head as she came round in pursuit.

Faulkner kept the Dutch colours hoisted and boldly held his course. It was clear the other ships were uncertain as to what was going on. The firing of a single gun from a flagship could mean anything, usually signifying a signal from the admiral was not being attended to and setting every quarterdeck abuzz with introspection. All they would see was Moulton's flagship swinging in the wake of an incoming Dutchman and, although the *Phoenix* was unmistakably not a Dutch-built ship, the fact that she was carrying full sail and heading confidently for the entrance to the Haringvliet flying Dutch colours was sufficient to inhibit any captain in the Commonwealth ships from using too much initiative.

What Faulkner did not know until later was that White had been correct and before the Dutch naval squadron departed the Haringvliet, the Dutch authorities had extracted from Moulton an undertaking not to interfere with the safe passage of Dutch merchantmen. Although several of Moulton's ships had entered Helvoetsluys and their men had suborned most of Prince Rupert's little fleet, many of the defecting ships had left their commanders ashore, sufficient uncertainty prevailed as to their fate that it was not until the *Phoenix* had almost worked inshore of the squadron that one vessel woke up to the advantages of her capture. Even now, however, luck favoured Faulkner, for the Commonwealth squadron was in some disarray as a consequence of the defection of the Royalist ships. Each had been assigned one of Moulton's men-of-war to stand guard over her in case her company changed its collective mind and these contemplated their charges, rather than a maverick King's ship sailing boldly through them. Added to this was the fact that a large number of Moulton's men were absent, for the squadron's boats had been sent into the Haringvliet to cut out the *Antelope*, as Faulkner would shortly discover.

Thus the *Phoenix* had almost won through when Faulkner called to his officers to prepare to engage on the larboard side.

'There's a ship of twenty or so guns bearing down upon us,' he called. She looked like one of the *Lion's Whelps*, one of which he had himself commanded. If so, while she might outgun the *Phoenix*, the weight of metal she threw would be less than their own.

'Make ready,' he called, holding his course. 'On no account fire until we are fired into. I have no wish to be branded pirate.'

'That you already are,' White called back, referring to their exploit of the previous day. The remark, though technically insolent, heartened the men and raised a cheer so that Faulkner knew its worth and mentally thanked White for it. He watched the approaching *Whelp* as her commander altered his course to drop across the *Phoenix*'s bow. A gun was fired to windward, the puff of grey-white smoke hanging in the wind as the concussion followed. The *Phoenix* stood on, ignoring the signal to heave to.

Faulkner watched as the *Whelp* drifted slowly to leeward. The distance between the two shrank and the foreshortening of the *Whelp*'s hull betrayed her commander's anxiety for her stern.

'Shift your men over to the starboard guns,' he called down to Lazenby, watching as the guns' crews quietly crossed the deck.

Turning on to a parallel course, she made sail as the *Phoenix* ranged up alongside and, under the muzzles of the *Whelp*'s larboard battery, they surged alongside for a few moments. Again Faulkner went through his little charade and again it seemed to do the trick until someone aboard the *Whelp* recognized him.

'Hey! That's Captain Faulkner! He's no Dutchman! He's a King's man under false colours!'

Faulkner thought fast. Hailing the *Whelp* he roared, 'Aye, this is Captain Faulkner but I am sailing under a warrant of the Seven United Provinces! Fire into me and I'll respond, as will all seven of the Dutch Admiralties!'

A perfect silence met this false claim and then he watched as the *Whelp*'s helm went over and she turned sharply, her bowsprit almost raking their rail, to come up into the wind under their stern. A moment later she was standing offshore on the starboard tack, heading to rejoin her consorts.

'Was that blind man's bluff, Captain Faulkner?' White asked with an air of amused whimsy.

One last drama was to beset them before the *Phoenix* fetched her mooring off Helvoetsluys and gave some clue as to the apparent incompetence of Moulton's attempt to thwart their entry. Barely a mile inside the Haringvliet as, under reduced sail and with a leadsman in the main chains, the *Phoenix* crept cautiously through the shallows towards her destination, they encountered the boats of Moulton's ships surrounding the captured *Antelope*.

To avoid complaints from the local admiralty, Faulkner had ordered the proper colours hoisted as they entered Dutch waters and, although these were concealed by the main topsail until they were almost abreast of the gaggle of boats surrounding the cut-out *Antelope*, once they were spotted, they produced shouts of abuse and derision. For a few moments Faulkner feared that the Commonwealth seamen in the boats might pursue and board them, but they were soon past and Faulkner realized that most of the attacking party were occupied carrying the *Antelope* to sea, Prince Rupert having previously removed her hands and distributed them among his own most trusted ships. Faulkner also realized that in cutting out the *Antelope*, Moulton's men had strained their undertaking not to molest the ships of the English Royalist far enough, and the seizure of the *Phoenix* – should they have achieved it, which was by no means certain – would be a provocation too far. Full comprehension of all these subtle but influential circumstances came much later and the sudden anxieties turned Faulkner's guts to water for a few fearful minutes. But the incident was soon over and, with beating heart, he gave the orders to make the shallow turn in the channel that brought the elaborate church spires of Helvoetsluys into view.

'From Hell and Helvoetsluys, Good Lord deliver us,' White intoned before turning to Faulkner. 'I'll go forrard and make ready,' he said purposefully. 'And may I congratulate you, Captain Faulkner, on a most successful cruise.'

With his innards still subsiding from the morning's excitements, Faulkner responded with a wan smile. 'I hope the men will not be disappointed at the lack of prizes. Moulton's fleet has had all the luck there.'

'Oh, they will, depend upon it, but the crop-head navy will soon be blamed for not defending the trade in the Thames and that will carry more weight in London town.'

Faulkner nodded. 'Stand by to clew up and make ready to moor.'

'Aye, aye,' said White turning away and raising his voice as Faulkner moved towards the helmsman. 'Main an' fore clew-lines!' White bellowed. 'And look lively there!'

Later that day Mainwaring clambered wearily aboard. Maintaining the outward flummery of appearing as Faulkner's admiral the old man eased himself into a chair and gladly accepted an offer of wine. 'Any news from Ireland?' Faulkner had asked, as he handed him the charged glass. Mainwaring shook his head.

'Nothing of import, but you have fared well if what I hear from the scuttlebutt on deck is anything to go by. Now tell me the truth of it . . .'

Faulkner made a verbal report, concluding that he thought he had 'annoyed the enemy in accordance with His Highness' desires'.

'So it would seem, Kit, and it is well done. While we may have lost a significant part of our power here, you have shown we are not without teeth.'

'Perhaps. But Moulton blockades us and will not let me out as readily as he let me in, distracted as he was with the seizure of the *Antelope*.'

'Aye, it was the news of his insolence that brought me here so fortuitously to meet you.' Mainwaring related how he had been at the head of a small body of cavalier gentlemen turned out of the *Antelope* as what remained of her defecting crew cheered the incoming boats of Moulton's squadron. It had been a desultory and futile business, a strutting and posing affair as the ship was seized by their enemy amid taunting cries of 'Wages and victuals!' – the promised advantages of serving the English Parliament. Mainwaring's old shoulders sagged as he related the circumstances. ''Tis a sad affair,' he concluded, 'and has cost us her purchase price, though Rupert took out her guns before the bill of sale was offered – which is a mercy of sorts, I suppose.' Mainwaring nodded his gratitude as Faulkner refilled his glass.

'That means more work for you, I presume.'

'What, the spoiled purchase?' Faulkner nodded. Mainwaring shrugged. 'It never ceases and the thinner our resources the greater the labour.'

'And what of the King himself, as I suppose we must now call him?'

'He talks about going to Paris.'

'Paris? To fall into Louis' arms? God save us!'

'To gain a pension, it is rumoured, or so Kate tells me . . .'

'And she would know the Royal mind, no doubt,' Faulkner remarked bitterly.

'Her lot is not an easy one, Kit,' Mainwaring said kindly. 'We outstay our welcome here at Helvoetsluys – there have been some ugly scenes here and the Dutch will be glad when we are gone for many of our men ran wild until Moulton's crop-heads carried them away. There are a few remaining; you'll find them begging and protesting their undying loyalty to King Charles, the scum that they are. As for the ladies at The Hague, where we are less and less tolerated, well, they have no option but to bide their time and eat humble pie. You know better than most that a woman, like unto a man, will do anything if her belly is empty.'

Faulkner gave him a sharp look and then his eyes softened. 'I am sorry, Sir Henry, I spoke . . .'

Mainwaring waved aside his protest. 'You spake as any man

might, but you have to realize affairs have been most difficult of late.' The old man fell silent and, looking at him, Faulkner realized he was exhausted.

'What's to be done, Sir Henry?' he asked, his tone softer.

With an effort Mainwaring heaved himself to his feet. His flesh seemed to hang from him and he stood with a stoop that Faulkner had never noticed before. 'When your men have been paid something we must to The Hague. I believe His Majesty has some opinions of his own and there will doubtless be orders – . . . We run out of all else, but there is never a shortage of stratagems and orders.'

A Successful Cruise

Spring – Summer 1649

Having travelled from Helvoetsluys with Mainwaring over a flat landscape bright with the promise of an early summer, Faulkner found Katherine in their lodgings at The Hague. Though thin with privation after a hard winter, her loveliness turned his gut with love and desire. She seemed less subdued than when he had left her, a change in mood he met with a swift resolution to put the past behind them. Her solicitude for him made it the easier for him in the euphoria of his return to forgive her all the agony she had caused him. It was clear from Mainwaring's casual but pointed remarks that any contacts she had had with Charles's threadbare court in exile had been fleeting. Faulkner certainly believed her when to his single query as to whether she had seen the King she gave a firm shake of the head.

'His Majesty was graciously pleased to send Sir James Verney to wait upon me but yesterday,' she had said in that formal manner that she had been taught, years earlier, as a young girl at the court of King James.

'Oh? On what business, pray?' he had asked.

'To say he had had word that you had damaged the trade in London's river and was pleased that you had struck a blow for the cause.' She hesitated a second, then added, 'As was, or so he told me, the King himself.'

'How the devil did he acquire that news so fast?' Faulkner enquired, surprised at the speed of the intelligence.

Katherine had shrugged. 'The packet boats run regularly and their skippers and mates make free with the news.'

Faulkner had been too intent in bringing the *Phoenix* safely into the Haringvliet to notice whether a packet boat from Harwich had been lying at the quay at Helvoetsluys, but he thought not. Besides, even had it been so, there had not been

time between his raid and any packet's departure from the
Essex port for the news of his exploit to be enshrined in even
the most superficial gossip, let alone the hastiest of despatches.

Faulkner shook his head. 'Even supposing the elapsed time
enabled a bulletin to be issued, the Parliament would scarcely
broadcast the affair to the satisfaction of its enemies.'

'Perhaps they are using pigeons,' she said. 'There is a loft at
the Maritshuis . . . What are you gawping at?'

'Pigeons?' he queried with an expression of genuine ignorance and enquiry.

'Yes. Did you not know? They are a homing breed and may
be trained to carry messages tied to their legs. You did not
know, did you?' She was laughing now and the revelation of
his ignorance melted the last of the reserve between them.

'Oh, Kate,' he admitted, 'I am such a fool; my education is
so wanting. I . . . pigeons! For the Lord's sake what a notion!'

She was sitting on his knee now and said, 'This is a land of
wonders, Kit; I heard that a tulip bulb can sell here for a
hundred guilders and some say far more.'

'Now you are gulling me and I am not such a fool as to
believe that and certainly not among these sober square-headed
dullards.'

'But 'tis true. Men make such utter fools of themselves over
money that a tulip is but an extension of the madness. It is
said some are set fair to ruin themselves in the business.'

'You speak the truth there, by God. And that is not confined
to these Hollanders.'

'And we must mind our funds. This cruise's success may
have reached the ears of the King by discommoding the
Parliament, but it puts no bread on the table nor tar upon the
Phoenix's stays.'

'Is that so terrible when we have each other?'

'We shall not have even lovers' short commons if one of us
should die from hunger, Kate. Thank God the winter is behind
us. As for the *Phoenix*, she is all I have besides thee and my
debts, and even she is pledged to the King . . .'

'As I am not, my love,' she said, breaking into his tirade
with the sudden affirmation.

Faulkner gulped, brought up short, like a curbed horse. 'And

I am grateful for it, Kate,' he said quietly. They fell into a thoughtful silence for a moment, then she kissed him, slipped from his lap and took a half turn by the table.

'And shall we take some bread and cheese? I have a little of that, at least, then you can make plans for your *Phoenix*.'

He brightened. 'Oh, she is in need of careening, though would to God I had the means to dock her properly.'

'If you are concerned we could take cheaper lodgings in Helvoetsluys and give these up.' She gestured round the bare room.

He shook his head. 'There is nothing cheap to be had there; commerce inflates rents and the English are no longer loved there, unless they have the Parliament's purse to draw upon.' He sighed and stretched, watching her bring food from the cupboard to the table. 'I am bound to say that if I do not take a legitimate prize soon, or loot something and make myself a pirate in the Parliament's eyes, we shall be in some straits. Anyway, poor Sir Henry, while he may labour occasionally at Helvoetsluys, persuades himself he is the King's admiral here in The Hague.'

'Poor Sir Henry,' she said sympathetically.

'And what about poor plain Kit?' he asked, standing up, making a grab for her and kissing her before she had time to respond.

Pulling away from him she looked up into his eyes. Her own were hollowed by hunger, her features fine drawn but her bosom rose and fell alluringly and she pressed her nether parts against his. 'For you, plain Kit, I have a devilish itch.'

The week that followed was blissful. Katherine's warmth drove the last remnant of hurt from him and, if he thought of her with Charles at all it was as a victim, trapped by the man's power and his arbitrary abuse of it. But there were other matters to distract him. The King's summons kept him kicking his heels overlong at The Hague when the repair and revictualling of the *Phoenix* required his attention, though he heard no news of it. He accomplished the refitting of the *Phoenix* with what remained of his slender means, but was obliged to attend Mainwaring in his visits to the money lenders of Amsterdam in order to raise funds for the underwriting of his next cruise.

True, his stock had never been higher; the news brought by pigeons or plain conjecture had been confirmed by the outraged tracts that finally spewed out of the London presses about 'Acts of Piracy' by the 'Malignant's successor's pretensions to naval puissance'.

As for the Malignant's successor, the uncrowned, unanointed King Charles II failed to summon the only naval commander available to him in Dutch waters who accomplished the refitting of the *Phoenix* with what remained of his private funds. Instead Faulkner was sent an order to expedite his departure on a second cruise 'in order that His Majesty's cause might be furthered by the utmost exertions to annoy His Majesty's enemies on the part of his Most Trusty and Well-beloved Captain Christopher Faulkner'.

Conscious of the burden laid upon him, Faulkner tossed the letter aside. The circumstances under which he would undertake his next cruise were very different from those that had attended his earlier venture. The year was sufficiently advanced for the Commonwealth navy to have fully commissioned the Summer Guard, and while Rupert might be active in the far west, the trade of the nation focused attention closer to home. The outrage felt in the City of London and the accusations against the men-of-war in the Medway who had failed to interrupt the raider overcame any reticence and were soon leaked to the exiled court. They encouraged Charles, profligate of the lives of commoners after his father had paid the ultimate sacrifice, to urge Faulkner to greater efforts, but Faulkner himself was only too well aware that while the Commonwealth's power grew daily, the King's weakened by the moment.

It was clear that Faulkner, should he fall foul of the Parliamentary authorities, would pay dearly for his insolence and these considerations, grasped only partially by himself, nevertheless made him plan his next cruise with great care, for he had no desire to lose his head like the martyred King.

Despite his congratulations at Helvoetsluys, privately Mainwaring was even less happy than Faulkner himself, for he thought that the exploit of The Nore had already compromised any compact either of them might in the future make with the Commonwealth. Any further successes could only worsen the situation. The old pragmatist grew daily wearier of the world in which he found himself but Faulkner, heady with Kate's loving, cast off Mainwaring's worst predictions.

''Tis me they will be after, Sir Henry. I mean no offence but your name is not noticed.'

'You have become too much the cavalier,' Mainwaring said, bristling. 'I am in no wise satisfied that the King's cause prospers to the extent of offering me the quietude to which — in less clamorous times — my years entitle me.'

'Then abandon the notion,' Faulkner advised, revealing an increasing irritation with Mainwaring. 'Settle for being here.'

'I cannot settle here. I am not a Dutchman.' Mainwaring sighed. 'You are too young to understand.' Mainwaring paused and then added, 'You owe me something, Kit, and I cannot go alone.'

'I owe you what you intended, that I should become a King's sea officer. If I accompanied you to London they would take my head for payment of lost cargoes while you might be mewed-up in the Tower. I cannot abandon Katherine and if she comes they will revile her for her kinship.' Faulkner began pacing the room. 'Must you go at all?'

Mainwaring nodded. 'D'you think a single success like you have achieved will amount to much in the end? The King's cause cannot prosper; it can only wither. These Commonwealth men, or whatever they call themselves, have judged and executed a King!' Mainwaring expostulated indignantly. 'They are not going to roll on their bellies like a fat cat and have the world tickle them, for Heaven's sake! Have they not shed enough blood to convince you that they wash their swords in it and will never sheath them while there are those like us to serve the successor to him they have dispatched to Abraham's bosom?' Mainwaring paused and then told Faulkner to sit down.

'Kit, I have secret communication with London.'

'The devil you have!'

Mainwaring raised a hand for silence. 'There is a constant to-ing and a fro-ing, Kit. You are a good sea officer but no politician. The nub of it is that I am informed that one might make a compact — there is talk of a composition to end the division in the country – and if this plays out I am desirous of settling my affairs in England before I die. I do not want to die an exile.'

He broke off as Kate came into the room. Talk of defection was dangerous and they had agreed the matter was not to be mentioned in her presence, though it occurred to Faulkner that he would be pulled asunder if Mainwaring did demand that he, Faulkner, accompany him. Kate would never go over to the enemy and would profoundly despise either of them for doing so; Kit feared it would part them. It was a dilemma that he had put from his mind and he hoped now that he would never have to confront it. Better a ragged loyalty to Charles and the security of his love for Katherine than his name be tainted with treachery. Had he become too much of a cavalier? Mainwaring certainly thought so, but then Sir Henry was on the horns of his own dilemma. The thought made him smile inwardly. Mainwaring had turned the course of his own life more than once. As for being a cavalier, he had met a few of those haughty gentry who hung about Rupert's skirts in their lace, slashed silk and half-armour. Fine-looking men under their wide-brimmed hats, bold as lions in battle but careless of their men, hopeless in discipline and ever ready to take offence at some imagined slight from an upstart. Even Mainwaring, with his long associations with the court, was held a parvenu. Faulkner inwardly dismissed the notion; only at sea, where a proper knowledge of the seaman's art could guarantee the success of even the most modest enterprise, did a man's ability graduate him.

'When shall you sail again?' Mainwaring asked, jerking him back from introspection. Faulkner guessed Mainwaring meant to steel him against the event of new separation from Katherine, for, sensing the sudden awkward silence, she looked from one to the other and he knew his answer would distress her.

'In a sennight,' he said, meeting Kate's widening eyes. 'I am sorry for it, Kate, but it must be done.'

'But a week's time . . .' she began and then turned and fled the room.

Faulkner sighed and glared at Mainwaring. 'That was ill done, Sir Henry, and unkind withal. Now I must placate her.'

And he left the room to Mainwaring who, shaking his head over the business of women, turned his attention to his pipe.

Faulkner's departure was a month later than he had said but the cruise upon which he embarked, though his most risky, proved to be his most successful. He had planned it with the utmost care and the delay fortunately ensured its success. True, Mainwaring's energies in assisting Faulkner helped, for the *Phoenix* was as well prepared as was humanly possible. Far from assuming the role of admiral, he took to that of ship's husband with all the gusto of a younger man, not least because it reminded him of happier times when he had been a ship owner. Leaving Faulkner to attend to the actual preparations of the ship herself, Mainwaring, having exhausted the resources of The Hague, travelled to Amsterdam with his Dutch servant as interpreter. Here he continued the rounds of the Jewish usurers so that, when the *Phoenix* dropped downstream on the first of the ebb on a fine sunny morning in late June, she had had the desired dry-docking, her rigging was all a-tanto and half her sails were brand new. During this, Faulkner had had the ship's name removed from her transom to better confuse any observer. Even better, her crew had been paid a modest advance and Faulkner had engaged a score of brawny Dutch seamen, of whom he had the highest opinion. To these he had added a number of waterfront loafers – mostly destitute English, some of whom were soldiers – whom he thought might beef up his prize-crews if he was fortunate in the matter of captures. Faulkner was less happy about the two additions to the after-guard, both of whom arrived on board the night before they were due to sail brandishing commissions as lieutenants under the King's sign-manual.

There was no doubt but they were cavaliers, for both men, though yet a year or so short of their majorities, bore notable names: the one a Hervey and the other a Digby. Neither had been to sea before and Faulkner sent them forward to observe the method by which the men, under the direction of White, unshackled the mooring.

'Captain Faulkner, we have come to *fight*,' Hervey protested.

'You are here to obey orders, Mr Hervey,' he said curtly,

nodding to Lazenby to let fall the topsail bunt and clew lines. 'The business of a King's officer at sea is of a thoroughly professional nature. There is no equivalence of a huntsman turning cavalry cornet on the deck of any ship, least of all, my own.'

Hervey stood his ground for a moment, his lantern jaw jutting truculently until, Faulkner was pleased to observe, Digby plucked at his voluminous sleeve and drew him forward. Later, after he had heard the two of them arguing while supposedly observing the mariners' evolutions, White good naturedly told them that Captain Faulkner had not only burnt several ships off The Nore under the eyes of the Commonwealth navy, but had so distinguished himself when a lieutenant in the *Prince Royal* that the late and sainted King Charles had given him a telescope. The royal largesse so imprinted itself upon the impressionable minds of the two young men that thereafter they treated their commander with a respect tainted only by the misgivings over his birth. Had they known the truth of that they might not have been so eager to serve under Captain Faulkner, but it had been intimated to them that, having missed Prince Rupert's departure, they might find favour with the King by serving under the only Royalist naval officer operating out of Helvoetsluys. Besides, the cost of their messing and accommodation, in falling upon the helpless Faulkner, did not fall upon the King.

Happily for all concerned aboard the *Phoenix*, the two were so soon prostrated by seasickness that all thoughts of aristocratic privilege were eroded by the ill-concealed amusement of the common seamen. Not that the weather at that season in the North Sea was bad, but the sea conditions, under a fresh and helpful south-westerly breeze, were lively enough to cause *Phoenix* to dance a lively dido as Faulkner took her north under Dutch colours, having given the slip to the two of Moulton's frigates he had left on the lookout by leaving at the dead of night. Faulkner had no intention of advertising his presence until he was far from his bolt-hole in the Haringvliet and it was three weeks before he took his first prize.

Towards the end of July the *Phoenix* had reached the latitude of Fair Isle and here, early one morning of light airs and fitful mist, they fell in with a homeward-bound whaler. The *Amity* of Hull was one of the few English whalers still working the Spitsbergen ground, the trade having been falling off prior to the Civil War, which, of itself, effectively killed what remained. Captain Norris, being a Yorkshireman, held firm in his belief that money might be made where others feared to go. Despite the usual presence of the industrious Dutch, which he left well alone, Norris stretched eastwards towards Kvitøya to where – unusually for so early in the season – he found open water and the feeding bowhead whales. In three short weeks he and his men had rapidly filled the *Amity*'s hogsheads with blubber. Norris landed the Shetlanders, of which his harpooners and most of his crew were recruited for reasons of fiscal prudence, and was soon heading south with only a handful of Hull men to sail the *Amity*. On the morning of his capture Norris was actually in his cabin calculating the possibility of making a second foray into Arctic waters before the end of the season. Considering this worth the effort he poured himself a glass of rum and sat in self-congratulation. An hour later he was a prisoner, the *Amity* of Hull was a prize and all Captain Norris' self-satisfaction had evaporated.

It would be weeks before anyone considered the *Amity* missing, whaling being such a speculative business and the season so little advanced, that Faulkner decided to continue north, taking two London vessels off the Lofoten Islands, both outbound for Archangel. Both were richly laden and he estimated the damage done to the Muscovy Company by their loss to be upwards of £2,000. Three days later he took a small Dundee ketch also heading for the Gourlo and the White Sea beyond. Holding his course to the north he lay off the North Cape of Norway in expectation of a further outward-bound ship or two, but was rewarded instead by taking a large timber-laden ship, also under charter to the Muscovy Company, which had been nipped in the ice before she could escape the previous winter.

They say a man makes his own luck and thus far Faulkner's provision of extra men to act in the event of success as prize-crews had paid off. The only clouds on his horizon in those high latitudes were his two cavalier officers whose desire to

fight the King's enemies was assuaged by this succession of easy
capture of under-manned merchantmen. Indeed, the ease with
which the unsuspecting vessels fell into their hands, added to
the brilliance of the weather, made the whole affair look so
like child's play that they began to murmur. They had, of
course, overcome their seasickness and were anxious to prove
themselves and Faulkner, aware of their chafing, had threatened
to send them away as prize-masters. This suggestion they
embraced with enthusiasm until he sardonically told them they
needed some knowledge of navigation to reach the Haringvliet
and must not, under any circumstances, let their charge be
recaptured unless they wanted to hang as pirates. Sobered, they
enthusiastically directed the guns when a few shots were thrown
at the approaching ships, forcing them to lower their colours.

By August the *Phoenix* was headed south. Most of the
Dutchmen and the English ragamuffins had been sent away in
prizes, the former in charge of them as masters under their
own ensign, and Faulkner was making his way south, intending
to fall upon the coastal trade between the Tyne and the Thames.
They made their landfall off Flamborough Head and within
hours had taken six collier-brigs all sailing in company. Faulkner
had sent off Lazenby as prize-commodore, with orders to keep
his little flock together for fear of losing any of them. That
evening White came to him with the muster-list.

'Given our run of luck it pains me to say it, sir,' he said,
'but another prize will leave us damnably short-handed.'

He had hardly uttered these words, indeed Faulkner was in
the very act of pouring out a glass so that the two of them
could discuss matters, when Hervey burst into the cabin.

'Captain Faulkner, a ship is coming up from the south-east.
The quartermaster advises me that she looks like a man-of-war!'

Faulkner and White exchanged glances and put down their
wine. 'Damnation!' White expostulated. 'And us with our men
all away in prizes.'

'A bold front. Hervey, you and Digby into seamen's clothes.'

'*What?*'

'Do as you're told. Mr White, English colours. Pass word
to the men that we are a merchantman.' He turned to his
satchel, searching for the papers of the ice-nipped vessel. 'The

Nancy of London and we have spent a weary winter in the ice. What news is there of the war . . . you can guess the rest.'

'Aye, sir,' White responded, his eyes aglow with admiration at Faulkner's quick-witted resource.

'And Mr White!'

'Sir?'

'Make sure those two popinjays understand.'

White grinned and was gone.

Faulkner made some swift dispositions in the cabin. He hid the papers of the other captures and congratulated himself on having the *Phoenix*'s name removed from her transom whilst she was in dock. It would not fool an intelligent observer who gave the matter some thought, but it might buy them time. At the last minute he remembered to stow his armour, sword and pistols away in his chest and then, casting a last look round his cabin, he went on deck.

It was a man-of-war, all right, and a big ship of forty or fifty guns. Faulkner needed only a glance to tell him that. It was more important that he had his own ship in order. He cast his eyes about the deck and aloft. The men were idling, White having clearly passed word of the intended deception among them. White himself was casually staring at the approaching man-of-war through his battered glass. At the peak the red ensign of England jerked at its halliards in the breeze. The watch tended the wheel and lookout; only Digby and Hervey looked out of place.

'You two,' he snapped, 'aloft and overhaul the main topsail buntlines. Stay up there until I call you down.' The two looked aloft, at each other and then at Faulkner. He swore then, seeing the junior seaman, a lad of no more than fifteen summers, coiling down a rope. He called his name.

'Jackson!'

The lad looked up, startled, wondering what he had done to catch the captain's attention. 'Sir?' he answered, his eyes wide.

'Take the young gentlemen aloft, Jackson, and show them how to overhaul buntlines. Mind you tell 'em why we do it too!' The lad was bright, and caught the captain's meaning. He grinned widely at the enormity of the trust vested in him and, seeing the two foppish youths in what they thought passed for seamen's clothing, fell in with the charade.

'Get them shoon off, m'lads and follow me oop the wind'ard rigging.' There was a moment of inactivity and then, aware that just for a moment all eyes had forgotten the approaching vessel but were laid upon their collective discomfiture, they complied. They had hardly got up on the starboard rail before the boom of a distant gun turned Faulkner's attention to their predicament.

'Clew up the courses!' Faulkner roared. 'Hands to the main-braces! Back the main topsail!' That would shake the young gentlemen as they made their unsteady way aloft in the wake of the monkey Jackson now was as he led them upwards.

'Rise tacks and sheets!' White called the supplementary order as Faulkner himself quietly gave the helmsman an instruction as the men ran to the pin-rails and belaying pins. The large lower fore and main courses were drawn up like a milkmaid's skirts, the yards on the mainmast creaked in their greased parrels and swung to bring the wind on the forward surface of the main topsail and main topgallant. In consequence, *Phoenix* ceased her onward rush and jibbed to a standstill, her bowsprit bobbing up and down as she drifted slowly to leeward.

Faulkner stared at the man-of-war and thought he knew her, though he could not yet see her name. She too hove-to and a few moments later a boat, its oarsmen toiling at their looms, was dancing across the sparkling sea towards them.

'Oh for a thick North Sea pea-souper,' White muttered beside him, 'and we might have got away with it.'

'Hold your tongue, Mr. My name is Bavistock and I command the *Nancy* of London. Go and meet the officer in the boat and pass the word.'

White moved off without a word, but his face bore a grimace that might have been a smile had not their situation been otherwise.

A moment later and a young officer in a plain buff-leather jerkin, a small round hat and a crimson sash of rank girt about him, threw a booted leg over the *Phoenix*'s rail. White brought him aft and introduced 'Cap'n Bavistock'.

'Good day, Lieutenant,' Faulkner said pleasantly. 'Is that the *Unicorn* yonder?'

'Er, yes, it is.'

'I thought so, didn't I say so, Mr?' he said to White, not waiting for a response before continuing to the Commonwealth officer, 'Come, sir, I imagine you wish to see my papers.' He began walking towards the cabin under the poop, drawing the lieutenant after him, throwing a conversational remark over his shoulder. 'We half expected to be stuck in that damned ice forever and a Russian winter is not to be recommended . . .'

In the cabin he went straight to his satchel and drew out the *Nancy*'s papers. 'A glass of wine while you . . .?'

The lieutenant held up his hand. 'Thank you, no.'

Faulkner restored the stopper in the neck of the decanter, affecting a certain discomfiture. 'I beg your pardon, Lieutenant, I should not have offered and, had we not come to rely upon it in the ice, it should not have become habitual.'

'Quite so, Captain . . .' The lieutenant was looking at the *Nancy*'s manifest; the most dangerous moment was upon Faulkner for he had no cargo of timber to show a curious stranger.

'What news is there?' he asked.

'Mmm?' the other responded abstractedly.

'What news? We have heard nothing, being stuck in the ice.'

The lieutenant looked up. 'You know the King was tried and executed?' he remarked, his interest diverted from the papers, distracted to see the effect this intelligence had on a man whose ignorance of so momentous an event was a curiosity in itself.

'The devil, I did not!' Faulkner blew through his lips and shook his head. 'Well, well, that is marvellous. So, the tyrant is dead! Ha! I lost a son under Essex at Edgehill. Good riddance! When did the Malignant meet his end?' To his intense relief the officer lowered the *Nancy*'s papers.

'He was beheaded in Whitehall on thirtieth January last. The Parliament governs a quiet country as a Commonwealth in which godly men may prosper.'

'Heaven grant that,' Faulkner said piously. ''Tis difficult enough at sea without a war of bloody faction.'

'Ah, yes. Well, there we may have trouble for there are Royalist ships at sea.'

Faulkner frowned. 'Royalist ships? How so?' he queried.

'The Dutch have given them sanctuary under Rupert of the Rhine. We have had word of them . . .' he finished rather lamely. It was impossible, Faulkner calculated, that news of his spate of seizures off Flamborough Head should have reached London and the *Unicorn* sent so rapidly in quest of them. Unless, that is, they had been seen from Flamborough itself and, he recollected, there had been fishermen about, bobbing in their cobles. Even so, the news could not have travelled that fast – unless pigeons were in wider use than he supposed. The thought, incredible though it was, turned a worm of anxiety in his guts.

He shrugged. 'We have seen nothing untoward,' he said, looking the lieutenant straight in the eye. The man held his gaze for longer than Faulkner liked. 'Something troubles you, sir,' he observed, his heart thumping in his breast.

'Yes. For a vessel fast in the ice, you are uncommonly well payed and oiled.'

Faulkner forced a laugh. 'Good heavens, Lieutenant,' he said, 'd'you think I would venture a laden voyage after a winter nipped by floes without putting the old *Nancy* in dock? A Russian dock is not to be had for the same price as one in the River of Thames, thank you, but English gold still commands in Muscovy. As for her upperworks, the minute we saw the sun and the wood was dry enough, my mate and I reckoned the men had had enough time to themselves! By heavens, I'd not have idle Jack about me, he always gets into trouble and trouble in Muscovy is treble the anxiety at home, Civil War or not. D'you know when I was first in the Company's service—'

'Thank you, Captain, I regret my own time is at the disposal of others. I must return and report to Captain Harris. Good voyage.'

'And a good cruise to you, sir,' Faulkner added as he followed the lieutenant out on deck where it struck him that a false or revealing remark by one of his own men might undo all that he hoped he had accomplished. But a glance at White, leaning over the rail and occupying the *Unicorn*'s boat's crew in idle conversation reassured him. White would not have suffered any of their own men to interfere.

The two stood together for a moment as the boat pulled away from the ship's side. The silence between them was eloquent: the deception appeared to have worked. Unless, of course, they came under a withering broadside the moment the lieutenant reached his own quarterdeck.

'He didn't ask to see the cargo, then?' White muttered.

'No, thank God. Now, let's get underway.'

'Mainbraces!' White called to the waiting men and, looking aloft, bellowed, 'Haven't you lubbers finished up there yet. Get a move on, or I'll take a rope's end to your pink arses!' And so the *Phoenix*'s men went to their stations laughing at the discomfiture of two cavalier gentlemen aloft, while their hunters returned to King Charles's old *Unicorn*, now flying the cross-and-harp colours of the Commonwealth. Half an hour later the two ships were almost hull-down from each other. There had been no withering broadside and after dark Faulkner gave orders to head for the Haringvliet.

Affairs of the Head and Heart

Autumn 1649

The *Phoenix's* success had preceded her, increasing as every prize arrived at Helvoetsluys where, with none too fine a regard for the law − a circumstance which in itself was to compound the *casus belli* that caused a war between the English and the Dutch Republics three years later − they were turned into ready money. For the time being the circumstances of the losses remained unknown in London, where most were underwritten or where their ventures had been capitalized. Only when the crews were let go, to dribble back home according to their initiative and resources, was Faulkner's name associated with yet another assault on the pockets of London's merchants.

Although Faulkner's triumph further imperilled and delayed Mainwaring's intended return to his native land, he was nonetheless not displeased at his protégé's success. Indeed, he concluded, though nurturing designs of his own which included Faulkner, that Faulkner's second cruise, though frustrating for the martial Hervey and Digby, had been of benefit to several. Besides topping up the Royalist coffers, His Majesty having rapidly approved the disposals as legitimate prize whatever the sober crop-heads and their bewigged attorneys in London might say about the matter, they also brought relief to his own stretched purse. As admiral, howsoever nominal the task, Mainwaring was − like Faulkner and his men, each in due proportion − entitled to a share of the prize money. Such a consideration, far from securing his sense of obligation to His Majesty, brought a very private consolation to Sir Henry Mainwaring. As for the King, he was so delighted with Faulkner's cruise that he summoned him to an audience, the news of which was brought by Mainwaring himself.

'I am charged to command you to accompany me and to

attend the King in person with Mistress Villiers and Lieutenants Hervey and Digby tomorrow at noon. You had better array yourself in your best finery, Kit. You too, Kate, for I am convinced this encounter with the King shall be of some significance.'

Faulkner looked up from his ledger where he was making up his accounts. 'What significance?' he scoffed, recalling Mainwaring's assurances months ago when he had returned from his raid on The Nore, that the King intended summoning him. Faulkner was learning not to put too much trust in such vague implications.

'Why,' Mainwaring waved his hand airily, 'some mark of the Royal favour, I don't doubt.'

'Oh, Kit, this might mean . . .' began Katherine, her eyes shining.

'I have been here three weeks,' he said sourly, 'during which His Majesty has not seen fit to send any indication of his approbation even though he has been enriched to the extent of –' he looked down at his books – 'some seven and a quarter thousand pounds.'

Mainwaring winked at Katherine and dismissed the matter. 'We shall see,' he said, 'we shall see.'

The morning in question came with heavy rain driven by a strong westerly gale and the little party arrived at the King's lodgings wet and dishevelled. Running repairs were effected in an antechamber before they announced their arrival and were summoned to the presence.

Faulkner, in a fractious temper, had seen the young King intermittently since his arrival in The Netherlands. On only one of these occasions had the King spoken to him, so he found the young man different from the boy he had taught to sail off the Isles of Scilly. Though the subsequent passage of time had not been great, much had happened in the young man's life, not least his assumption of his executed father's claim to the throne and the opening of diplomatic negotiations with any court in Europe that would entertain them. The change in Charles was subtle, something in his bearing and the decisive manner in which he spoke. Whatever it was, it commanded

Faulkner's instant respect. Unlike his nervous and vacillating father he seemed at ease, even in the extremity of exile; or perhaps because of it, Faulkner thought as he footed his bow and uncovered his head with Katherine curtseying at his side. As he cast his eyes down he noticed that the hem of Kate's dress was not only soiled and damp, but ragged with poverty. Hervey and Digby, their boots creaking, swept their feathered headgear to the floor.

'You have excelled yourself, Captain, and I congratulate you upon your recent cruise. I consider it something of a phenomenon.'

'Your Majesty is most kind.' Faulkner was conscious that this was the man who had toyed with his mistress, yet – almost against his will – he found himself placated by the pleasing condescension, at least to the extent of soothing his temper.

'Tell me, sir,' the King went on easily, 'how exactly you bluffed the *Unicorn*.' Faulkner did as he was bid with as much bluff modesty as he thought became him. 'And what of these two?' The King indicated Hervey and Digby.

'They will make good sea officers in time, sir . . .'

'But not yet?'

'Not yet, sir. I do not impugn their courage or character, but, as Your Majesty well knows, the conduct of ships, especially ships-of-war, requires certain skills.'

'Ah, the arts and mysteries of navigation, cunning and seamanship,' the King remarked, looking at the two young men. 'You would do well to attend to Captain Faulkner, gentlemen, he is well versed in these arts. He was my first instructor in the business of handling a vessel in a seaway.' Sensing there was even more to Faulkner than they had as yet been informed of, the two murmured their eagerness to place themselves entirely at the good captain's every whim. 'And what did you two do when the *Unicorn* boarded you?'

'We were aloft, Your Majesty,' Hervey said with a quick opportunism and some indignation, 'dressed and acting as common seamen.'

If Hervey had sought at least the King's sympathy, he miscalculated. 'A right and proper place for a King's officer to learn his business,' Charles said dismissively, turning his attention to

Katherine. 'Now, Mistress Villiers, I see having your Perseus home has cloven your chains and you are as handsome as ever. You are a fortunate man, Captain Faulkner, but it would be better if you were married.'

Astonished at the turn of the King's conversation, Faulkner flushed, unaware of where the King's discourse was leading, though his gentlemen-in-waiting were all smirking as the King went on.

'Of course we all live in unusual circumstances but I can . . .' The King paused, reaching out his right hand behind him. Faulkner, his eyes remaining lowered, heard the rasp of sword blade on scabbard rim and caught the dull gleam of light on steel. A moment later the long blade wavered before him.

'Come, Captain, on your knees if you please.' Only half comprehending what was happening Faulkner obeyed. 'That's well . . . I can dub thee knight but cannot thereby make Mistress Villiers Lady Faulkner – at least, not until . . . but no matter.' Faulkner felt the blade pressed upon each shoulder, stirring his hair as the King passed it over his head from one to the other. 'Now, rise, Sir Christopher. Or shall you be Sir Kit?' The King handed the sword back to his gentleman-in-waiting as Faulkner rose. 'Well, sir,' the King went on, waving Mainwaring forward. 'Sir Henry has orders for your next foray for which I wish you good fortune. You are making our name feared again, just as my cousin does in Ireland.'

'But it is a trap!' Faulkner said furiously. 'And I am damnably cozened by it, by Jupiter!'

'For heaven's sake, Kit,' began Katherine, rolling her eyes at Mainwaring. Faulkner saw the communication between them.

'You two knew of all this, didn't you?' His tone was outraged. 'Why, you had a hand in it! This is infamous! I am dubbed knight one day and sent to my slaughter the next.'

'Oh that is preposterous, Kit, quite preposterous!' Mainwaring said, angering. 'You are growing too big—'

'What? For my boots? God damn it, don't you see what he has done? He has obliged me, just as he obliged me to feed those two young bloods! God, the House of Stuart does not lack cunning. And I thought him a better man than his father . . .'

'What is it that so disturbs you, Kit?' a puzzled Katherine enquired. 'He does you great honour.'

Faulkner looked at her as though stunned. 'What? You don't see it? You would rather have me dead Sir Christopher than good old plain and living Kit? Yesterday you were weeping at my departure, now you speak eagerly of honour!'

'I don't understand . . .'

'He sends me into the Thames under orders so precise that I have no hope of commanding my fate. And in mine own ship too! A ship I put at his disposal.' Anger and outrage robbed him of further words and he bit at his own crooked index finger with such fury that it drew blood.

'I think you grossly overestimate the risk, Kit,' Mainwaring said. 'Why, His Majesty requires only that you repeat your success off The Nore arguing, quite logically, that you cannot yet repeat the success of your cruise to the northwards.'

'The enemy knows that I am back in The Hague; the place is full of spies,' Faulkner said with contempt but calming himself with an effort to match Mainwaring's argument with his own. 'If this is your stratagem, Sir Henry, then I deplore it and admit I am too big for my boots. Moreover, I have little doubt but that word is already on its way to London that another attempt is going to be made on the Thames and Medway.' He looked at Mainwaring, a sudden suspicion entering his mind and growing in an instant with the certainty of conviction. 'If this plan is so easy to undertake, Sir Henry,' he said, fixing the old man with his gaze, 'would you not condescend in hoisting your flag and accompanying me as the King's admiral?'

'I have every intention of so doing, Sir Christopher,' Mainwaring said archly, steadily meeting his interlocutor's eyes. Faulkner nodded. 'I divine your purpose,' he said, shooting a look at Katherine who was none the wiser. Mainwaring intended to carry Faulkner, the *Phoenix* and all her people into the hands of the enemy and make his compact with them.

Faulkner lay that night beside the sleeping Katherine, his thoughts in turmoil. He felt torn in his loyalty to Mainwaring, unable to understand the imperative that was driving the old man. Faulkner had supposed Mainwaring had no roots in

England, and misunderstood the other's complex intellect and the compulsions of a man of Mainwaring's subtle character. He himself had sundered his present from his past, retaining the cunning and opportunism that had kept him alive as a child in the gutters of Bristol along with his clear vision of what he conceived as right from wrong. It was indeed true that he owed Mainwaring a great deal, but he had himself accomplished much by his own efforts. Now he felt betrayed; Mainwaring wanted to play on his obligation and compel Faulkner to facilitate his own return to a welcome Faulkner guessed Mainwaring had secretly arranged.

But the implications of Mainwaring's plan were compounded by other complexities. What could be his motive in going over to the Commonwealth with his flag flying in the *Phoenix* other than to betray Faulkner and all his people, to hand over the last Royalist ship in these home waters capable of dealing an effective blow against the trade of England? It was not credible that he, Faulkner, could make such a compact as Mainwaring had, presumably, made provision for. Faulkner was a wanted man and they would make an example of him; what was more he would be seen of by both sides as a gullible dupe, fooled by the old man who had been pirate, courtier, admiral and Judas!

Faulkner had no friends in England. He could scarce revive his association with Nathan Gooding who had been not merely his former business partner but his brother-in-law, any more than he could claim assistance from Judith herself. She would be so steeped in her Puritan victory that she would never forgive him sufficiently to save him from the noose she would conceive he deserved.

And what of Kate stirring beside him? To fall in — even blindly — with Mainwaring meant her abandonment. And that in turn would drive her directly into the arms of the King. The thought brought him wide-awake. He lay for a moment thinking fast and then, having rapidly come to a conclusion, he slipped out of bed. Waiting to ensure Kate remained fast asleep, he then left the room, crossed the landing and, without knocking, entered Mainwaring's chamber.

The room was close and stank of the old man's breath. 'Sir

Henry,' Faulkner said in a low voice, shaking the old man so that he started awake and sat bolt upright in bed.

'What the devil! Is that you, Kit?'

'Be quiet. I would talk with you. You mean to defect by carrying yourself into the Thames in the *Phoenix*, with me and my people as an earnest of your good faith and reformation,' Faulkner hissed, his voice low but strident with passion.

'Yes, but you do not—'

'Do not, I beg you, tell me that I do not understand. On the contrary, I understand you all too well and I am reluctant to be hanged as a pirate on the evidence of another such.'

'You think I would do that?' Mainwaring's tone was outraged. 'After all I have done for you, you think that I would thus throw you away?'

'What else?'

'You, among the finest of sea officers, would be of great value to the Commonwealth. You think that you have risen far, to a trumpery knighthood . . .'

'I think nothing of my knighthood.'

'Ah, but Kate does.'

'Ah, yes, Kate. And what use is my knighthood to Kate? I cannot marry her; the King said as much. He received her out of his own desire because her curtsey afforded him a good view of her bubs. And what of Kate? Where does she come into this complex intrigue of yours? Shall she bob her hair and sign on as my boy? Perhaps you would have me turn pretended sodomite like the great Buckingham himself that I might smuggle her in as my bawd in breeches?'

'Don't be a fool, Kit! D'you think that I have not thought of her? Why, I am as fond of her as of you – fonder perhaps, if only because she has better manners. She shall remain here; we have, thanks to you and Providence, sufficient money to maintain her. Then, when we have made our compositions, we shall fetch her over.'

'Does she know anything of all this?'

'No, of course not.'

Faulkner fell silent for a few moments and Mainwaring left him to his thoughts. Then he said, shaking his head in the darkness, 'No, it will not do.'

'Think about it, Kit. The King's cause is doomed. I did not think that they would cut His Late Majesty's head off but having done it there is no turning back. England will not die like even the young Charles will do sooner or later, as we all must. England is a rock, her people stolid. They are reaping the advantages of their new order. See how the Dutch have prospered since they threw off the yoke of Papist Spain. Why, one can scarce believe it: the riches of Madrid in every burgher's chamber. Likewise England will do well, believe me.'

'You are no necromancer; you can see the future no more than any other man,' Faulkner said, adding sarcastically, 'You only believe you can, thanks to your earlier composition with King James.'

'That is as untrue as it is unkind, Kit,' Mainwaring responded.

'Be that as it may, it shall not fall out as you wish.' Faulkner drew away and without heeding any more of the old man's argument he withdrew.

Back in his own room he gently shook Katherine. She woke confused from a deep sleep. 'Hush, my love, but I must be away tonight. I would have you remain quiet here. Expect me back in ten days, if God wills it, and I will yet make you a duchess.'

'But . . . Why the sudden departure?'

He put his finger to her lips and she grasped his wrist tightly. 'I am in dispute with Sir Henry,' he whispered, 'the details of which need not concern you but are of importance to us both in the long run. If I am to obey the King, I must move with great speed. If I am successful then much may flow in consequence.'

'If not?' she breathed.

'Let us not consider that.' He paused, gathering his clothes and cramming his portmanteau. Thank heaven he travelled light from Helvoetsluys and habitually left most of his effects aboard the *Phoenix*. Having completed his preparations as far as he could, he bent over her. She was weeping.

'Will this business of separation never end?'

'Soon,' he said, kissing her. 'Soon, by God, it must.'

Outside he waited in silence before trying the door of Mainwaring's chamber. From inside came the snuffling of an old man fast asleep. 'Incredible!' he breathed to himself. Then, his boots in one hand, his portmanteau in the other, he descended the stairs.

'Spithead,' he said to White and Lazenby. 'We can carry the tide westwards, strike at any shipping off Portsmouth under cover of night and escape by way of the Solent.'

'What if the wind is westerly?' White asked.

'We drop through St Helen's Roads and double the Wight by way of St Catherine's Point. Either way we retreat west, the inference being we are one of Rupert's raiders.' Faulkner looked up at the two men. 'Are you game? For I'll have none here that aren't.'

'I'm game,' said Lazenby. White nodded.

'Then roust the men out of their whores' beds, I would leave before noon.'

'Why the hurry?'

'Because there are spies in The Hague would betray the orders the King thinks he has given me.'

'Do you not act at some risk, Sir Christopher,' White asked with punctilious regard for Faulkner's change of status, 'in disobeying the King?'

Faulkner looked up at White, seeking some superciliousness in his expression. Instead he found the man's concern moving. 'If I read the King like I read other men, and I confess that may not be possible, but, if I do, then His Majesty will be pleased with such success as we bring His Majesty's arms. He would have me strike at London's trade at The Nore.'

'What? Again, and so soon?'

'Just so. Instead we shall strike at the heart of the enemy's naval power: at Portsmouth.'

It was a bold plan, and with Rupert active in the Irish Sea and drawing some of the Commonwealth forces to the west, stood fair to succeed. The *Phoenix* avoided Moulton's single frigate whose captain, with only a single ship to blockade but well supplied with spies' information as to when the *Phoenix* was preparing for sea, failed to take his task seriously. By winkling his men out of their beds and leaving with all haste, Faulkner compromised his endurance, having only stores for nineteen days on board, but he proposed to be no longer than ten, if he was to keep his word to Kate.

Whatever he might have neglected in his haste to be away before either the King or Mainwaring realized he had gone, he had not neglected his preparations. It was a strong tide that carried the *Phoenix* down the French coast, well clear of The Downs so that she passed through innumerable fleets of French fishermen as Faulkner followed their littoral. Not crossing the Channel until nightfall would find the tide about to ebb to the west after he had passed the Nab. Again they pitched short-fused shells into two small men–of–war lying at St Helen's but, finding nothing anchored at Spithead beyond a hoy, Faulkner's run of luck began to falter. At three in the morning the wind fell light and the *Phoenix* drifted on the tide, passing the Mother Bank and approaching Cowes with but bare steerage way.

Arguing that the three or four hoys, bilanders and ketches lying off the Wight's major port were not worth cutting out and eager not to be caught within the Solent at daylight, Faulkner held what course they could make for the western entrance, off the Needles. It was therefore almost daylight when they passed the guns at Hurst Castle without disturbing the garrison and had, by providential grace, passed the narrows off the ragged chalk stumps of the Needles themselves, out into deeper water.

With the dawn coming up astern of them they only saw the approaching ship at three miles' distance, emerging from a light mist caused by the lack of wind. She was heading for the Needles passage where, by the time she made it, the tide would be slack and then turning in her favour.

Despite the dispiriting calm, when summoned, the men ran to their stations willingly enough, encouraged by White's assertion that the strange vessel was almost certainly a merchantman. Not only that, she bore with her the bones of a breeze which, White assured all within earshot, would soon 'fill in and they'd have the to'gallant yards on the caps afore noon'.

The news that a potential prize was bearing down upon them put them all on their mettle. Faulkner had had an anxious night of it and had to admit to a sense of disappointment that his stratagem, though fulfilled in one sense, had conspicuously failed in another. Although two men–of–war ketches afire was a feather in his cap, the little victory came with no money and money was the thing to please the King as much as his own creditors. The prospect of a prize was therefore welcomed by all.

Faulkner passed word for his sword and baldric. There was no time to don a cuirass; besides, he did not think he would need it.

'They'll have seen us,' Lazenby remarked to no one in particular and stating the obvious, but those aboard the on–coming vessel seemed unafraid that the *Phoenix* might prove hostile. Unfortunately none of the growing breeze that bore her along as yet filled the *Phoenix*'s sails, even though her helm was hard over and her yards braced to avoid it taking them aback. Faulkner impatiently paced the deck, pausing every so often to stare at the oncoming vessel, then stare aloft at the slack and slatting sails before crossing the deck, staring at the compass and glaring at the helmsman as though that unfortunate could remedy his plight.

The stranger came closer and closer. 'We'll miss her by Jupiter!' he hissed furiously.

'Sir, might I suggest . . .' White began, but Faulkner was one jump ahead of him.

'Square the yards!' he snapped and the parrells groaned and the blocks clicked as the yards came round, making a right angle with the ship's centre–line. 'Lie low you gunners, but all to the starboard battery and blow on your linstocks,' he called in a low voice to Lazenby at the guns in the waist. 'And you there,' he instructed the topmen, his voice still muted, 'keep below the rail, but stand by, ready to brace up on the larboard tack. D'you understand, bosun?'

'Larboard tack, yar, yar, sir,' the big Dutchman replied and not for the first time Faulkner congratulated himself on engaging so fine a sailor.

Faulkner turned to White and addressed him with a quick instruction, following which the first lieutenant, who grasped exactly what Faulkner intended, went and stood by the helmsman.

'We'll be caught aback,' whispered one of the guns' crew.

'Aye, and that varmint'll smoke us,' one of his mates added, but Lazenby also divined his commander's stratagem.

'Silence there,' he said in a low voice. 'You watch us put in a stern-board and . . .'

The stranger was therefore almost abeam and Faulkner had hoisted himself in the mizzen rigging, hat in hand to hail the incoming ship in a friendly manner when first the topgallants and then the *Phoenix*'s topsails were caught aback.

'Ahoy there!' he called, and then in mock fury he swung round and shouted, 'What the hell! We're caught aback!' The slap of the canvas against the masts made the ship shudder and Faulkner jumped down on the deck as though about to belabour someone on deck and the helmsman, convinced that he was about to be assaulted, was only steadied by White's curt orders. Faintly over the water they could hear the watch on the strange ship laughing at their discomfiture as they began to move astern.

'Helm over now!' hissed Faulkner, watching as the *Phoenix*'s head swung to starboard as White ordered the rudder put to larboard. Aloft the sails began to shiver and in the waist Lazenby took a look over the rail and passed word to his gun crews.

'Haul all!' Faulkner ordered in a voice loud enough to suggest the most routine of orders. The stranger was no longer approaching their beam; the alteration of the ship's head had brought her round, broad on the *Phoenix*'s starboard bow as she began to gather headway.

'Stand by, Mr Lazenby,' Faulkner said with almost casual disinterest, looking across the diminishing gap of ruffled water that separated the two ships and waiting for the suspicion to dawn on the other that all was not quite what it seemed. For a moment or two nothing happened and then an officer clambered up into the other's mizzen rigging and hailed them.

'Ahoy there! What ship?'

Faulkner waved his hat. 'The *Nancy* of London, Captain Bavistock!' he shouted. There was a flurry of activity and, in the first of the day's sunlight coming over the Isle of Wight, he caught the flash of a telescope glass. Then, with the chuckle of water growing louder alongside as the *Phoenix* heeled to the breeze and increased her speed, he quite distinctly heard someone say: 'That ain't the *Nancy*! She's in the Archangel trade!'

'Up helm, starboard two points, braces there . . .'

White and the bosun acknowledged their orders and the *Phoenix* turned further to starboard. It was clear now that her intention was to cross the stern of the stranger, clear that this was a hostile act and the reaction on the other vessel was courageous but too late. Unbeknownst to them until later, two men ran down into the cabin and, dashing the glass out of the stern windows, poked two loaded matchlocks out of them.

'Now, Lazenby! Fire!' Faulkner bellowed.

Both of the men died before they could aim their weapons. The rest of the stern glass was smashed in as the *Phoenix*'s starboard guns, emerging from their suddenly opened ports as their crews strained at the breechings, opened fire. The strange ship was viciously raked as they passed across her stern.

'Up helm! Lay us alongside!' Faulkner roared, lugging out his sword, as the *Phoenix* resumed her starboard swing and, in a moment or two, ranged up alongside her shattered quarry. In the waist, Lazenby's gunners were furiously reloading. 'D'you strike?' Faulkner bawled the summons. There was no reply and he was conscious that, as the tide turned, it and the wind would carry them on to either the Shingles Bank to the north-east, or the Needles rocks to the south-east. And if they passed safely between them without the present matter being settled, they would soon come under the guns of Hurst Castle a few miles further on. It was inconceivable that the gunfire had not been noticed from the castle's low ramparts.

'There'll be no quarter unless you strike at once!' he shouted. Then turning to his own men he shouted, 'Boarders make ready! Stand by, Mr Lazenby!'

'All ready, sir!' Lazenby replied.

'To whom do I strike?' a voice called.

'To Captain Faulkner of the King's Navy!'

'Captain Christopher Faulkner? Of the *Phoenix*?'

'The very same!' Faulkner suppressed the half-smile that appeared on his face, flattered by the realization that his name was known among his enemies.

'And what ship are you and who commands?'

'You are my father!' came the unexpected response. 'This is the *Judith* of London, Nathan Gooding, owner, and Nathaniel Faulkner commanding!'

Faulkner stood as though stunned, his entire crew staring at him.

'Lay off to starboard, Captain, and steer south,' bellowed White after a tremulous moment. 'You are our prize and I will board you when we lie two miles south of the Needles. Now haul your yards and mind you do as I say!' White turned to Faulkner. 'Are you all right, Sir Christopher?'

Faulkner had steadied himself at the rail and looked at White as a man come out of a fever. 'The *Judith* . . .' he murmured.

'Aye, of London. Your son is in command, I take it?'

'Apparently so.'

A Turn of the Cards

Father and son stood staring at each other in silence. The cabin seemed to Faulkner full of ghosts as well as the living presence of his offspring. The name of the captured ship – *Judith* – had struck him like a matchlock ball as much as the revelation that his son, young Nathaniel, named after his uncle and looking like his handsome, opinionated and headstrong mother, was in command of a ship. The whole thing seemed surreal, impossible, a coincidence of such gross proportions as to be unworthy of even Shakespeare, or Marlowe, and yet . . . and yet it was quite possible. He had left Gooding a thriving business, the possession of several ships and what made more sense than Nathaniel should be bred to them, command one for a few years before taking over the principal's place as Gooding grew long in years. And what more natural that they should be successful, and invest in new ships, and name one for Nathaniel's mother and Gooding's sister? Why, it may have been a consolation, to make her part-owner as she had been before, to put money in her purse as he – her husband – should have done, had it not been for the beguiling Mistress Villiers. And there was not much remarkable about their encounter, when one came to think of it: a successful shipping enterprise, a state of civil war at sea, and he a licensed pirate.

It was Nathaniel who broke the awful silence, precipitating Faulkner to fill two glasses and hand one to his son.

'My mother said you had been bewitched,' the young man said, shaking his head and refusing the proffered glass. 'Is it true?'

Faulkner swallowed a large draught and stared at his son as the two ships stood steadily over towards the French coast, the *Judith* under command of Lazenby and a prize-crew. Beneath their feet the *Phoenix*'s rudder stock groaned. He shook his head.

'No, I was not bewitched,' he said slowly. 'I do not expect you to understand.'

'I was a boy,' Nathaniel breathed in a low, emotional voice.

'What else did your mother say?'

'That you came from nothing and would become nothing and that I should forget you as she intended doing.'

'And has she?'

'She does not speak of you.'

'And yet you bear my name.'

'As does she. Besides, whatever my father is, I am no bastard.'

'And what *do* you think your father is?' Nathaniel hesitated. 'You knew me, knew of me and of this ship.'

'The whole of the Pool of London knows of you and your ship. That I do is not because I am your son but that I am a ship-master.'

'And yet you called me father.'

'To put a stop to your cannon. My men are but plain seamen and innocent; you, on the other hand, are drenched in blood.'

'As are those who decapitated a King.'

'A tyrant!'

'But a King, nonetheless.'

'That is a matter of no importance now. The people of England have dispensed with a King and find that the world still turns.'

'You have a ready tongue,' Faulkner said, refilling his glass. 'I'll say that for you, boy.'

'I am not your boy. It is my misfortune to be your son.'

'You have suffered from it?'

'What do you think?'

Faulkner shrugged. 'Ours is not the only family to be set at odds by civil strife.'

'But we were sundered by something more pernicious; we were set at odds by vice.'

Warmed by the wine, Faulkner was recovering from his shocked state. 'Be careful how you employ that ready wit of yours. What your mother poisoned you with was not necessarily the truth. Have you never been in love such that the mere thought of a particular woman turned your guts to water?'

Nathaniel drew himself up. 'Such a feeling I would ascribe to lust; as for love – I am married.'

'And have children?'

'Aye, a small son.' He hesitated, then asked, 'And have I bastard half-brothers and half-sisters?'

'No, you may tell your mother that God punished us thereby.'

'Shall I see my mother again?'

'If she lives.'

'She does, and is well.'

'Then I shall parole thee.'

'And my ship?'

Faulkner stared hard at his prisoner. 'That I cannot let go. She is mine since you surrendered her. That was a consequence of your action, or lack of it, as commander.'

The remark stung. 'I was tricked,' he responded indignantly.

'You were fooled.' Faulkner paused, seeing Nathaniel's discomfort. 'But 'tis not a thing to take too much to heart; 'tis but the fortune of war, a mere turn of the cards. But then, I don't expect you play cards if Judith raised you a Puritan – which I take to be the case from your refusal of wine.'

'I am proud of the fact and England is the better for it.'

'Perhaps.'

'What I find most extraordinary is that you think that any advantage can accrue to your cause, which is irrecoverably lost, by persisting in this war at sea. You cannot win it, Father, you must see that.' Nathaniel stopped abruptly, sensing he had assumed an intimacy that was at once importunate and unfounded.

Faulkner smiled. 'You are a fine young man, Nathaniel, and, while you may be ashamed to have me as your father, I am not so to have you my son.' He saw the other swallow hard and sniffed away his own sentiment. 'I am bound upon a course you cannot yet understand; perhaps one day you may. I should like to think so, whatever your mother says. I do not deny that I treated her badly any more than I can exculpate myself from any charge of neglect you level at me, though I left her means enough. Upon occasions we are caught up in stronger winds than we can resist.' He broke off for a moment then added, 'No matter now. You must be hungry. Will you take meat with me?'

The invitation was met with an indecisive silence before Nathaniel said, 'I must see to my men.'

'There is no need for that. You are my prisoner, alas. Now sit, and I shall summon meat and drink; will you take small beer for I do not commend the water?'

'And as your prisoner . . .?'

'You will give your parole not to do anything foolish. Do you agree?' The younger man nodded. 'And with what were you laden? Come, your manifest?'

'Very little. We are on a state charter as a storeship to the naval squadron in the West Country and were returning to Portsmouth.'

'I see. And what . . .' Faulkner got no further for the cabin door opened and White's head poked round it, his expression one of extreme agitation as he shot a look at the stranger in Faulkner's cabin. 'Yes, Mr White?' White hesitated and required a brusque prompt from Faulkner. 'Come, sir, what is it?'

'A man-of-war, sir. A large one, coming up from the west-ward hand-over-fist.'

'That will be the *Resolution*,' Nathaniel remarked coolly, 'of sixty-four guns.'

White whistled.

'Moulton's flagship?' Faulkner enquired and the younger man nodded. 'Captain Richard Blyth commands.'

'I'll be up, directly,' Faulkner said to White. He then turned to his son. 'You may sit here quietly, or come on deck if you desire it.'

'I shall stay here, Father; I have no wish to see your final humiliation.'

On deck Faulkner discovered that White was cramming on sail and had hailed Lazenby to follow suit in the *Judith*, but one glance to windward showed Faulkner that they were unlikely to outrun the powerful man-of-war as she bore down directly for them.

'She cannot have been ten miles astern of the prize,' White remarked.

'We'll make a chase of it,' Faulkner said, wondering whether he should jettison his precious – and expensive – cannon to lighten the *Phoenix* and give her half a chance.

White must have divined something of his indecision as he remarked, 'I doubt the prize will escape, even if we do.'

'No, God damn it.'

'And the wind's freshening from the westward all the time.'

'I know.' Faulkner looked aloft. White was too good a seaman not to have set every sail to maximum advantage. 'Set up extra backstays; that at least will allow us to carry a press for longer.'

'Aye, aye.' White went off to do as he was bid and Faulkner raised his glass and studied his pursuer. He felt uncharacteristically empty of energy, like a half-filled pig's bladder with which apprentices played at football. The presence of Nathaniel below brought home the ambiguities of his life and all sense of resolution seemed to have deserted him. He felt the warmth of the sun on the deck through the worn soles of his shoes; the sunlight sparkled on the sea creating a brilliant contrast with the darker clouds massing to the westwards. The roiling of the wake as the *Phoenix* forged ahead, rising and falling in her headlong rush, but there, her bright work and gilding twinkling in the sunshine, her sails taught and drawing, her whole array made splendid against that looming bank of cloud, came his nemesis – of that he was suddenly certain.

Already the *Judith*, a slower vessel than the *Phoenix*, was falling astern and there he would have to leave her, allowing Lazenby and his men to fall into enemy hands. The very thought seemed to dull him, as though he should not abandon his men, that to do so would be an evil he could not bear.

'Mr White!'

'Sir?'

'Send the men to their quarters. I'm damned if I'll abandon Lazenby. I mean to fight.'

'To fight? Very well.'

As soon as the men were at their battle stations, Faulkner put up his helm and shortened sail.

'Rise tacks and sheets! Clew up to'gallants!'

The *Phoenix* slowed and then, upon Faulkner's orders, turned to slew across the *Judith*'s stern whereupon Faulkner hailed

Lazenby. 'God's speed! Make for Helvoetsluys! I'll try and buy you an hour or two, until nightfall if God wills it!'

'God save the King!' Lazenby called back, his voice faint, but his waving hat evidence of his spirit and relief.

'What do you intend to do, sir?' White asked, then added, 'The men may not—'

'I know the temper of the men.'

'She's a ship of force, sir. Sixty-four heavy cannon; more than our match.'

'If we last till night falls, I'll run under cover of darkness. Tell the men that.'

'That's long odds, Sir Christopher.'

'Be so kind as to do as I say.'

White went forward without a word. Faulkner watched him going from gun to gun and then addressing the topmen standing by to work the ship. He noted a few of them took the information calmly; others showed so obvious a reluctance, staring aft with hostile glares, that Faulkner turned away, raised his glass and made to study the Commonwealth man-of-war.

She was little more than two miles distant now, stretching out to range up on her quarry's larboard beam. He could see a little knot of men clustered above her gilded figurehead as she dipped into the blue seas, a white bone in her teeth. Moulton's flag flew at her fore-masthead and Faulkner realized that there were many aboard the *Resolution* who would recognize the *Phoenix*, notwithstanding the fact that he had had her name removed from her transom. It would be a sweet revenge for them, he thought bitterly.

As he watched she veered to larboard and a puff of smoke appeared; a second later a column of water rose up on the *Phoenix*'s starboard quarter, fifty yards away. What the devil was he to do? Clewing up the courses was clear evidence that he intended to fight. He spun round and gave the helmsman an order. 'Stand to!' he called to the men at the guns. 'Man the larboard battery, knock out your quoins, load bar or chain-shot and aim high, reload and fire as you will as soon as your guns bear!'

There was a scurrying on the deck where men ran with no obvious sign of reluctance, Faulkner was pleased to see as he waited. The men from the starboard guns crossed the deck to double the guns' crews on the side with which he proposed to engage. When he judged them ready and White gave him a grim but confirmatory nod, he turned to the helmsman.

'Now, quartermaster, carry her head round to larboard!'

The *Phoenix* swung almost, or so it seemed, under the bows of the *Resolution*. She lay over to the wind as the braces swung the yards and at the top of her leeward lurch White, sensing his moment, bawled the order to fire. Out of the smoke that blew back across the deck Faulkner saw the black and spinning projectiles as they climbed into the sky and lost them a split-second before several rents opened in the *Resolution*'s sails.

'Keep your helm over.' Faulkner spoke in a steady tone as the *Phoenix* sailed an arc around the big man-of-war as she came onwards, ever shortening the radius. The guns, or some of them, fired again and Faulkner saw splinters rise from the *Resolution*'s upper-works. A brace parted and one yard swung so that the sails which were served above and below it began to flog, but there was no tumbling of topmasts, and then they were past with only the whistle of matchlock balls about their ears to say that the enemy had responded. Now they would cross the *Resolution*'s stern into which a few of the *Phoenix*'s guns fired raking shots. It was well enough done, but to work it had to be decisive and affect the manoeuvring ability of the bigger ship, thus reducing the odds against them. In this it had fallen short.

One thing they had achieved was a measure of surprise, for apart from half-a-dozen marksmen, they had provoked no heavy gunfire.

'They weren't ready for us,' White observed, coming aft. 'Shall you haul your wind? It occurs to me that we might make off to the south and use the recovery of the prize to lure her off.'

It was a clever notion and White was prompting him to let fall the courses, harden up the tacks and braces and stand away before the *Resolution* could come round in pursuit. For a moment it looked as though Moulton had every intention of carrying on to recover the *Judith* as White had thought, but Faulkner feared otherwise, and was proved right. The *Resolution*'s helm went over and they could see her yards coming round. A moment later the flicker of fire along her side was shrouded in smoke before the balls slammed into the *Phoenix*'s hull.

'Aim high. We cannot do otherwise,' he snapped and White ran forward. Several gun captains were traversing their gun carriages with handspikes but more shots hit home and the noise of the first discharge rolled over the water towards them. Then there was a loud crack aloft and someone yelled, 'Main topmast is shot through!' Slack ropes looped down, canvas, spars and splinters tumbled on to their heads and men were screaming.

'Aim high, lads.'

Then White was back at his side. Faulkner saw that he was bleeding from a wound in the scalp, a laceration from which blood poured down the side of his face. 'The men won't answer, sir. You must strike!'

And before he could make a reply, Faulkner felt a sensation of fire pass through his right thigh. He dropped on to one knee, vaguely aware of the quartermaster being blown from the wheel and his mate's shattered body lying over the abandoned helm. Somewhere forward more spars, blocks, ropes and sailcloth fell to the deck and the pitiful cries of the wounded and dying assailed his ears. Above the wreckage and the accumulating smoke he could see the loom of the *Resolution*, her sides twinkling with points of fire that marked her gun muzzles and punched the hot breath of passing iron balls over his head. Strange noises of impact, the darting whirr of splinters and the confusion of utter defeat rose up all about him. White had disappeared until Faulkner, trying to move, slithered in what remained of him and thought not of White but of Nathaniel below, in a cabin that must by now resemble a shambles.

Summoning every ounce of strength that remained to him he yelled, 'I strike! I strike!'

He came-to some time later, uncertain of his whereabouts. Someone had tended his leg and he had a bandage about his head. A raging thirst was on him and he called feebly for water. A figure, blurred in the half darkness leaned over him.

'You are lucky,' a vaguely familiar voice remarked.

'Who are you?'

'Nathaniel, Father.'

'Nathaniel? Are you hurt?'

'No, thanks be to God and no thanks to you.'

'Where am I?'

'Aboard the *Resolution*. The surgeon has attended you. You are a prisoner of Vice-Admiral Moulton and I am obliged to inform him that you have recovered your wits.'

'Does he know . . .?'

'Who you are and what I am to you?'

Faulkner nodded.

'Of course,' came the response, accompanied by a short, bitter laugh.

Faulkner closed his eyes. It was the end. He would likely hang before they reached Portsmouth. Nathaniel rose and moved away. His father lay still in the gloom, listening to the groans of others, the wounded of, what, both sides? He lay thus for some while and drifted into an uneasy doze. Later he was started awake, aware of men about him. He caught the gleam of a glim reflected on half-armour, the crimson of a wide sash. Looking up he saw the filigree of fine lace above which the short, almost fashionably Caroline beard and moustache marked the otherwise heavy features of Robert Moulton, Vice-Admiral of the Commonwealth Navy.

'Well, well, so now we have the devil's nephew in our hands. Welcome aboard, Sir Christopher, or are you Sir Kit?' Moulton's sarcasm ended in a mirthless chuckle. 'You acted boldly, but foolishly. I am still undecided as to whether it was entirely admirable, but then you have built a reputation on stratagem and subterfuge, I am given to understand.' He paused, as if making up his mind, and turning to a younger man beside him, asked, 'It is him, is it not?'

'No doubt of it, sir.'

'Good. Have you anything to say, sir?' Moulton asked and Faulkner shook his head. 'You are not curious about your future?' Faulkner tried to shrug his shoulders. 'Are you affecting indifference, Sir Kit? If so 'tis unwise for I surmise we have plans for you . . .'

Faulkner felt his blood run cold. It was clear they knew all about him, even down to the trumpery knighthood he had been saddled with. Whatever they charged him with, be it piracy or even treason – for if they charged the late King Charles with treason, they could most certainly nail Kit Faulkner on the same grounds – they might not merely hang him, but castrate him, draw his entrails and quarter his body before the noose had choked the life out of him.

'I feel sorry for your son, Sir Christopher. He is a good and loyal man.'

'It is a matter of regret that his principles are not mine,' he murmured.

'Indeed they are not, and it will be a matter of regret for him that that is the case. Are you there, Mr Faulkner?'

'Yes, sir.'

Faulkner shifted his eyes from Moulton to his son. 'Your father is careless about his future. You may tell him he is an especial prisoner of the State and you may tell him that we shall find him a fine lodging – in the Tower, I'll warrant.'

Moulton and his small entourage turned away, leaving Nathaniel standing next to his father. 'The fortune of war, Father, I think you said. A mere turn of the cards.'

Part Two
The Prisoner

1649–1651

The Tower

They put him in an enclosed carriage for the journey from Portsmouth to London. The windows were fastened and curtained, but the movement of the coach allowed him fitful and fleeting glimpses of his surroundings He had as a clip-clopping escort a troop of crop-head cavalry with their iron helmets, leather jerkins and strong bay horses that stank of sweat and leather. Straight swords were scabbarded at their left hips and they all bore wheellocks in holsters at their saddlebows. From time to time one would ride close alongside and peer in at him, shouting something to the effect that the prisoner was within and well enough. A cornet-of-horse commanded, a man of middling years whose face bore a scar that ran across his nose and formed an ugly purple notch in it. He breathed with a sibilant hiss that added menace to the creak of his heavy topboots and the faint jingle of his spurs as he opened the door to check his charge when they stopped. Otherwise he made no other noise towards Faulkner, addressing not one word to his prisoner during the long journey. These were seasoned campaigners intent on their charge and they paused only to change the horses hauling the coach and feed and water their own mounts. Both horses and dragoons seemed as tough as years of war could have wrought them. These were men of Oliver Cromwell's New Model Army and, for Faulkner, used to the negligently martial elegance of cavalier officers in exile, they brought the changed state of England vividly to his notice.

He received one beaker of small beer on the journey; otherwise he was left to bounce around in the equipage, every jolt of which set his teeth as his wound tormented him. He was in a mild fever by the time they reached London and had no very clear notion of the time other than that the darkness proclaimed it night. It was raining and the flare of torchlight gleamed on dark wet stone walls as, after an exchange of challenges and passwords, they passed beneath the Lion Gate and entered the chief fortress of the state.

Taken out of the coach at the doorway of a grim tower he was led inside, two troopers holding his arms and the middle-aged cornet clumping along behind him as they followed a gaoler, a sober-suited man with a gleaming bundle of keys and a lantern that threw shadows hither and yon, up a staircase and into a bare room. The door was open, the gaoler stood aside, the troopers thrust him inside and one threw a bundle in after him. As he turned he saw only the disfigured face of the cornet as he held up the lantern he had taken from the gaoler, as if verifying his prisoner had been well and truly cast into durance vile. Then the officer spoke for the first and last time.

'God have mercy on you.'

Then the door slammed shut, keys turned twice in their locks and he was left to himself. For perhaps ten minutes he stood stock still in the darkness, his beating heart slowly quieting. His leg hurt, his head ached. He was exhausted, hungry, thirsty and . . .

And what?

It came to him suddenly that he was the same starved little boy that Sir Henry Mainwaring had discovered on the quay at Bristol, trying to purloin an apple core to keep body and soul together. Nothing connected the two, no interval of time, no voyaging to the Mediterranean, no marriage to Judith, no children, no Katherine, still less a King who gave him a telescope or an idle Prince that fondled his mistress. He was not Sir Christopher at all; he was Mr Rat, just as Mainwaring had said all those years ago.

He felt the tears start to his eyes, not tears of weakness but tears of profound regret at the passing of the intervening years, of the living of his life, and with the tears came the shock of his predicament. He fell to his knees, indifferent to the pain it caused his leg, or the start of blood from the half-healed wound. Sobbing uncontrollably he wrung his hands before grinding his filthy palms into the sockets of his eyes. He remained thus for some few minutes until he calmed himself and began to think clearly. He could expect no mercy from his captors; it remained only to reconcile himself to death. But what death? The terror of that question caused his heart to flutter and his guts to churn to water. What death?

The straightforward hanging of a pirate, after which his body would be left to rot on the tideline at Wapping?

Or the formal horrors of a traitorous execution, the ritual but partial hanging, the castration, evisceration and quartering?

He found himself shuddering as much with cold as fear and became aware of a small window and the faint light from a cloudy night sky. He remembered the bundle that had been thrown into the cell and realized it was his few remaining effects, containing a cloak which he found and wrapped about him, sitting on the cold flags, in a corner of the room he judged opposite to the door. He had, in the space of just over an hour, become a feral beast, a literally cornered creature whose fate had brought him to this pass.

He must have fallen into something of a stupor for he suddenly seemed to awaken to a change of circumstances and noticed the pale parallelogram of light that revealed an emerging moon. Stiffly, he rose to his feet and stood to look out of the window. There, far above, the passing clouds were like waves which the moon, like a ship, rode; from time to time they obscured the moon's face and the light faded. Then it shone out again, lighting up the massive keep of the White Tower, pallid and yet solid, like a gigantic fist slammed down in the centre of the curtain walls and defensive towers that circumvallated it. It was William the Bastard's mark, the mark of absolute monarchy that had stood for almost six hundred years. He saw the irony of his situation. He, Kit Faulkner, who had thrown in his lot with a monarch as absolute in his conceit as The Conqueror, now found himself, Sir Christopher by act of that King's son, imprisoned in the same Tower. The irony saved him from himself; armed him a little with fortitude, for he saw himself as one among many and drew a cold comfort from the knowledge. He was, in that midnight hour, alone, alive and contemplating not merely the works of man but – and here he looked again at the sailing moon – also those of the

Maker of All Things. He drew a strange consolation from the thought and held it tight against his soul, recalling a phrase from the scripture that referred to the 'whole armour of God'. He was to think of that numinous moment many times in the succeeding weeks.

For a month he saw the gaoler twice a day when he admitted a man who brought him a wooden platter with some hard black bread, a bowl – also of wood – containing a thin soup, and a horn beaker of small beer. The man also removed the slop pail that Faulkner had first discovered by a more practical use of the moonlight during his first night of incarceration.

At first he had no desire to speak with either the gaoler or his myrmidon. It seemed that, once established, this twice-daily routine might be kept up indefinitely. They brought no news of his fate and, under the trying circumstances in which he found himself, no news was good news. Neither man gave any impression of recognizing him as a sentient being. They were neither unkind, nor gloating; neither kind nor cruel. He might have been a horse, or a patient ox. Once the gaoler gave his assistant some murmured instruction and the man went off, to return with a broom, which he silently held out to Faulkner, making a motion that he should sweep the flagstones. Faulkner took the broom and nodded.

After some ten days he felt compelled to ask whether he might shave and when the gaoler shook his head, he impulsively asked if he knew what would become of him. The man shook his head again, then raised his gloved forefinger to his lips. Faulkner realized he was under orders not to address the prisoner on any circumstances. The realization troubled him. As long as he could persuade himself that the routine would go on indefinitely he could endure the incarceration – or thought he could. But once the notion that specific orders had been given relative to his conditions, the blindfold that he had wrapped himself in was torn away.

Oddly, however, it was not so much anxiety about his own future that concerned him, though that ate relentlessly at his innards during the sleepless hours of the night, as anxiety about Katherine. Would she hear what had happened to him?

And if she did – and it was difficult to think that the word would not somehow reach Helvoetsluys – what would she do? Throw herself into the ready arms of His Royal Highness? And who could blame her if she did? She must eat and he could do nothing for himself, let alone for her. He felt, in those first days of his captivity, like the cock in a game of battledore, flung first one way and then the other, between deep concern for Katherine and the sheer dread of his own, appalling death.

On the evening of the nineteenth day of his captivity he wrapped himself in his cloak as usual and lay down on a straw-filled palliasse that had been provided for him a fortnight earlier. He had drifted off into an uneasy doze when something woke him. It was black as pitch and there was no moon. The window casement rattled slightly. He was disturbed by a soughing wind and the scuttle of a rat, which made him draw his feet up so that he lay like a child. But something else had caused a noise, something unusual: the sound of men's voices. Abruptly, the noise of keys grinding in the locks was followed by a sudden blast of cold air as the door was flung open. Faulkner leapt to his feet as, partially lit by the gaoler's lantern, two cloaked and hooded figures came into the room. Scuttling round the three men came a boy that Faulkner had never seen before. He bore a candlestick and a guttering candle which he placed on the floor. As Faulkner stood stock still, staring at the intruders, his heart hammering with the certainty that his last moments had come, the boy ran out, returning seconds later with two rush-seated chairs each of which he placed either side of the door. Then the boy withdrew, followed by the gaoler. The key ground only once in the door as the two men sat down and a voice commanded Faulkner to sit before the candle where they could observe his features.

He did as he was told.

'Now, if thou value your life any, keep thy eyes upon the candle and we shall see if the game is worth its expense.' He had no idea which of them spoke, but the voice was deep and not unkind. It was clear that even if he did involuntarily raise his eyes, the candle flame's effect upon his retina would prevent him seeing their features. Moreover, neither of his visitors threw back their hoods. He lowered his eyes as he had been commanded.

'State your name.'

'Christopher Faulkner.'

'From whence come you originally?'

'From Bristol.'

'And more recently?'

'I was in the service of King Charles—'

'There is no such personage. Do you mean that man who pretends to the throne, the offspring of the Great Malignant lately executed for High Treason?'

'I suppose that is who I mean.'

'You would do well to do more than suppose. And were you lately commander of a ship called the *Phoenix*?'

'I was.'

'And were you also the owner of the said *Phoenix*?'

'Yes.'

'And did you take up arms in the said ship against this Commonwealth, and take or destroy ships and vessels belonging to the said Commonwealth?'

'I waged war.'

'In a private ship, sir?'

'Under commission of the . . . Of the man of whom we spoke a moment ago.'

'You are a pirate, Captain Faulkner.'

'I would plead otherwise.'

'Would you now! On what grounds?'

'On the grounds that a state of civil war exists and that I was in arms against the late King's enemies as many others have been and some still remain so.'

'And you consider that a legitimate claim to assist you to escape execution for piracy?'

'If there is honour still in England.'

'You are damnably bold, upon my word.'

There was a pause and then the other took up the interrogation. He had said nothing up to that moment and his voice was harsher than his fellow.

'You look for honour, Captain Faulkner. From men you presumably regard as regicides? Is that not a little trusting of you?'

'I have no other means, sir. I conceived myself to fight as an honourable man, I never fired a gun under a false flag, nor turned aside a call for quarter, nor treated any man without due regard.'

'You sound like a pillar of virtue.'

'I do not wish to, sir. I merely wish that my part in this is fairly regarded.'

'And do you really think that your part in this, whatever you think this is, is to be fairly regarded. On what grounds, pray?'

'That I was loyal to my King and to his son.'

'So much so,' broke in the first man, 'that you placed your ship at his disposal.'

'What else was I to do?'

'Well, you could have remained in London, kept your wife and children, and laid your talents and your vessels at the service of Parliament, could you not?'

'I was not inclined to do that.'

'No, Captain, you abandoned your loving wife to run off with a whore of that most detested clan of my Lord Buckingham, the Villiers whore!'

'It is true that I abandoned my wife and I am not proud of the fact. I do not expect you to understand my motives, nor why Mistress Villiers and I—'

'Enough! That is a subject that lies between thee, your wife and Almighty God and for which you will be called to judgement in due course.'

A silence fell upon them for a moment, then the first who had spoken, addressing him in an altogether different tone asked, 'You are an experienced mariner, Captain. A man misguided in your loyalties but, by all accounts, a man cool under fire, bold in your enterprises and firm in your resolution.'

Faulkner sensed a trap. The smooth tone, the complimentary words seemed unlikely in these circumstances and surroundings. He remained silent.

'You are – or were – a member of that Fraternity known as the Trinity House, are you not?'

'I was. I hear that the Parliament put a stop to its charity.'

'You were and still are an —' the man paused, as if finding the noun distasteful — '*associate* of Henry Mainwaring, sometime Master of the said Trinity House.'

'I am sure you are aware that I have been long in the service of Sir Henry, who has been like a father to me and to whom I owe my life, and that he is presently safe in The Netherlands.'

'Is that so?' There was sarcasm in the voice.

'How competent a mariner are you, Captain, by your own reckoning?'

'You reveal yourself a landsman, sir, by your question.'

'How so?'

'There are several types of mariner; those who toil in the merchants' service, those who serve a king or, as of now, a state or commonwealth, those who work in their own private interests, and among these you shall find men who command, men who swab, men who hand, reef and steer, but I take you to mean mariner as in the context of those who lately formed the Fraternity of Trinity House, in which case they serve both the merchant and the, er, state. Lately some served the merchant and the late King.'

'Yes, yes, I did not intend the question to produce so didactic a response. You refer to those who sailed for the coast of Morocco some years past.'

'As an example, yes.'

'And among which you were.'

'I was.'

'And do you know where your fellow Brethren now are?'

'Some are dead; some have fallen during the late disturbances; some serve under the Prince Palatine.'

'Meaning Rupert?'

'Meaning Rupert, and some serve the Parliament.'

'How do you feel about men of your acquaintance and Fraternity serving the Parliament, Captain?'

'That they follow their consciences as I follow mine.'

'And would you fight them?'

'I do not know that I have not already done so.'

'Indeed not.'

There was a low exchange between the two men, then they rose, making the candle flame gutter and, quite without thinking, Faulkner looked up, only to find he could see nothing but the glow of the flame before his eyes.

'Gaoler!' one of them cried and the key rasped in the lock, the door opened to lantern light and the swirl of cloaks as the men departed. On the threshold the first who had spoken turned. 'I wish you goodnight, Captain. We shall leave you the candle.'

Then the door closed and he was alone with only the noise of his own blood rushing in his ears for company.

Faulkner did not sleep that night. He lay on his straw mattress, the image of the glowing candle flame still burning his retina, ruminating on the turn events had taken, trying to reconstruct the interrogation as best he might. At first it was his own answers that preoccupied him as he sought to determine whether he had placed himself in a worse position at the termination of the interview than he had occupied at the start. The problem was that he had no idea where he had stood in the minds of the two visitors and this led him to cudgel his brain to recall the questions in detail. As far as he was concerned he realized that, without thinking about it, he had been absolutely straight in his conduct. Honesty was the only legacy his long-dead and all but forgotten mother had left him with. It was this straightforwardness – along with a quick and obvious intelligence – that had so impressed Henry Mainwaring some thirty years earlier. The question of whether it had had a similar effect on his recent interlocutors did not cross his mind. It was unimaginable that they had been probing for his sole virtue, not least because it was innate honesty that had led him to abandon Judith. This, it had been made abundantly clear, was but one of the list of crimes with which he was being judged. Moreover, he thought, Judith's conspicuous Puritanism would have commended her to the authorities even more than his own conduct towards her.

At first there had been the probing of his alleged piracy, then the charges of infamous conduct before that strange request for self-examination as to his qualities as a mariner. And then there was the tone of the interrogation. It had been strict, but not cruel, not even harsh. There had been no deep probing, no threat of torture to extract whatever they might have thought he knew of matters concerning King Charles's plans. Why?

The only reason he could deduce was that he was being lulled into some state of half hoping matters might not be as bad as he thought. Indeed, it struck him that being left so alone for almost three weeks was a perfect preparation for such a strategy. What else could he think? And what else could he think, but that the outcome of the visitation would be prejudicial to him? Eventually, convinced of this and that further visits would follow – inevitably of a less congenial nature – he fell into an uneasy slumber.

Nothing further happened for a month, although imperceptibly his conditions improved. He at first attributed this to the onset of a cold winter. A fire was set in a small grate by the gaoler's boy who now became a regular attendant. He was allowed two blankets, one of the rush-seated chairs and a small wooden table. Once the gaoler made the passing remark, mumbled more than properly articulated, that these 'comfortable emoluments' would be charged to him, refusing to expand or enter into any subsequent dialogue. This puzzled Faulkner. He had been removed from the *Resolution* with only a purse of small change and if trial and execution were to be his fate, he saw little chance of being able to repay the Tower's governor for the 'comfortable emoluments'. This puzzlement increased when, two days later, the boy set a stump of candle on his small deal table, along with a wispy spill with which to light it from the fire.

'I want but paper, pen and ink,' he observed with an almost cheerful smile at the gaoler waiting by the open door, conscious that he had been compelled to live in the moment and that sense that if only such a routine persisted, all would be well. That he must die sometime, he acknowledged, but better to die in this bleak place in private than screaming with terror and pain as he regarded his bollocks in the executioner's hands to the cheers of London's citizenry.

It was at Christmas, to the sound of the bells of All Hallows and St Olave's, that he received his next visitor. The short mid-winter day was drawing to its close and Faulkner had just decided to delay lighting his candle until full darkness had fallen, when he heard steps outside. He was not expecting his evening broth for another hour, the appointed time when his fire would be doused and kicked out. Instead the gaoler introduced the boy who brought a fresh bucket of sea-coal, made up the fire and then scuttled out. Watching him disappear, Faulkner saw the gaoler turn and jerk his head to someone obviously waiting outside. The gaoler's gesture was impatient, from which Faulkner deduced his next visitor was reluctant to enter. A figure shuffled in, head down, his face shielded by the brim of his plain black hat. Only when the door slammed behind him and the sinister sound of the double lock turning emphasised that he too was locked in a cell in the Tower of London, did the stranger look up.

'Nathaniel!' Faulkner stood and stepped towards his son, intending to embrace him, but the young man stiffened, arresting the impulse. Faulkner drew back, confused. The two men stood regarding each other in silence before Faulkner, in an almost pathetic attempt to break the impasse, drew the upright chair forward, towards the now leaping flames of the fire and requested his son to sit.

Nathaniel shook his head, so both continued to stand, the younger relaxing insofar as to cast his eyes about his father's accommodation. However, even this inspection produced no reaction and Faulkner rapidly gathered his wits. It was clear this was no filial visit, so it therefore followed that it had been contrived. He drew himself up and, quite unconsciously, fell into his quarterdeck manner.

'Well, sir, if thou cannot accept the miserable hospitality that I can offer, perhaps you will tell me your business, following which I shall do what I can to have you released from what you clearly conceive to be an impossibly awkward situation.'

'Father, I . . .' The young man watched as Faulkner accompanied this speech with the lighting of the solitary candle. By the combined light of it and the fire, Faulkner could see his son's face working with emotion. This was not easy for either of them.

'Sit down, my boy,' he said in a softer tone, 'and tell me what you have been sent here to tell me.' Nathaniel shook his head. 'Have you come to tell me I am to be tried for piracy or treason?' Faulkner continued and took the sharp look his son gave him to think he had divined the reason for Nathaniel's reluctance to speak. He felt his own blood run cold. So, it was to be death and they had sent his own son to inform him. He stood, swearing. 'A pox upon it all!'

'No, I have not been sent to say anything of the kind,' Nathaniel said hurriedly.

'What? Not that? Then what?'

'That I am to see that thou art in spirits, warm and fed.'

'Is that all? Then thou canst depart and inform them that I am as well fed and warm as they allow in this benighted place.'

'They? What do you mean "they"? I am sent by my mother.'

'Your mother?' Faulkner was astonished. 'God's bones, and why should your mother take any interest in me?'

'I have no idea, Father. I know only that a few nights ago a man waited upon her and informed her of your situation. He asked if there was anything she wanted communicated to you and she told him that she would defray reasonable expenses . . . and whether you could accept visitors.'

'And that is why you are here?' Faulkner dropped the formal tone, mollified by Nathaniel's explanation but suspicious of Judith's ultimate motive.

'It is.'

'That is kind of your mother.' It occurred to him that it might be otherwise, more especially as apart from abandoning her he had taken one of her ships. The thought persuaded him to alter the course of the conversation in an attempt to thaw his son as much as improve his own understanding of the whole rigmarole. 'And what of the other *Judith*, the one you commanded?'

Nathaniel shrugged. 'She was retaken by the *Resolution* within hours of your capture. I thought that you knew.'

'No, I was told nothing, not even by you.'

'No. You were feverish. How is your wound?'

'Fully mended, I am glad to say.'

The thought of bodily disfigurement led to both men contemplating Faulkner's future and both spoke at once, the frost between them finally thawed.

'Have you heard . . .?' Faulkner began.

'What will happen . . .?' Nathaniel asked.

'You do not know what is intended for me then?'

'No. We are puzzled that no mention of your taking has been mooted abroad. You were vilified as a pirate after your last raid on The Nore. Now there is nothing but silence.'

'And you and your mother are reluctant to probe the reason?' Faulkner asked, his face twisted in an ironic smile.

'It has not been easy, knowing that it was you who was thus signalized.'

'Indeed, I suppose it has not.' There was a moment's silence and then Faulkner asked, 'Why has your mother taken an interest in my welfare? Would she see me in good condition to hang?'

Nathaniel shrugged. 'I do not know; she did not say.'

'You are here reluctantly, upon her urging?' The young man nodded. 'And upon no others'?'

'Only my Uncle Nathan's.'

'And how is the good Nathan?' Faulkner asked with a smile, playing upon Judith's brother's surname of Gooding.

'He is well and sends you greetings.'

'I seem to recall he was not the loser by my going,' Faulkner remarked drily. 'Your mother and her brother were always square in their dealings,' he added. Again Nathaniel shrugged; such matters were not his business, it struck his father. Clearly he had detached himself from moral questions of his parents' generation. Faulkner concluded that, had he been in Nathaniel's place, he would have done something similar and this explained much of his son's ambivalence.

'Well, my boy, although it is good to see you, you have executed your commission and, if it pleases you, I give you leave to depart.'

Nathaniel nodded and half turned to the door, realizing he could not go without the gaoler unlocking the door.

Seeing him hesitate, Faulkner asked, 'Shall you come again?'

The young man looked up at him and their eyes met properly for the first and only time during their awkward meeting.

'Would you wish that I should?'

It was Faulkner's turn to shrug. 'Not unless you throw off that Puritan gloom. A man facing death has need of cheerful company and if wine is forbidden then a pipe of tobacco and a jest or two. Even news of the follies of mankind would stir me and divert me from contemplating my end.'

'Father! Please . . .'

'Ah, you are too young.'

'I am not too young! Damn it, sir, I stood to arms against you in defence of my ship. Thou shall not cozen me with that kind of bravado. My mother acted out of Christian charity. She said that once a woman had lain with a man and borne him offspring he owned a corner of her heart, and even though she would watch you hang in the knowledge that you deserved it, she could not promise that she would not shed a tear, if only for herself and the children you abandoned for your Villiers whore!'

Even in the poor light, Faulkner could see the colour in the younger man's cheeks. Here, at last, was spirit. Now he understood the moping emotional aspect of his son, for he had entered Faulkner's presence with a weighty burden and no clear means of delivering it. Impulsively Faulkner reached out and grasped his son's arm.

'Well said, Nathaniel, and all as charged beyond your reference to Katherine as a whore.'

''Tis said she is, Father, and that she lies with . . . with the man over the sea.'

Faulkner's mood was pierced. Such thoughts were among those that tortured him at any state of the day or night. 'How know thou that?' he spat.

'Father, thou knowest little of matters in England. There are those who make it their business to learn such things.' Nathaniel hesitated, as though considering something – perhaps the consequences of what he was about to say – before he went on. 'Although the Trinity House is in disarray there is a commission to administer its affairs and those of us who still confer.'

'Us?'

'Yes, Father, as a mariner I am admitted to their confederation.'

'You are made a Younger Brother?' Faulkner asked with a smile.

'We do not call ourselves by that name.'

'And how does this touch me? Surely you cannot utter the names of those unworthy dogs who kept true to their oath of allegiance in your confederation?'

'My own admission near stumbled upon the block of thine own intransigence.'

'Is that what they call honourable adherence to an oath nowadays? God's bones, perhaps I am best out of it then.' Faulkner gave a short, bitter laugh.

'Father,' Nathaniel said assertively, 'try and understand that matters are in great flux. New ideas and principles displace the old; they must if progress is to be made. Do you want to lick the boots of men like Goring and that venal sack of putrefaction, Buckingham?'

'I lick no man's boots.'

'But those of Henry Mainwaring.'

'He is as a father to me and I am not his creature.' Faulkner paused. A cold suspicion had him by the entrails. 'But what of him?'

'He is among those who keep us informed.'

'How dost *thou* know that?' And he knew the answer immediately he had asked the question. Holding his tongue, he awaited Nathaniel's reply.

'From those mariners whose business they discuss among themselves.'

Faulkner knew well that the Brethren of Trinity House were not merely inveterate gossips, but gleaners of commercial intelligence along with which came news of associated affairs. He knew too what was in Mainwaring's mind.

'Does Sir Henry know of my incarceration here?'

'I do not know for certain, but it is likely. Did he speak of such matters to you?'

Suddenly it was as though a curtain had been rent from before Faulkner's eyes. Nathaniel had been coached to determine Faulkner's relationship with Mainwaring's state of mind. The thought made him turn away, for the question arose as to why. Why on earth was a triumphant Parliament, or even its paranoid servants, interested in an ageing man clinging on to an increasingly precarious life in exile? For the intelligence he gleaned at the threadbare court of the would-be King Charles II of England, which seemed likely to consist of little other than with whom Charles lay at night? For the moment he must concentrate upon an answer to Nathaniel's query. Mainwaring had made no secret of his desire to return to England, if only to die in an English bed. Would the news that his protégé, Kit Faulkner, languished in Commonwealth hands persuade him to do so sooner or later? And would the fate of Faulkner condition his decision?

That still left the question of what interest the authorities could possibly have in old Sir Henry. And then it dawned upon him, spurred by the recollection of the strangers' question about the quality of himself as a mariner: Mainwaring had possessed a formidable reputation as an organizer, of a supervisor of ships, of the preparation of men-of-war. And, if his two visitors were in some way connected with matters of admiralty, they would know that he and Mainwaring were connected and that, alone among the exiled captains, it had been Faulkner and the *Phoenix* who had been left behind when Rupert sailed for Ireland. The reasons were simple enough when reviewed in The Hague, but they might not look so simple when seen from London.

These thoughts tumbled through his mind like lightning descended through a tree. Such quick, intuitive linkages allowed him to respond with barely a hesitation and a disarming candour, confident that he did not do disservice to his old mentor.

'I was, until I sailed on my cruise, as close to Sir Henry as it is possible to be.'

But Nathaniel pressed his case, revealing the gravity of his mission. 'Your discussions were in confidence and intimacy?'

'It would be hard to conceive them closer.' Faulkner wanted to ask whether his reply satisfied the brief with which Nathaniel had been charged, but he held his tongue. The younger man, though mature enough, was still gauche in such matters. Silence again grew between them and Faulkner realized that the younger man, having achieved his goal, lacked a means of leaving without it seeming too obvious. He added, almost ruminatively, as though cast into a study but the better reinforcing what he divined Nathaniel had been entrusted to discover, 'We were, as I say, as close as a fond father is to a son, though I could, alas, not expect you to understand that.'

'I could have wished to understand it, Father.'

'Yes, yes. But pray leave me now. It grows late and the gates will be locked ere long.'

'The gates are long since locked. I have lodgings prepared.' Nathaniel broke off, realizing he had been indiscreet and lest Faulkner should notice. He had, but fobbed off the suspicion, remarking that, 'The gaoler must make money somehow and I am precious little use to him.'

Faulkner saw a way to divert Nathaniel and added, 'And please thank your mother for her kindness. Tell her that when a man has lain with a woman and the twain have produced a fine son, they are not quite sundered, for all the attractions of others. Can you remember that?'

'You forget I am married myself, Father.'

'Of course! And made me a grandsire, by Heaven!' Faulkner clapped his son on the shoulder and called for the gaoler.

As Nathaniel was let out, Faulkner wished him goodnight and asked that the gaoler returned before he retired for the night. When the man came back, Faulkner asked for wine. It was clear the strictures on what he might have had been lifted by Judith's underwriting of his expenses and, without a word, the gaoler brought him a tankard of passable claret. Faulkner drank slowly, composing his mind as best he might with the news of Katherine's infidelity, trying to persuade himself that Mainwaring had hoped to communicate the news to him but that it might not be true. It was possible, just, that Mainwaring had invented it to convince Faulkner that there was nothing left for him on the continent and that he must throw in his lot with Mainwaring, who was now intent on carrying out his plan to return home. And in the emotional exhaustion of his mind the wine seemed to establish this as the most likely thing, if anything in this insane business bore any logic in its train. It was an encouraging thought, though to what extent it was the action of wine on a constitution deprived of all but bread, beer, and thin gruel was uncertain. Nevertheless, it was consoling enough to give him his first good night's sleep.

From that day Faulkner's conditions improved. He was

allowed cheese and meat, taking wine, but occasionally, for fear of frightening off Judith's largesse. Then, towards Lady Day at the end of March and the New Year, he received a further visit. It was just after noon and he heard the approach of the gaoler accompanied by a man whose boots struck the stone steps with a ring. He did not at first recognize the newcomer for he was older, and dressed in some opulence, wearing an orange sash of commissioned rank, a baldric and sword and a hat that was stylishly un-Puritan. The ostrich plume put Faulkner on his guard, fearing he was an *agent provocateur*, until he bethought himself that no such person would dare to enter the Tower in broad daylight. Besides, it was notoriously difficult to enter the fastnesses of the fortress without the accreditation of the state.

'You do not recognize me, God damn your black soul!' a vaguely familiar voice cried as the man turned to the gaoler. 'Come, man, bring us a bottle or two of your best claret, if any such thing is to be found hereabouts.'

'Harry? Harry Brenton, is it you?'

'Who else, my old cock, but Honest Harry?'

'I am astounded that . . . No, no, perhaps not, you were never a King's man entirely, I recollect.'

'I was as loyal as the next man while His Late Majesty paid my wages but when he placed his privy purse above his public duty I began to detect cracks in the divinity of kings. Mind you, Kit, I should not have you think me a black-garbed Puritan, though they have their stolid virtues in the right place.'

Brenton's monologue trailed off as the gaoler brought in wine, ready in anticipation of Brenton's *douceur*, which he palmed with an altogether admirably polished expertise. The boy brought in a second chair and as the two sat on opposite sides of the little table Faulkner took quick stock of his old friend and shipmate from long past days when they had both served as lieutenants under Mainwaring in the *Prince Royal*. It had been on a voyage to northern Spain to embark the then Charles, Prince of Wales, and his dissolute companion, the first Duke of Buckingham, after their failed attempt to woo an *infanta* for His Royal Highness. It was during the voyage home that the Prince had noticed the impoverished Faulkner had no glass, and afterwards sent him a telescope.

Brenton threw his hat on the table, handed the wine to Faulkner and drank deeply of his own before looking at his old shipmate squarely. 'They are,' he said, after wiping his mouth and resettling his moustache, 'trying to decide what to do with you, Kit.'

'Has your presence here anything to do with their deliberations?'

'Of course. I shall not pretend otherwise, but I should have been here sooner had I not been on service, if only to tell you that you had cost my sister her husband in your infernal raids.'

'I am sorry for that.'

Brenton held up his hand. 'I do not blame you. Besides, she claimed he had the pox and is well rid of him, though to hear him you would have thought him cousin to John the Baptist, such was the sanctimony of his discourse.'

'And you? What of you, Harry?'

'I fought at Marston Moor and commanded a company of foot in the absence of its captain at Newbury. More recently I have been serving in the State Navy under Blake off Kinsale, where we bottled your Prince Rupert until he escaped to Lisbon, where I am lately come from with the General-at-Sea's despatches. Hearing you were here, and who could not? I engineered this visit.'

'I had heard that my presence here is not well known.'

'True, but that is so only among the populace. Those of us in the State's service at sea are aware of you and are much pleased by your confinement. You were becoming likened to another Drake, believe it or not.'

'I had no idea.'

'Which begs a question . . .' Brenton paused, his eyebrows raised.

'I do not understand. What question? What is to become of me?'

'More or less.'

'More or less? Am I not as good as condemned by mine own actions?'

Brenton nodded. 'Oh, aye, but these are fractious times and, between the two of us, though the King's head was struck from his shoulders, there are those who fear our new and experimental realm may not be as secure as we should like. There is trouble brewing with the Dutch. The Scots have proclaimed your young puppy King of Scotland, and King Louis sits like a patient spider in Paris pulling the strings of his web of spies that have, I am given to understand, also ensnared His Majesty the King of Scotland.'

'And why are you telling me all this, Harry? Is it because I am shortly to be arraigned, condemned and executed, and it matters little what I know?'

'It may well be, indeed. But it depends.'

'Upon what?'

'Upon you, perhaps, and as much as upon others, for the Council of State – when it has the liberty to discuss your case – is divided in its opinion as to your value. You must have realized that after you had been here some months and seen nothing of the rack or the wheel.'

'Pray God not that. I should rather thrust mine own neck into the noose, and cheerfully too.'

'I will be frank with you, Kit, this may yet be your fate which, for the moment at least, hangs in the balance for reasons I cannot tell you. I am allowed to see you on the grounds of sounding you out and this I refuse to do, though I shall not tell those who sent me that, for I would not see you sell your soul. What you do you must decide for yourself, for I know you to have been bewitched by Mistress Villiers and I do not know how you stand thus. What I shall tell those who sent me is that you are undecided, and crave another month to determine your future.'

'Stop, Harry, for God's sake! What are you offering me? Amnesty? Pardon? A chance if I come over to you?'

'Of course! Think of your future. Your skills could be put to better use and, if it consoles you, better men than you have come over to the righteous cause of a beleaguered people.'

'And if, having been sent here for an answer, you do not take one back . . .'

'I am dealing with men of conscience, Kit. Too hasty a

decision, though welcomed by some who are, if not your friends, are not yet your enemies, would seem hasty enough to cast you in the liking of a wind vane,' Brenton said. 'Especially to those who would rather you swung for your crimes.'

A silence fell between the two men and then Faulkner observed, quietly, ''Tis like to walking along a sword blade on its edge.'

'Very like.' Brenton refilled the wine cups. 'Do not let Mistress Villiers too much influence you. You will not survive unless . . .'

'What must I do?' Faulkner asked abruptly.

'Write an expiation. I shall not call it a confession.'

'And offer my services to the Parliament?'

'If that is what you wish.'

'And if I do not?'

Brenton shrugged. 'I doubt they will hang you after all this time. They will want you forgotten and are the more likely to condemn you to serve at sea in an inferior capacity which you will be compelled to bear as a humiliation.'

'You would recommend this, as a friend?'

'You are too inquisitive, my astute friend,' Brenton said, standing up and picking up his hat. 'Gaoler!' He lowered his voice. 'I return to the fleet. The General-at-Sea recalls you from the fighting in the West Country.'

'The General . . .?'

'At-Sea. It is what we term the senior admiral nowadays. Robert Blake – a man who wants watching, for he will do great things if he lives long.'

If he lives long. The words tumbled about Faulkner's brain long after Brenton had gone and night had fallen. Glad as he was to see a friendly face, of all his odd visitors Brenton's had been the oddest, leaving him both confused and yet certain there was, if he decided to seize it, a way out of his predicament. In contrast to the first time he had taken wine in the Tower, he was unable to sleep after imbibing several cups with Brenton. He had no reason to suppose Brenton had not been honest towards him, nor could he have been admitted to Faulkner's cell had he not come armed with the necessary papers, so he must take Brenton's words at their face value.

But what was he to do? On the one hand it was blindingly obvious that to throw his lot in with the Parliament meant that he could at least come home, though what did he do about Katherine? Was she abed with Charles, or was that a fiction of Mainwaring's? And if it was not, did he care if he got her back? And if he did accept that he might serve as a common seaman, might not that at least give him an opportunity to desert, to escape and reach Kate? The longer he thought about the matter, the more confused he became. The weeks of isolation had disturbed his reasoning powers because his world had become so circumscribed that the personal was so conditional, unaffected by greater events owing to his imperfect understanding of them, such was the insulation afforded by the massive ramparts of the fortress.

And there was always that tricky subject of honour upon which he had stood so defiantly when first interrogated. What did an honourable man do in such circumstances? An honourable man, he assumed, would rather die than turn his coat. Had he not as good as said so to his son over the business of the Trinity Brethren's oath of allegiance? He spent several days and nights in this mental turmoil so that, as the last frosts of winter gave way to spring, he fell foul of a quinsy and then a fever that had him tossing, sodden in sweat and a stinking funk on his straw palliasse. Delirious for eleven days, his life was feared for by the gaoler who had discovered his prisoner to be a modest but steady source of additional income. He was visited again by his son and one of the two strangers who had first disturbed him. This last asked for a daily report to be sent to the Palace of Whitehall, addressed to Mr Fox, an assumed pseudonym. Even when he recovered from his fever, Faulkner remained weak and listless. His mind shied away from any anxiety and, when reporting on him, his gaoler described him as having descended into 'a decline, a want of spirits and a general disinterest in life occasioned by some agony of conscience'. Keen to retain the weekly monies that arrived for Faulkner's comfort, it played into the gaoler's hands to maintain this state of inertia for as long as possible. Indifferent to death, a weakened state of life was less troublesome and more profitable to him and in this way the weeks passed, a spring became summer, and soon that too showed signs of fading.

Faulkner's mind seemed to have given way. Five times he called for pen and paper and five times he drew up the heading of 'An Expiation'. Five times he drafted a paragraph and on each occasion it was different. Five times he contemplated a false start, taking comfort only in what appeared the solid fact that while he did nothing, nobody seemed inclined to do anything to him. This unreal conclusion was conditioned in part by his institutionalization, but also by his distant past. As a guttersnipe he had learned to lie low and take advantage of whatever offered a thin subsistence. Thus, what would have driven another man mad, simply called up reserves of experience known to few, for few rise as Faulkner had done.

And, as the time passed, it seemed that he was correct, that the authorities had forgotten him, having other, more pressing, matters to attend to. While this was only partially the case and his occupancy of a cell in the Beauchamp Tower was regularly noted by a sub-committee of the Council of State, the overtly bureaucratic minds of which it was largely made up did not question the decision to leave him there. The expense of his incarceration was small and, at least for the time being, the wisdom with which England was governed by its Parliament called for few prisoners to be sent into the Tower while the melting down of the Crown Jewels meant it was less frequented by the public than heretofore. Fortunately for Faulkner, the eyes of England were turned upon the slaughter being wrought by Cromwell and his army in Ireland, where the forces brought together under Ormonde were crumbling under the onslaught. Now Ormonde himself was on his way to join the exiled Charles. With such weighty events in train and in this wise, Faulkner had been imprisoned a year before anyone bethought themselves to ask what *was* to happen to him.

That person was his wife.

Judith

Judith Faulkner had been left substantial shares in two East Indiamen besides lesser interests in several lesser vessels when her husband deserted her. She had clung to a right to be regarded as a wronged woman, respectable by her own efforts, by becoming a force in business. Although she relied upon her husband's business partner, her own brother, Nathan Gooding, as the public face of their joint enterprise, there were few in the rather circumscribed circles of London's ship owners who did not know that, shrewd though Gooding was, his sister was the more canny.

Her original decision to pay a moiety to maintain her estranged husband in the Tower was a form of revenge. In spite of his very depredations against her – for one of the East Indiamen he had attacked at The Nore had been a ship in which Judith had an interest – she was wealthy enough not to miss a few pence a week. A woman of deep but repressed passions, a legacy of her Puritanism, she enjoyed a perverse, almost visceral pleasure in knowing Faulkner's very well-being depended upon her. However, such pleasure waned as time passed and he, it seemed, was likely to become a permanent drain upon her income. Besides, any pleasure that she might derive from the knowledge required that she confront him and made him abase himself. Only then could the investment pay off with the dividend of his humiliation. For many weeks she contemplated this event, playing versions of the fantasy in her imagination, and these ranged from the severe and heartless – in their most extreme form she plunged a righteous dagger into him – to curiously erotic imaginings wherein she took her pleasure of him while he – for darker reasons that it would be proper to relate here – was unable to similarly enjoy. These were nasty midnight excursions which, in the severe austerity of the chapel services among a congregation of the righteous, she confessed silently. Indeed, during those devout years of the Rump of the Long Parliament, there were those people among her congregation who were apt to remark that Mistress Judith – for these souls, being most sympathetic to her, avoided the use of her married surname – always bore a high colour when she came from her witness. Such, they claimed, was clear evidence of the workings of God among his chosen flock.

However, there came a late November afternoon when, the day having drawn in, but when her eldest son Henry was still assisting Nathan in the counting house, her daughter Hannah was visiting a neighbour and Nathan was back at sea in command of his old ship, Judith called for her private ledger. The household expenses rose alarmingly at this time of the year and the cost of a chauldron of sea-coal reminded her that its price was artificially high because of the risks attending its carriage from the Tyne to the Thames. It also reminded her that such a price was first caused by a certain Captain Kit Faulkner but that the said filibuster was now mewed up in the Tower of London. The thought caused her to turn to the untitled column at the rear of the ledger where a list of disbursements made to a certain John Fitchett, Gaoler, when added up, came to fifteen pounds, twelve shillings and three ha'pence.

The sum shocked her; she had not thought it amounted to more than eight or nine pounds and had been so confident that that was the case that, of all her various payments and expenses, she had neglected its addition. Somehow, she recalled, every time she had intended to, she had fallen instead into a fantasy of contemplating their eventual and, for her, delicious confrontation. Now she considered the matter with a more singular purpose, recollecting the manner in which the payment was made by application, Fitchett sending his boy with an itemised list. Of course, this usually only bore a few times which she paid promptly from her purse, but it now struck her that the boy's appearances had been more persistent than prudence dictated. True, there had been the circumstances of her husband's prolonged indisposition, relief of which mollified Judith as an act of disinterested Christian charity spiced with a righteous compassion. Even so, she chid herself, the boy's regular appearances ought to have warned her of the rising expense and she was not so stupid as to realize Fitchett must needs take his ample rake-off.

'Well, Mr Fitchett,' she said to herself, closing the ledger resolutely, 'you have been long about your business and, if my husband is sick I must see for myself the extent of his illness.'

Had she not been seen as something of a martyr of the late disturbances by the most charitable, she might not have been able to gain access to her husband. As it was, she had been visited several times by a man introducing himself as 'Mr Fox' who asked for certain details of her estranged husband's character and the extent of his interests in London and Bristol. Mr Fox had paid her several subsequent visits and, Judith had convinced herself, had she not had a husband living, might have made himself more familiar with her. Happily both parties recognized the presence of the Devil when they saw it, though there was little doubt on either side that had anything happened to Faulkner, both would renew their acquaintance. Judith did not know that Mr Fox was active in promoting the view that Faulkner ought to have been called to account and the only outcome of any trial would have been death. However, he was prevented from carrying the argument to this conclusion in part by the opposition of others who put affairs of state – even minor matters as to the usefulness of an accomplished sea officer – above personal considerations, and in part by the reflection that he was already married, a fact he had carelessly concealed from Mistress Judith.

These complexities did not prevent either party from flirting, nor from making veiled hints and suggestions, all of which were quite improper given their religion, so that Judith had no compunction in calling upon Mr Fox – by way of a messenger, of course – to provide her with an entry permit to the Tower to visit her husband. Mr Fox delivered it personally. He was a handsome man, some five years older than Judith, and the night he chose was filthy with rain. What passed between the two in the privacy of Judith's chamber must remain conjectural, for she took him there for purposes of discretion, not wishing to advertise her intentions to her daughter who lived with her. However, had one observed Mr Fox leaving the house that night, one would have remarked that he had been at least three-quarters of an hour doing a task that took no more than three or four minutes, even when accompanied by the utmost ceremony. As for Judith, she could not sleep for some hours after retiring, recollecting that she was still a comparatively young woman, still capable of bearing a child, and thankful that she was not quite in danger of carrying Mr Fox's. The encounter nevertheless sharpened her appetite to see again the only man who had lain with her and she restlessly plotted to that end.

Despite the easing of his conditions, Faulkner felt the chill of the afternoon and sat in a corner wrapped in his cloak when he heard the key turn in the lock. He looked up into the eyes of a woman he had not seen for years.

'Judith!' he exclaimed, struggling to his feet and wiping his face with his hand, only to find the rasp of thick stubble; it had been a week since he had been allowed to shave. Seeing him in his dirty clothes, his face unshaven and careworn, almost vacuous after his weeks of mental distress and physical illness, he was not the figure she had conjured in her imagination.

'Husband . . .' she said uncertainly.

'Pray, er, sit down.' He drew forth a chair and, turning to the gaoler who was curiously watching this encounter between the twin components of his sideline, ordered wine and meat 'if there was any to be had'. Whereupon Fitchett, with a lopsided grin, assured him there was a plentiful supply.

Faulkner remained standing, embarrassed by the stink of the slop bucket and the state of his appearance. 'I am sorry that . . .' he began apologetically and then pulled himself together, suddenly aware of how far he had fallen in body and spirit since the meeting with Brenton. Clearing his throat, he asked, 'What are you doing here?'

She caught the noisome smell of his breath that presaged scurvy. 'I have come to see you and how you spend my money,' she said, both her words and her voice harsher than she intended, for he seemed piteous and she resolved to steel herself against any feminine weakness. In that she found the stench of his ordure vaguely helpful.

'Your money? How so?'

'Who do you think pays for your wine and your plentiful supply of meat?'

He disdained any explanation that meat was not, at least not until this very afternoon, in any way plentiful and leapt immediately to the right conclusion. 'It was you who paid for my comforts. Great God, I thought it Nathaniel.'

'He is at sea. How could he . . .?'

'I don't know, I simply thought that it was him, that he left a sum with the gaoler. I had no idea it was you.' He hesitated. 'Well, I suppose I must thank you.'

'I suppose you must, though I had hoped for more grace in it.'

'I am sorry, Judith. I did not mean it like that. I am most sincerely grateful. I know that I did you a great wrong and that you appear to have borne it with the fortitude I so admired in you.'

'Admired. So all is in the past, husband.'

'Where else? They want me hanged as a pirate; there is only past for me, for the present grows intolerable and the contemplation of my short and shortly to be curtailed future does not bear scrutiny.'

'That is not what I hear. And where is that uprightness of purpose I supposed you to possess? Why, I find you . . . not to my liking.'

For a moment he stared at her uncomprehending. 'I did not expect you to come here *liking* me, whatever charitable notion you may have entertained over the past weeks.' She remained silent, repenting that, had he chosen to see it, her words had all but betrayed her. Although he was too confused and surprised to divine the deeper meaning of her odd remark, it prompted him to repeat his first question. 'Why are you here?' She shrugged. 'Did you come to gloat? To see me upon the edge of ruin? To damn me and my Villiers whore.'

'What of her? Dost thou still rut with her?'

'What is that to you?'

'You told me that I was your first.'

'What of that?'

'You were mine.'

'I know, I know . . . and God knows I wish we had never met for I was smitten by her long ere I set eyes on you.'

'Then you married me without love.'

Faulkner shook his head. 'Judith, this is old ground. We tramped it years ago and nothing is to be gained by going over it again.'

She stared at him, her fine features full of fire and indignation, yet she was intelligent enough to realize what he said was true. He watched her ample bosom heaving with repressed emotion and the sight awoke in him those longings a man cannot escape for long, no matter to what extremity fate has reduced him.

'For Heaven's sake, Judith . . .' But she was now reacting against her own impulses, wondering what had driven her here and how she could escape. He misread her and lowered his voice. 'Judith, you can stay here the night.'

'No!' She stood, for looking at the state to which he had been reduced the very notion revolted her.

'Judith, please,' he said hurriedly, 'I meant nothing by it. I . . . I am in low spirits as anyone would be.' He stopped, hearing the bells of All Hallows. 'What day is it? And what is the month?'

She told him and he ran his hand through his long hair, clearly unaware of the details. 'November. God's bones!'

'Desist from such blasphemy, if only to please me.' A thought seemed to strike her. 'Hast thou turned papist?'

'What?'

'Was not your whore a papist?'

'Not to my knowledge,' he said with an air of exasperation.

'And you?'

'Am I a papist?' He shook his head. 'No, of course not, but then,' he added with a touch of irony, 'neither am I a Puritan as you well know.'

She rose, stately and handsome, her face composed and resolute. 'Husband,' she said pointedly, 'I know not what you are.' Then she turned for the door, recollecting herself and swinging back to him to ask that he call Master Fitchett that she might be let out.

Faulkner did as he was bid and a moment later was again alone in the cell with only her faint aroma to say that she had been present, and that rapidly succumbed to the stench of the bucket. For a few moments he stood at the window and caught a quick glimpse of her as she passed into the outer bailey, accompanied by 'Master Fitchett'.

'So she knows his name as I suppose she must if she has had dealings with him.' He spoke out loud, though softly, unaware that it had become habitual. The visit, though it had left him confused, had at least caused him to reassemble his wits. Judith would never understand that her visit, profoundly unsatisfactory to her, had been the saving of her despised husband's life.

Mr Fitchett and Mr Fox

Winter 1650 – Spring 1651

As she vanished from his sight, Faulkner felt a great relief that at first confused him. A moment's reflection, however, made him realize that he longed for the fresh air of a ship's deck. A ship's deck was greatly to be desired – at any price. He moved swiftly to the door and called through the shut grill. After a few moments the gaoler appeared.

'You might have had her lie with you for a price,' he said.

'No doubt,' Faulkner replied coldly, 'but that is not in my mind at the moment.'

'She is a comely woman. I'd not toss her out of my bed were I lucky enough to have her in my room.'

'Likely your room does not stink of your shit and you have means to shave when you wish it, not to mention apparel of some cleanness.'

'Captain, these things can be had, you have only to ask.'

'I would ask you something else.'

'Have you the means to put a farthing or two up for it?'

'You know damned well you stripped me of every coin I possessed within a week of my arrival. Debit whatever compact you make with my wife.'

'What is it you wish to ask for?'

'Dost know the names of either of the two gentlemen who were the first to visit me here some twelvemonth past?'

'What if I do? I cannot tell thee.'

'But thou knowest?'

'I did not say so.'

'Mr Fitchett, I do not need to know their names, I need to know only that you will pass a message to them, either of them, it does not matter.'

'It might matter.'

'How so?'

Fitchett shrugged. 'Well the one might be up for you and the other down upon you.'

'I cannot trouble about that. Now, can you do it for me?'

'Not for a farthing; perhaps a crown.'

'A crown then.'

'But I have orders to deliver only your confession and you have yet to write it.'

'No matter about that. No, wait, I shall write that I am composing it and you will take this news, together with my desire — no, my humble supplication — that one or both of the gentlemen who favoured me with their attentions might come again and talk with me. Will thou do that for me, Mr Fitchett?'

The gaoler stood regarding Faulkner for more moments than seemed comfortable. 'Have you considered, Captain, that by drawing attention to yourself, you may find . . .'

'That I am hanged for my pains? Yes,' Faulkner responded with more cheerfulness than he felt, but with such a sudden liberation of his spirit that he felt careless of the consequences, so brimful was he of sudden resolution. 'Now, will you do as I ask?' Fitchett nodded. 'Good, then come to me in an hour and I shall have the paper ready.'

An hour later, sealed with candle wax, Faulkner placed into the hand of his gaoler a letter upon which his future depended.

Faulkner was never certain when Fox received his letter, though Fitchett protested it had been delivered the day following that in which Faulkner had put it into his hand.

'You took no receipt for it?' Faulkner asked irritably.

The gaoler shook his head with a chuckle. 'Is not the word of a gentleman enough?'

Faulkner desisted from an argument in which the quality of a public turn-key, even one practising his dark art in the Tower of London, was sufficient claim to gentry. And although he returned to questioning Fitchett as the days rolled into weeks and the weeks into months, the man persisted in his story, advising Faulkner from too much troubling Mr Fox by sending a second missive, he having important business of state to attend to. Faulkner received no other visitors during this time and, to his chagrin, it appeared that some at least of his comforts were withdrawn. Fitchett refused him wine and meat on several occasions, pleading a lessening of his fee from 'that handsome wife of yours'. Moreover, he let it be known that, unless payments resumed at their maximum level by the autumn, Faulkner could forget about a fire during the next winter.

Apart from the mysterious arrival of a case of books, he was left to his solitude as winter gave way to spring and the year turned. The diversion afforded by the books, which included Sir Walter Ralegh's *History of the World* and, of greater significance, Selden's *Dominion of the Sea*, undoubtedly preserved Faulkner's sanity. There had been a snowfall at Christmas and, careless of the loss of heat, he had opened his narrow, barred window to put his hand out and catch some snowflakes. The falling snow deadened the sound of the surrounding city so that he distinctly heard the raucous cawing of the ravens and a sad, desultory roaring of a lion in what was once the Royal Menagerie. Somewhere else in the grim fortress another prisoner had opened a window and was singing a yuletide air that threatened to start tears from Faulkner's eyes. He was on the point of shutting the casement when he reflected the singer, whoever he was, had been motivated to open his window and express his own wonder at the phenomenon. Nonetheless, there were bleak moments when, for example, the church bells of All Hallows, St Olave's and diverse others within earshot of the Tower, rang in the New Year.

He was not left alone forever. Without warning, and on a propitiously sunny morning in early May of 1651, Fitchett threw open the door with a flourish and a triumphant expression that challenged Faulkner to mistrust his honesty, notwithstanding the interval of time that had passed, to admit the man Faulkner had come to regard as Mr Fox.

'I trust I find you well, Captain Faulkner?' he asked abstractedly as he uncovered, sat at the small table and briskly removed some papers from his satchel as though he had paid a visit only recently.

Faulkner forbore replying; the question seemed ridiculous for the symptoms of scurvy were an increasing torment and Fox, if that was his real name, was pointedly avoiding the foul breath that was an indication of Faulkner's distemper. Fox drew a tobacco pipe from a pocket, called for a light from Fitchett, who was hovering in the doorway, and indicated for Faulkner to sit opposite. With the pipe alight and himself settled, Fox stared at Faulkner, tapping the papers before him. Faulkner recognised them as his 'expiation'.

'These are . . .' Fox pulled a face. 'Adequate. At least the Council of State, which has had your case under constant review, has decided not to bring you to trial but to require you to serve out your adjudged sentence of five years.'

'How can I be adjudged and sentenced without first being tried?' Faulkner asked.

Fox smiled. 'You were tried in absentia, my dear Captain, shortly after your exploit at The Nore.'

'Why was I not told?'

'In case we wished to charge you thereafter with treason. As I say, your case has been under constant review and has caused some little flurry in Lincoln's Inn.' Fox's tone had a certain charming levity, as though the entire matter was of no great moment but a teasing challenge for the lawyers. Beyond the laws of prize and reprisal, in which Mainwaring had coached him, Faulkner's unusual past denied him any understanding of the wider common law. 'Your expiation, though unremarkable, has stayed the Council's hand in respect of treason. If you are willing, at the termination of your sentence and upon your affirming by oath your loyalty to the state, we may have some employment for you. Part of that affirmation will be your further good conduct under the beneficent care of the good Fitchett.' Fox stared at him. 'Do you understand?'

Faulkner was certain that he did not. There seemed something odd about the whole affair, something peculiarly irregular. True, some walked out of the Tower with their heads still set firmly upon their shoulders, but more left in two distinct parts concealed in a coffin.

'Well?'

'I, er, I greatly appreciate the clemency of the Council,' he said hurriedly, 'and will do whatever I can to justify its confidence.'

'I would not put it that high, Captain,' Fox remarked drily, sorting some documents in his satchel, 'but I note your remark.

Now, I wish you to attest to this document drawn up in your behalf.' Fox passed a single sheet of paper across the table and proffered a short quill and a travelling inkpot.

'I have my own,' Faulkner said, as he began to read.

'Of course,' said Fox, watching him. The document was short; a simple repudiation of his oath of allegiance to King Charles and his heirs. He knew an instant's hesitation would utterly ruin his case, and why Fitchett had remained in the room. He signed immediately, whereupon Fox spun the document, witnessed Faulkner's signature and held his quill out to Fitchett to act as second witness. A moment later Fox was on his feet, the papers scooped into his satchel and his hat upon his head.

For a long moment after Fox's departure Faulkner wondered what consequences would follow. After a little reflection, however, he realized he was one of many who had renounced the King, most he suspected for reasons of self-preservation. And did he not have all the more reason if Prince Charles had seduced Katherine, as he had been led to believe?

After the long and wearying months of isolation, Faulkner's life now entered a new phase. Despite the years of incarceration he had yet to endure if he was to regain his future at all, within a week of Fox's visit he was allowed to walk in the Tower grounds. At first he found the full sunlight agony to his eyes and his muscles ached abominably from having to climb the steps of the Beauchamp Tower but, of all things, a few apples – upon which, he noticed, both his own fate and that of Adam turned – had ended his incipient scurvy and all but fully cured him of his noxious breath.

Ten days after he was first allowed to exercise in fresh air he was awakened one morning by Fitchett and another, a superior officer in the Tower who conducted him to another part of the fortress. The man said little beyond informing Faulkner that he was being permitted an interview with another prisoner, one but recently arrived. On enquiring the other's name, the constable's officer merely smiled, saying, 'I am sure you will not need to ask after you have seen him.'

Faulkner was at a loss, but knew the face that turned towards him as he was ushered into a room not unlike his own. 'Sir Henry!'

'My boy! They told me you were here, I had not thought
. . .' Mainwaring, who looked much older than his sixty-odd
years, broke off choking. He was visibly moved by their
encounter. Faulkner himself was overcome as the two men
clasped each other.

'Have you been well treated?' Mainwaring asked, holding
Faulkner by the shoulders at arm's length.

'As well as I suppose I had a right to expect,' Faulkner
replied. 'But what of you? How come you too are in this
place?'

''Tis a long story, Kit, and not entirely disconnected with
you, for much happened after your departure and much, I
suspect, has a bearing on your own fate and your long
imprisonment.'

'I do not understand. Surely you are in England, as you
intimated was your intention, of your own accord? Why should
you be sent hither?' Faulkner, who had persuaded himself that,
whatever the vagaries of their politics or religion, the
Commonwealth authorities prided themselves on a less arbitrary
form of government than the late King. If they had thrown a
willing supplicant for mercy into the Tower, what did that
make of Fox's reassurances to Faulkner himself?

Mainwaring shrugged wearily. 'My long negotiations are not
yet sufficient but that I must pay some penance by time in this
place. I have reached what they are pleased to call a "composition" with a committee for compounding the estates of
"Malignant Royalists" and have admitted to owning a few
effects to the value of eight pounds. My case is being decided
and I have been warned to expect a forfeit of one sixth of this
estate.' Mainwaring paused, looking at the younger man who
seemed to need time to digest this intelligence. In his eyes,
Faulkner looked older, thinner, his face lined, his beard, though
not long, neglected, as though he shaved infrequently.

'You did not apply for *habeas corpus ad subjiciendum*?'

Faulkner looked blank. 'I do not understand . . .' he said
again.

Mainwaring smote his forehead. 'Of course! You had no
knowledge of it! I neglected to give you legal education necessary to . . . God rot me, Kit, but I am so sorry. Damn me,

but 'tis too late now. But tell me, what is the state of your affairs?'

Faulkner, realizing the Latin expression articulated by Mainwaring was some legal process for which the time of application had long expired, told him what had passed between himself and Fox a few days earlier. Mainwaring nodded, asked a few questions and then agreed that he had done the only thing he could. 'They made me sign a repudiation, too. Does it trouble you?' he asked, referring to Faulkner's broken oath of allegiance.

Faulkner shrugged. 'Perhaps. But that rather depends upon what you are going to tell me by way of news from The Hague.'

Mainwaring blew out his cheeks, as though deciding where to start, but avoiding addressing the question Faulkner most wanted answered but feared asking. 'Well, the King, having gone into France secretly, is now in Scotland.'

'Raising an army?'

Mainwaring nodded. 'He left McDonnell in The Hague to answer awkward questions. Rupert is God knows where by now, but probably the Mediterranean. When I learned of Charles's advances to King Louis, which followed hard upon definite news that you had been taken, I determined to make my peace with the Commonwealth. It was not easy, for the Parliament's agent in The Hague, a man I think you met named Isaac Dorielaus . . .'

'Yes, I knew him, but did not trust him.'

'Well, he was murdered by someone acting for Charles, or those advising him, which is the more likely. That put my own plan behind hand, for it had of course to be a most secret undertaking otherwise those who slit the throat of Dorielaus would have despatched me with as little regret. Indeed, it entirely unravelled and I had then to reconstruct it without it being known to those close about me.'

'And was Kate among those close about you?'

'She was . . . for some of the time.'

'And did you intend that I should learn she had been bedded by the King?' Faulkner found he could ask the question without his voice betraying his emotion.

Mainwaring nodded.

'And was it . . . is it true? Or did you wish me to believe it so that I too might be of the same mind as you and make my composition with the Commonwealth?'

'Both; it was true and I strove to get the message to you indeed to induce you . . .'

'To turn my coat.'

Mainwaring shook his head. 'No, Kit, no. These are not the times for such crisp distinctions. Why, half the Fraternity of the Trinity House, men you and I loved like brothers, have bethought it best for themselves and their country to throw up the old order and embrace the new.'

Faulkner was not listening. He was musing on his numbness at the news of Katherine's undoubted infidelity and discovered that it pained him less than he had thought it would. After the loneliness of the recent past he found himself almost indifferent. She, like he in his extremity, must make the best of things as they stood, not things as they might desire. Perhaps Judith had been right, and Katherine was nothing but an elegant whore; perhaps Katherine had had no alternative with him gone and Mainwaring lacking in income once he, Faulkner, had ceased taking prizes. Eight pounds' worth of personal effects said all there was to be said about exile.

'Kit?'

'Eh? Oh, yes, yes. Truth to tell, I am not greatly troubled any more. If I escape this place with my head upon my shoulders I shall consider myself well served.'

'More closely touching yourself,' Mainwaring said, lowering his voice, 'you have money in the hands of a banker in Amsterdam. Some two thousand pounds.'

'Great God!' Faulkner paused, puzzled; he had not thought the proceeds of his privateering career had yielded so much. 'Why did you not use it for yourself? Or for Kate?' he asked, as Mainwaring put his index finger to his lips.

'Because, my dear Kit, whatever I may have been and whatever the world may think of me, I did not raise you from the gutter to rot here or anywhere else. I am old, a dying old fool, but I would yet see you acquit yourself in this benighted country's service. There is a war brewing, if not with the Dutch

or the French, while Charles and his bloody Scots are likely
to march south to raise those Royalists still to be smoked out
of a few corners of the kingdom.'

'Perhaps that is not the correct term,' Faulkner said, with a
smile at his old mentor's enthusiasm.

'They would have a king in the Channel Islands and the
Scillies – and London too, if Charles succeeds in his mad
enterprise.'

'Do you think he will?'

Mainwaring shook his head. 'No, the army of the Parliament
is a force to be reckoned with for it has grown in stature during
these last years, whereas the King's dwindled in proportion.'

Faulkner recalled the tough old cornet-of-horse and the
troopers of his own escort to London. 'Happen you are right,'
he said, 'but if we fight the Dutch, what of my money in
Amsterdam? And why so much? I thought the sum remitted
to the King.' He paused frowning, the revelation occurring to
him as he studied Mainwaring's wry expression.

'You! You have been manipulating . . .'

'It was only necessary for Charles and Rupert to tax your
efforts to the extent that I thought necessary,' said the shrewd
old man. 'I was, after all, in charge of refitting Rupert's ships.'

'You put money by!' Faulkner said, his eyes wide with
wonder. 'But you, Sir Henry,' he paused, thinking of those
eight miserable pounds that represented Mainwaring's entire
fortune. 'What of yourself? After all you have done for me, I
would have had you well provided for.'

'I know that, my boy, I know. But what was the point? The
old have fewer wants and needs than the young and would
you have me forfeit it to the Commonwealth, notwithstanding
the fact that it was derived from their shipping?' Mainwaring's
watery eyes twinkled. Twisting his mouth he added ironically,
'Besides, what would you have an old pirate to do, eh? Honest
broking is too straight for these twisted times.'

'And the money now?'

'Oh, it is safe enough.' Mainwaring rummaged in a pocket
and brought out a small sealed packet.

'You know the man, Johannes van Oven?' Faulkner nodded,
Van Oven had, from time to time, acted as a prize agent on

his behalf. 'This is a letter of credit which will allow you to refit yourself in London. There are also papers lodged with Meneer Goudsmit.'

Faulkner recollected the Jewish banker and his fine house on the River Ij in Amsterdam. Shaking his head, he remarked, 'You have considered everything.'

'Up to the point where matters must take their course. What shall you do about your future?'

'I must serve out my sentence before my expiation is effective.'

'It was not I who sent for you today, Kit,' Mainwaring said pointedly. 'I was asked, in that way that a room in the Tower makes plain, to indicate to you that, if you are to be of any value, you must commit yourself — and soon.'

'How is that possible until my sentence is passed?'

Mainwaring smiled. 'How well do you recall Jersey?'

'Jersey?'

'Aye. We were there some months before His Royal Highness passed into the Low Countries. And you know the Scillies well enough.'

'You mean . . .' Faulkner responded, Mainwaring's meaning becoming clear. 'You think my services as a pilot might be of value to an expedition to these places?'

'I am told,' said Mainwaring, 'that a certain Captain Henry Brenton is fitting out the *Basilisk* at Deptford and has yet to complete his complement.'

'Why could they not have made this matter plain?'

'Because you are under a sentence and because the notion has to come from you as proof of your honourable intentions.'

Faulkner shook his head. 'They have a rum way of doing business.'

'They wish to be taken for honest men, Kit. It is best to accept them at their own valuation. I do not know that they will accept your offer, but —' Mainwaring shrugged — 'who knows in this uncertain world?'

'Was it Brenton who was in touch with you?'

'No. Others, who come by night, and do not reveal their names. And now, for all our sakes, my lips are stopped.' Mainwaring patted Faulkner on the shoulder. 'Now let me send for wine and then you must to your own place and summon your wits with pen and paper.'

On returning to his cell Faulkner stood for some time staring unseeing out of the narrow window. In his mind's eye he conjured up the image of Katherine and was filled with an immense regret so deep that the tears started to his eyes. And yet, circumstanced as she was, with news that he had been taken into the Tower of London and scarce a farthing to her name, how could she not have accepted the protection of the uncrowned Charles. He would cast her aside when he had had enough of her, when another pretty ankle, roguish eye, or pert bosom had taken his fancy. For all Faulkner knew, she may already have been thrown over but he also knew that for all his carelessness towards the emotions of those in his service, he would see that Katherine did not starve. Women had little choice in this world, he concluded, and with that thought he turned from the window and reached for pen, ink and paper, bawling for Fitchett's boy to bring him a light. An hour later, having sealed the missive with candle wax, he called for Fitchett himself and, for another crown – 'the last I hope, Master Fitchett, that you will demand from my wife' – had the letter taken to Mr Fox.

Three weeks later, shortly before noon on a chilly day of mizzling rain and swirling mist which might have been either autumn or a wet spring, Fitchett brought him a note from Mainwaring which informed him that he had been released and gone to Camberwell. He regretted being unable to part properly from Faulkner but declared that, should matters fall out to his advantage, Faulkner would be most welcome at his lodgings.

The following morning, with a great jingling of his huge bunch of keys, Fitchett opened the door to admit Mr Fox who bore his satchel. Placing this on the table he withdrew a heavily sealed letter, which he opened with a penknife and, having waved it under Faulkner's nose, handed it to Fitchett.

'Your discharge, Captain Faulkner, and –' he withdrew a second paper which he passed to Faulkner – 'a warrant to act in the State Navy. You are to be congratulated. Captain Brenton has requested your services as pilot aboard the *Basilisk*, frigate.'

Part Three
In the Service of the State

1651–1659

The *Basilisk*

Faulkner drew his cloak closer round him, bracing himself against the heave of the frigate as she led the squadron towards the low table-land that extended itself across a wider arc of the horizon ahead with every hour that passed. It no longer bore the appearance of a blue bruise in the growing light of the new day. Increasingly he could make out differences in tone along the shore of Bouley Bay where the land dipped and rose, culminating in the western extreme of Grosnez Point. Turning, he looked abaft the starboard beam where the island of Sark was dropping reassuringly astern. This was their second attempt to reach Jersey, the first having been frustrated by a gale that had forced the squadron to lay-to and afterwards anchor off Sark.

Turning back to regard their objective, he judged they had sufficient offing to round Grosnez Point without running foul of the extensive reef three miles north of the headland known as Pierres de Lecq, even though they were hard on the wind which blew from the south-west with post-equinoctial ferocity. The bearing of the white water he could just make out breaking over the rocks was slowly opening out on the bow and the tide, he knew, was then setting to the west, also assisting them. Reassured, his own poor physical state impinged upon his senses.

God, but it was chilly! He moved reluctantly, the disturbance in his wrappings necessary to bestir the blood in his cramped limbs. The legacy of long imprisonment hampered him; the lack of exercise and the want of good food had transformed a man in the peak of condition. Faulkner felt, for the first time in his life, the impact of hard usage and advancing years. Not even the wound in his leg had confronted him with death as a reality, although – after the many months of inactive incarceration in the Tower – it had left him with a slight limp. He tossed the personal reflection aside as Brenton came on deck.

'I give you good day, sir,' Faulkner said, doffing his hat to the *Basilisk*'s commander before jamming it securely back on his head.

'God's grace to you, Captain Faulkner,' Brenton replied with his friendly smile. It was a measure of the man that he had insisted on calling his pilot, a man under a certain subtle supervision, by his former rank. Although any mention of Faulkner's knighthood had long been buried, Brenton insisted this courtesy was extended to him by all the frigate's officers. For his own part, Faulkner had determined to keep his own council and to execute his duties with a scrupulous attention to detail. Brenton had offered him no special favours, though he was always friendly towards the man that some aboard the *Basilisk* regarded as a cuckoo in their nest while the inhabitants of the lower deck were more inclined to regard him as a Jonah. This owed more to the delay in getting the *Basilisk* refitted than to any misconduct on Faulkner's part, but his identity was well known to all on board and the failure of their frigate to join General-at-Sea Robert Blake's squadron for the taking of the Isles of Scilly from the Royalists under Sir John Grenville had to be ascribed somewhere. God-fearing men, as all who served the Commonwealth now regarded themselves, could see no other reason than that of the cavalier officer foisted upon them by some quirk of authority. Indeed, Brenton himself risked some criticism for insisting upon Faulkner's engagement as the *Basilisk*'s pilot, but Faulkner began the work of self-redemption by producing some new charts of their destination.

When the *Basilisk* joined Blake's flag in early August, news of the fiasco of the mismanaged attack on the Scillies, due largely to the failure of the pilots to land in the appointed place, became common knowledge. There were those on board who recalled Faulkner before the Civil War, who spoke of his straight dealing as both commander and ship owner and his part in the raid on the Moroccan port of Sallee. It began to occur to some among the ship's company that if, with God

on their side, matters might still miscarry, as they had at Tresco
in the Scillies, then perhaps harnessing the reformed spirit of
a Malignant might the better manifest God's will. Thus, the
chilly atmosphere that had prevailed during the passage down-
Channel began to thaw and, if they thought much about it at
all, both officers and men began to regard Faulkner with less
hostility.

Now, as they approached their objective, the Royalist strong-
hold of Jersey, it became clear to many, especially the *Basilisk*'s
officers, that Faulkner's qualities were about to be put to the
test. Few among them failed to recognize that landing on the
rock-and-reef island in the face of opposition was going to be
difficult. Fewer still did not know that those difficulties would
be compounded by the late season of the year and the fact
that the Channel Islands were not merely surrounded by rocks,
but subject to exceedingly strong tides. Not only was there a
large rise and fall of water, a matter making the landing of
boats uncertain, but the strength and speed of the tidal streams
had a profound effect on the conduct of a vessel, particularly
if the wind fell light. Not that there seemed much prospect
of that at the moment, with a stiff breeze coming up from the
south-west. But that in itself posed problems for, while it gave
the men-of-war the power of manoeuvrability, when tide and
wind ran in contrary directions their opposing forces cut up
a vicious hollow sea, making boat operations impossible.

'We shall be off Grosnez Point in three hours,' Faulkner
remarked to Brenton as he turned to look astern and out on
the starboard quarter at the squadron spread out behind them.

'The post of honour, Kit,' he said in a low voice, turning
back to stare ahead. 'May I have the use of your glass?'

'Of course.' Faulkner handed Brenton his telescope. 'You
will see the white water on Les Pierres de Lecq a little to the
left of the end of the land . . .'

They fell to discussing the run of the tide in the coming
hours and the best way of making the approach, which they
had been worrying over ever since they had received the order
issued by the Council of State on 20th September, to take the
Channel Islands.

★　★　★

...ase from the Tower of London, Faulkner had
...k with Mainwaring in Camberwell assembling
...lothes, arms and instruments to resume his career
...Mainwaring's prudence in securing a means of accessing
his money had greatly eased this task, reminding Faulkner of
the older man's generosity in first equipping him for sea.
Divining the Council of State's likely strategy, it had been
Mainwaring who supplied Faulkner with some new charts of
the Channel Islands. These had come from 'some old friends
from the Trinity House', Mainwaring told him when he
enquired. But that was not all Mainwaring had done for him,
for it became obvious to Faulkner that Mainwaring's coming
over from the Low Countries had been largely dictated by his
own situation, and that Mainwaring's objective had always been
the promotion of his protégé.

It was not easy to understand all this, particularly as following
the then Prince Charles into exile had been so palpably the
wrong course of action. It was only later, when Faulkner had
the liberty to consider these things, that he realized that for a
man of Mainwaring's age, background and uncommitted and
undeclared religious affiliation, the repudiation of a legitimate
monarchy in the face of rebellion had been a step he felt unable
to take. That he had repented at leisure, while making the
matter more difficult, only made it more necessary. Despite
their long intimacy, Faulkner had never fully understood the
reasons for his patron's conduct, especially in respect of himself.
Long ago Mainwaring had told him the country was desperately
in need of good sea officers, but that was back in the reign of
King James when the century was a not a quarter old. Later
conversations had been less clear-cut but, on the eve of his
return to London to join the *Basilisk*, Mainwaring had made
a remark that Faulkner had turned over in his mind ever since,
and was perhaps the best explanation he would ever have from
the old man.

Amid a rather emotional eve of leave-taking, after a good
dinner during which each of them had downed the better part
of two bottles, Mainwaring had stoked up his pipe and lay back
in his chair, wreathed in smoke, his voice thick with fine feeling
and the slur of wine, musing on the nation's predicament.

'Once the Royalists are overcome, we shall likely fight the Dutch,' he had mused. 'That will be a tragedy for both countries, for both share a religion and neither has territorial ambitions over the other. We shall fight for trade and, I believe, the victor has the potential to become the most important maritime power in Europe.'

'What of France?' Faulkner had asked. 'Or Spain?'

Mainwaring had considered the question for a long while and then said, 'Both will be dangerous, especially France as long as *Le Roi Soleil* governs her, but neither has the same predatory instinct for trade as the Dutch and they have proved that they can measure their swords against both. If they prevail at sea over us, then we shall be nothing but an offshore island with a population that will sink into barbarity watching the ships of others sail past our southern coasts, whose abler sons take to prosecuting piracy like the Irish.' He had paused again as Faulkner had seen the logic swim out of the blue clouds of tobacco smoke wreathing the old man in the form of the full sails of a score of ships. Wrapped in the fanciful illusion, Faulkner studied the swirls, watching the chimera dissolve with an almost childish delight. Suddenly Mainwaring set aside his pipe, whipped off his full-bottomed wig and flung it on the table beside him. Vigorously scratching his pate he had declared with a conviction that Faulkner was later to recall many times, 'Kit, if the Commonwealth survives as a strong centre of power, it could achieve great things and it can only achieve great things at sea.'

Now, as he watched the coast of Jersey take on a distinct appearance, the details of its church towers, the grey flecks of cottages, the white of sheep, the autumnal green of a pasture dotted with brown cattle, the rich russets of turning trees, he wondered if they were on the eve of a great thing, or not.

Blake's operations off Jersey were not helped by the lateness of the Council of State's order, a demonstration that it was dominated by soldiers rather than men acquainted with operations at sea. True, it had been hoped that the appearance of the squadron would induce Sir George Carteret to surrender and – as they later discovered – it had so rattled the rank and file of the defenders that, in the end, with the exception of Carteret's withdrawal into Elizabeth Castle, the fortress at St Helier at the extremity of its long mole, once ashore resistance soon crumbled.

It was the landing that proved difficult, calling from the assembled squadron some minor prodigies of seamanship as the squadron anchored first in St Ouen's Bay. This extended from Le Grande Etacquerel to the south-west corner of the island, Corbière Point, which extended offshore some distance in the form of a jagged series of rocks and reefs. These were exposed at low water and lurked not far beneath the surface at the top of the tide. Rounding the point, one encountered the smaller and easily defended St Breland's Bay, beyond which was the long curved stretch of St Aubin's Bay upon the shores of which, behind the dark mass of Elizabeth Castle, lay the principal town of St Helier. But seaward of these bays, cast about the island of Jersey like the devil's necklace, was an extensive litter of rocks, reefs and shoals, within which an invading force must operate. And while the interposition of this natural barrier broke the worst of the powerful surge of the sea itself, the prevailing wind from the south-west quarter could blow with gale force, making the coast a lee shore.

As the squadron stood inside the outer shoals, passing within long cannon shot of Le Grande Etacquerel, it was immediately obvious that Carteret had fortified the shoreline of St Ouen's Bay with earthworks. A boat from the flagship, the *Happy Entrance*, was ordered by Blake to land an officer with a flag of truce, but the offer of terms was rejected by Carteret, who hoped the autumnal weather would defeat Blake. In this he seemed correct, for although the boat bearing the flag of truce got off the beach, all hope of a rapid landing evaporated as the wind increased and Blake ordered Richard Badiley in the *Paragon* and the two frigates, including the *Basilisk*, to sail up and down the bay, bombarding the shore.

Had the Commonwealth forces seen the terror this induced among the Royalist troops they might have taken heart, rather than be disappointed at their own frustration. As it was, the provocative bravado of the Royalist officers, some of whom ostentatiously caracoled their horses, made a brave enough show to conceal the uncertain state of their men's morale. At sunset the signal was made to anchor and next day, with *Basilisk* again in the van, the squadron doubled the Corbière rocks and made as though to land in St Brelade's Bay. Although commanded and enfiladed – the narrow bay was a death trap – Blake's bold move induced Carteret to abandon his positions at St Ouen's and march on St Brelade's Bay. But Blake had no intention of sending his men into trouble and cruised the whole of that day, 22nd October, under easy sail along Jersey's south coast, sending the frigates into the anchorages to annoy the anchored merchant shipping there. The *Basilisk* played her part in this, Faulkner ensuring that at no time did Brenton run his ship into shoal water.

But such manoeuvrings were mere demonstrations and Blake was playing a waiting game, appearing back in St Ouen's Bay by daylight on the 23rd. Unfortunately, he was matched in cunning by Carteret who had counter-marched his men and was ready for a landing that was, for a second time, abandoned for fear of a rising wind and heavy surf. Instead Blake hoisted his boats and under easy sail the squadron sailed north, passing Le Grande Etacquerel, throwing shot ashore and again drawing off Carteret's force by detachments. In this *Basilisk* again led, Faulkner being unequivocally burdened with the pilotage. He knew that were anything to go amiss he would be held responsible and possibly charged with treason. He also knew that there was no one in the squadron as familiar as he was with the coast in question for here, in the autumn of 1648, he had taught Charles, Prince of Wales, the finer points of sailing, and they had several times circumnavigated the island in the craft in which the Prince had escaped from the Isles of Scilly.

The feint to the northwards was carried out under low cloud, with frequent rain squalls and a strong onshore breeze, but at dusk they put about and the *Basilisk* followed the other men-of-war back to their anchorage off St Ouen's Bay where the troopships had remained. Soon after dark, the wind began to drop and orders were passed to make ready to land the troops, the men-of-war sending their boats to the transports, but high tide had passed before a boat ran alongside the *Basilisk* and an officer with a written order came up the side. When he had read it, Brenton sent the men to the capstan and summoned Faulkner.

'The General has ordered an attack on the ebb,' he said, clearly anxious. 'He wants us to stand inshore as close as we dare and give covering fire.'

Faulkner nodded. 'The tidal stream, though ebbing, loses much of its strength. Besides, with the wind dropping the moment the boats are emptied of troops, their crews will get them off.'

'Yes, I know,' Brenton said uncertainly, but it was clear he was both anxious and nervous. Just then, the low call from the bow indicated the anchor was a-trip and then aweigh.

'Let fall the topsails and sheet home!' Brenton called and Faulkner went forward to be near the leadsmen who began calling out the diminishing depth. Between the two rocky headlands of Le Grande Etacquerel and Corbière Point, St Ouen's Bay was a sandy strand that sloped gently into deep water. When they had but ten feet under the keel, Faulkner ran aft and told Brenton they could go no further. The helm was put over and the *Basilisk* rounded-to and dropped her anchor. A few minutes later she lay brought up to her cable, gently resolving the forces of wind and tide. A lantern was hung to seaward where the pale shapes of other ships' topsails could be made out against the cloudy night sky and within twenty minutes small black shapes, looking like huge insects, could be seen crawling across the ruffled surface of the sea. The wind had all but fallen away as, led by Captain Dover of the *Eagle*, the first boats touched the shore. Dover's forlorn hope consisted entirely of armed seamen sent to secure a beachhead for the less agile troops – a lesson learned after the debacle of landing on Tresco in April.

To his chagrin, Faulkner was left aboard as Brenton, in common with all the captains in the squadron, accompanied their men and the troops embarked in their ships. Aware of the approaching enemy, Carteret had mustered his men, but his infantry's spirit broke and only a small force of cavalry answered his orders. Cavaliers to a man, they rode down on to the hard sand and slashed left and right among the seamen and crop-head infantry, who scrambled out of their boats as soon as the first scratch of sand was felt under their keels. Some leapt out prematurely and had to swim ashore, or drown in the attempt.

For half an hour vicious fighting went on in the small breakers as horse and foot struggled for mastery of the water's edge. Dover was wounded, as was a lieutenant supporting him. But when the Royalist cavalry commander, Colonel Bosville, was shot out of his saddle by a matchlock, the exhausted and outnumbered cavaliers withdrew, leaving the strip of sand to the invaders.

'It was suddenly all over,' a cold, wet Brenton recounted two days later, nursing a glass of coddled wine back on board the *Basilisk* as she lay snubbing her anchor while Faulkner was as anxious as Brenton had been on the evening of the assault. 'Once the horse broke, we struggled up the beach and found the entrenchments all but empty and we marched for St Aubin's, chasing the Malignants all the way to St Helier.' Brenton paused, knowing his friend was paying more attention to the view of Elizabeth Castle and St Helier, judging whether the frigate's anchors still held in the seabed. 'But you have had your share of troubles, I hear.'

'Yes,' Faulkner replied, abstractedly. 'As you see, the weather worsened while you were enjoying your walk ashore.' Brenton snorted derisively. 'And we lost the *Tresco*, frigate, with all hands.'

'All hands? Dear God. That means . . .'

'Aye, Captain Blake, the General's cousin is lost.'

Blake withdrew the greater number of his ships a few days later. Badiley left for the Mediterranean, another departed for Virginia while the *Basilisk* remained for a few days to support the siege of Elizabeth Castle in which Carteret had barricaded himself. Lying off and throwing shot at the ramparts, the *Basilisk* did what she could to harry the few remaining men loyal to Carteret and King Charles. Meanwhile, they learned that the King, crowned in Scotland and at the head of a Scots army had been utterly routed at Worcester in early September. The Royal personage was, once again, a fugitive, and the news caused Faulkner to fret over Katherine, a mark of his general anxiety rather than his true feelings for his erstwhile mistress; or so he thought at the time.

Bad weather drove them off station and they followed Blake to Portsmouth, arriving on the 17th November.

Before he went ashore and his flag as General-at-Sea was hauled down two days later, Robert Blake sent for Captain Brenton and 'the chief pilot to the squadron'. It was thus that Faulkner followed Brenton up the side of the *Happy Entrance* as she lay at anchor at Spithead. They were met by Blake's flag captain, John Coppin, who bid them welcome and pointed out the irony in their recent operations.

'Did you know, Brenton, that Carteret used to command this ship? Hah! Bet he was less than entranced by the appearance of the *Happy Entrance* off the Jersey coast, eh?' Pleased with his own jest, Coppin led them under the poop and into the great cabin where Blake sat at a table covered with papers, a secretary busy writing at one end. Faulkner had heard a great deal about Blake, of his rise in the Parliamentary army and his transfer to the Commonwealth's navy. He was popular with his crews, but less so with his captains, making stringent demands upon them, unwilling to suffer fools gladly, so he was as anxious as Brenton about the nature of the unusual summons, particularly as he himself had been singled out in such a formal fashion.

Blake was in his shirtsleeves, a plain waistcoat over the white lawn, a bunch of plain lace at his throat. He wore his dark hair long, his round face with its strong features, straight nose and firm mouth looking up at the intrusion.

'Captain Brenton of the *Basilisk* and his pilot, General,' Coppin said, making a small bow as Faulkner followed Brenton's example, sweeping his hat from his head and footing an elegant bow.

'Not *his* pilot, Coppin, *the* pilot, but thank you. Please sit down gentlemen.' Blake indicated two upright chairs that would have served for dinner had Blake invited them to dine with him. As Coppin withdrew, Blake ordered a servant in a side cabin to produce two glasses of *oporto* and Faulkner recollected he had been at Lisbon the previous spring.

'So,' Blake said, raising his glass to the two of them and fixing Faulkner with a steady gaze. 'This is the infamous Sir Christopher Faulkner.'

Faulkner made no move; no one, least of all himself, had used his title since he had landed in England a prisoner and he returned Blake's survey, trying to divine the General-at-Sea's purpose at using it now.

'You do not use your title. Why is that?'

'It does not seem appropriate, Your Excellency. Besides, I am more attached to my reputation as to infamy, than to a knighthood awarded me in previous existence.'

He thought a smile briefly crossed Blake's face. 'You object to being referred to as infamous?'

'I did my duty as I saw it at the time.' He paused a moment, gauging Blake's mood. Blake was ten or twelve years his senior, but they had seen the same changes and might have some things in common.

'I have no doubt as to either your courage or your competence, Sir Christopher. I rather thought your reputation for infamy rested upon your moral state.'

'My moral state, Excellency? Why, what is that to you?' Brenton stirred uneasily beside him, but Faulkner felt a sudden liberation, as though, despite being freed from the Tower, he had been serving some penance at the direction of dark and nameless men. Now, face to face with a man of the Commonwealth elite, he felt the compulsion to make his mark for better or worse.

'Those are bold words, Sir Christopher.'

'Excellency, I do not think—' Brenton began but Blake held up his hand, the left corner of his lips curling upwards, and Brenton fell silent.

'Oh, I do not object to a man standing his ground. Tell me, Captain Brenton, how you addressed our pilot aboard the *Basilisk*? You have been previously acquainted, I believe.'

'We served together aboard the *Prince Royal*, General.'

'And what name do you use after this previous amity?'

'As my . . . as our principal pilot, General Blake, and knowing his rank in other service, I allowed him the courtesy title of Captain.' Faulkner noticed Brenton's left hand was shaking and wondered if he had, on some earlier occasion, been a victim of Blake's wrath.

'Did you now? Well, well.' Blake turned to his secretary who had been busy writing the entire time. 'D'you have that commission, Joseph?'

'Excellency . . .' The clerk laid his quill aside, lifted a paper and handed it to Blake. Looking at it briefly, Blake leaned forward to pass it across the table to Faulkner.

'It seems Captain Brenton has anticipated me, Sir Christopher.' Blake's eyes twinkled with irony. 'I do not have a ship for you at present, Captain Faulkner, but you may count on having one before winter is out. Come, sir; take it, take it.'

Faulkner took the proffered document. Although covered in writing and sealed with the enwreathed emblems of the St George's Cross and Harp, it took him but a moment to realize he was a commissioned captain in the Commonwealth's State Navy.

'My congratulations, Captain Faulkner, upon the faultless execution of your duty. We could have done with you at the Scillies. Now, gentlemen, if you will excuse me . . .'

Scrambling to their feet, Faulkner tucked his commission into his gauntlet. The two officers withdrew after a second, fulsome bow, emerging on deck to find Coppin talking with his first lieutenant. He looked round as Brenton and Faulkner crossed the deck. 'I understand you are one of us, Captain Faulkner,' he said matter-of-factly.

'So it would seem, Captain Coppin,' Faulkner replied, 'so it would seem.'

The Kentish Knock

January – September 1652

Faulkner spent the winter with Mainwaring at Camberwell. His pay enabled him to ease the increasingly frail old man's pains and penury during the cold weather. Mainwaring was pathetically grateful. Faulkner declared it was the very least he could do for a man who, with no more motive than a philanthropic desire, had encouraged a demonstrably able lad to be metamorphosed into a sea officer. What Faulkner was able to tell him of the Commonwealth Navy seemed to please Mainwaring, setting him nodding by the fire of sea-coal that Faulkner ensured was kept in by a husband and wife he hired to attend the old man's wants.

Faulkner mentioned names from the past, some from the Trinity House as it had been before its replacement by a committee, some the names of men now executing the offices of the former Brethren, whose talents for opportunistic ship-owning and timber-supplying were not dissimilar to the pasts of both Mainwaring and his protégé. Although open to charges of corruption, the likes of Nehemiah Bourne, Thomas Smith and Richard Badiley – then commanding the Commonwealth squadron in the Mediterranean – at least ensured that the navy wanted for nothing. It was even known that the victor of Dunbar and Worcester, Oliver Cromwell, supplied timber to the navy. Mainwaring brushed the references to venality aside, maintaining the end justified the means. 'Was not the poor's box at Trinity House filled with the products of sin, Kit?' he was fond of asking. 'And our charitable bequests prompted by bad consciences?'

Here they learned of the recapture of Jersey where the siege of Elizabeth Castle had proved a wearisome business until Carteret, aware of the disaster that had overtaken his Royal Master, capitulated on 12th December. A week later his example was followed by the remnant Royalist garrison on neighbouring Guernsey, likewise mewed up in the island's fortress, Castle Cornet at St Peter Port. Looking at Mainwaring dozing before the fire, Faulkner recalled his words. Great things indeed seemed to be in train.

Although they had spent Christmas that year on their own, in mid-February they were paid a visit by Brenton and his petite blonde wife. Fresh from London, Brenton brought news both of further extirpation of the Royalists, and more closely touching Faulkner.

'Of course, with Rupert at large in the Mediterranean, we have yet to dispose of the canker,' he said, 'but the Royalists at Barbados have surrendered to a squadron under Sir George Ayscue, by Heaven, clear evidence of God's good grace towards our cause.'

They had drunk a bumper to Ayscue and his men, after which Brenton informed Faulkner that he had been ordered to take command of a new ship, the *Dunbar*, then fitting out at Deptford, and hinted that Faulkner might thereby find himself appointed to the *Basilisk* in his room.

'I think, Kit, Blake will prove as good as his word.'

'I never doubted it,' put in Mainwaring, calling for a refill of his glass. Sure enough, three weeks later a letter arrived instructing Faulkner to report to the Naval Commissioners 'upon his appointment to the command of the *Basilisk*, frigate'.

'Great things are afoot, Kit,' Mainwaring had said at his departure. 'Great things.'

A man cannot be everywhere at once, but it seemed to Faulkner in the following sixteen months that he was swept up in the great things that Mainwaring had predicted, for he beat about the Narrow Seas at the behest of either one or another of the Commonwealth's Generals-at-Sea. True, he missed several of the actions with the Dutch, being occupied in other duties which took a frigate elsewhere, but he found himself in the line of danger on more than one occasion and played his part in the first clash between the Protestant powers. In later life he recalled those tumultuous months as a kaleidoscope of impressions which encompassed the howl of the wind, the anxiety of shortening sail on a lee shore or of watching from the quarterdeck the straining gear aloft as he pressed the *Basilisk* to make the best speed she could, for she oft times bore despatches from Blake and Monck to their subordinate admirals, went in chase of a strange sail, or ran before a superior force to bring word of their coming to the nearest English squadron. There was, too, the thunder of the guns, the noise and confusion of close action as the fleets of the two nations clashed off Dover, in the Thames Estuary, off Dungeness, off Portland and, finally, off the coast of Holland. And in the aftermath of action, the pitiable condition of the wounded, for which there was precious little succour, kept the spectre of death before their eyes even as they licked their wounds after defeat, or rejoiced in their victory.

In the spring of 1652, Faulkner was with Nehemiah Bourne's squadron in The Downs. A Dutch fleet under Maarten Harpertzoon Tromp had been reported close inshore off the South Foreland with forty sail and Bourne, with a small squadron of nine, became alarmed when a messenger arrived from Dover with news that, despite a warning gun from the ramparts of Dover Castle, the Dutch refused to dip their colours in respect of England's sovereignty over the narrow strait. The following morning boats from the Dutch men-of-war had pulled close inshore and fired musketry to no good purpose other than to raise an alarm. The intentions of the Dutch were unclear, and while in fact Tromp was awaiting the arrival of a convoy of seven East Indiamen, Bourne sent Faulkner to slip past Tromp during the night, and carry word to Blake who lay off Rye.

Having word from a Dutch frigate that the expected convoy was off Beachy Head, Tromp weighed anchor and hauled offshore against an easterly wind, expecting the convoy's topsails to come over the horizon. What he saw was Blake, his ships on the starboard tack, coming up from Dungeness, so Tromp, with the wind on his starboard quarter, bore down to cut across the head of Blake's two divisions which were parallel to each other. Although neither side intended action, the contentious matter of respect to the English flag provoked an exchange of fire, following which a fierce fight developed. The concussion of the guns and the clouds of smoke rolled ashore over the little town of Folkestone so that the houses shook and the fishermen on shore spoke of a fog on the waters of the Channel, the like of which they had never previously seen.

The *Basilisk* played little direct part in the main action, being sent to locate the expected convoy and harry it with such success that two Indiamen were taken while the rest hauled their wind for the French coast. As Faulkner came up from the south-west with his prizes he witnessed the last phases of the action, with Bourne falling upon the Dutch rear from the north. On a lee shore Tromp, in the *Brederode*, extricated his ships with the loss of three of them, giving Faulkner the opportunity to fire at the retreating force as it stood away out of harm's way.

The battle off Dover, fought on 19th May, caused a declaration of war between the two countries. No one was surprised, for the difficulties of maintaining trade during the long Civil War had encouraged the Dutch to make up for the lack of English merchant ships able to serve the collective needs of the North European markets. The loss of trade to the Dutch, who had thrown off the Spanish yoke, made such inroads that English ship owners were threatened with bankruptcy, particularly those engaged in the Baltic trade. With little to fear from the English navy, divided as it was by civil strife and engaged upon a war against itself, the Dutch thought little of any opposition. The navy of the Stuart kings had been unimpressive, despite the magnificence of a handful of its ships, and the Dutch rested upon the certainty of being the better seamen. It was this weakness that had preoccupied Mainwaring for most of his life and he had striven wherever possible to reverse this, both in terms of ships and men, particularly officers. Kit Faulkner was a product of Mainwaring's private project and, as he made his way up the side of Blake's flagship, the *James*, anchored in The Downs at the end of the day, he considered he had played a small part in the great event that precipitated the war. The *James* had taken a battering and Blake had little time for pleasantries, instructing Faulkner to carry his despatch to London.

The *Basilisk* rejoined the fleet a few days later with orders to take Blake north, to intercept the main convoy from the

East Indies which was expected off the Orkneys. Faulkner himself was left with Admiral Sir George Ayscue, and missed the unsatisfactory encounter between Blake and Tromp off Fair Isle which was spoilt by bad weather. Instead, the *Basilisk* took part in Ayscue's destruction of Dutch ships off Calais before being sent to the westward in search of another homeward-bound convoy, which, they had learned from their captives, was expected to be entering the Channel. Ayscue's squadron, consisting of the sixty-gun *Vanguard* and *George* and eight lesser men-of-war, was also charged to cover English shipping. To this end they were in Plymouth Sound when word came that a Dutch squadron was somewhere off shore, intent on meeting the silver-laden homeward convoy from the West Indies. The Dutch men-of-war made their rendezvous before Ayscue, who had by now been reinforced to a strength of some forty sail, weighed and headed south to intercept the Dutch, known to be under Michel Adriaenzoon de Ruyter. To his chagrin, Faulkner took no part in the action in which De Ruyter succeeded in warding off Ayscue, saving his convoy and compelling Sir George to withdraw into Plymouth. Instead, he had been sent to seek the Dutch to the westwards, in case De Ruyter decided not to hazard his valuable convoy through the Strait of Dover but passed it north of Scotland.

Thanks to detached duty seeing English merchantmen safe into port, Faulkner missed further actions and manoeuvrings in the Channel between the main contending fleets. Nevertheless, he acquitted these tasks with a brisk efficiency that ensured his name began to be noted by the merchants of Liverpool, Bristol, Plymouth and London as a reliable commander who perfectly understood the ways of merchantmen, he having first been to sea in the *Swallow* of Bristol. There were those who asked if this could possibly be the same Captain Faulkner who had caused such a flutter on the London insurance markets a year or two previously but, being assured that it was, remarked that God's redeeming powers were wonderful. Those of a more practical bent agreed that former poachers made the best gamekeepers, remarking that a former privateer commander of any note ought to know where best to intercept incoming ships, whether they were from the East or West Indies.

Unaware of this gossip, Faulkner was in Portsmouth in early September where he rejoined Blake's fleet, sailing east with it when the General-at-Sea ordered his ships to proceed to The Downs. Although the Dutch had succeeded in bringing in most of their trade, some two hundred of their merchantmen were outward bound for the following season's cargoes and, Blake reasoned, would pass the Strait of Dover before the onset of winter. Blake's fleet of over sixty men-of-war was led by the first-rates, *Resolution* and *Sovereign*, the latter formerly King Charles's over-gilded, one hundred-gun, *Sovereign of the Seas*, and the greatest warship in the world.

The weather in late September was blustery, with intermittent gales and short steep seas made worse when wind and tide were in opposition. Thus, while word came that a large Dutch fleet was at sea, Blake hesitated, aware that to better his opponents he must be able to use his superior firepower, particularly the heavy guns on his largest ships' lowest decks. These could not be fired in a heavy sea, for opening the ports led only to flooding. But at daylight on the 28th, the conditions appeared propitious and Blake hoisted the signal for the fleet to weigh and proceed through the narrow Gull Channel so that, once off Ramsgate and clear to the north of the Goodwin Sands, they could form up in their respective divisions.

Passing a fleet of three score men-of-war through a channel fit only for one at a time led to a certain amount of confusion off the North Foreland. The three divisions – the first under the General-at-Sea, Robert Blake, the second under Admiral William Penn, the third under Rear-Admiral Bourne – took hours to debouch to the north of a shoal, Bourne's lagging far behind Blake's and Penn's.

On rejoining the fleet, the *Basilisk* had been ordered back under Bourne's flag and although one of the first ships to be under weigh, Faulkner was obliged to heave to off the North Sand Head and watch the others head away to the north as they came up with their flag officers. Far away, over the lumpy grey-green water, they could see the westering sunlight, shining occasionally through rifts in the rapidly moving clouds, catching the topgallants of the Dutch as they came in from the east, beating up against a brisk south-easterly.

Faulkner paced his quarterdeck in frustration; the day was slipping away, the Dutch had been in the offing for three days and he felt the quickening of blood that was nigh irresistible. Where was Bourne? Beside him his first lieutenant, Matthew Stockton, was in a similar state, almost beside himself with eagerness to get into action and it was the near fury of the younger man that cooled Faulkner.

'We must save the hot-headedness for action, Matthew,' he said with an easy familiarity, raising his glass and staring astern.

'I suppose so, sir,' Stockton responded, 'but I confess to being in a damned fizz.'

'Ahh, here comes Nehemiah, by heaven.' He could see Bourne's flag flying from the mizzen mast of his flagship as, with three other men-of-war, she altered course round the inner extremity of the Goodwins and passed close to the Brake Sand. 'I think that we might haul the mainyards now. Keep the courses in the buntlines while the flag catches up.'

'Aye, sir, I'll inform the master.'

Faulkner nodded and turned his attention to the north where, at last, Blake, his flag now flying from the *Triumph*, and Penn in the *James* were almost up to the southern tail of the Kentish Knock, a large sandbank that lay athwart the outer Thames Estuary. A cloud of sail was storming in from the east, their yards braced sharp up, the dark mass of their hulls still just below the horizon. Faulkner studied the enemy. He had been out in the strait two days previously and had seen the Dutch fleet come out of Calais Road, like themselves, in three divisions. Their chief commander was Witte Corneliszoon de With, a hard republican, hated by his men; but he was a brilliant seaman and ably supported by De Ruyter and De Wildt.

The dull thump of a distant gun rolled across the water as Bourne's flagship cleared the shoals, bunting bright at her mastheads, summoning his squadron.

'All sail, Mr Clarkson,' Faulkner called to the master, shutting his telescope with a snap. 'I am going below a moment,' he said, dropping smartly down to his cabin where his servant buckled on his half-armour over a leather jerkin. The cabin was cleared of all furniture and a gun's crew occupied each quarter, looking at him curiously as he stood in their midst, making his final preparations by settling his sword on his hip. He took up a small hat, devoid of any decoration and as like Puritan garb as anything he had ever worn. Clapping it on his head he looked about him.

'Well, men, I wish you God's blessing on your work today. Serve your guns well and trust in the righteousness of our cause.' He was uncertain of the righteousness of their cause, or of too frequent a reference to God, but he knew their sympathies and knew they were still getting the measure of him as a former Malignant. He was therefore pleased with the enthusiastic 'Alleluias!' that greeted his little speech. Nodding to his servant as he took up the wheellock pistol that Brenton had presented him with on taking command, he stuck it into his crimson sash. 'It's charged and loaded. God bless you, sir,' the servant said.

'And you, Jackson. And you.'

Although he had been below for only ten minutes it seemed they had significantly closed the distance on Blake and Penn as Bourne's division came up from the south. The Dutch fleet, though no more than the English, seemed numerous, stretched out on the starboard bow. Faulkner stared out on the larboard bow, trying to see whether there was white water showing over the Knock but the horizon was obscured by the English men-of-war.

'Have you seen the Knock, Mr Clarkson?'

'No, sir, but I've a man in the larboard chains to keep an eye on the depth.'

'That is well done. If the Dutchmen press us too far to the west . . .'

'We'll be in trouble,' Clarkson finished the sentence, as anxious as Faulkner. 'The tide ain't helping neither.'

'Look there, sir!' Stockton called, pointing out on the larboard bow. 'The general's engaging!'

Now up with the enemy, the *Resolution* had altered course to starboard, across the line of the Dutch advance, her yards squared off before the wind and leading Blake's ships into action. At this distance, the prickling sparks of her gunfire seemed innocuous and nothing could be heard in the thrash of the sea alongside the *Basilisk* and the soughing of the wind in their own rigging. Smoke clouds began to form and then drift to leeward while answering flashes came from the bow chasers of one or two of the Dutchmen. Then, like distant thunder as the wind carried it away from them, they heard the noise; already men lay dead and dying as the fleets exchanged their opening shots.

'They're tacking!' Stockton called excitedly.

Faulkner raised his glass, watching the leading Dutch ship turn across the wind and head south-south-east. He did not think she was the *Brederode*, but she was flying De With's flag from her main truck, the horizontally barred red, white and pale blue of her ensigns flickering brightly from her stern. The last of the sun caught the gilding of bow and high stern, sparkling as she swung, and flecked the fluttering luffs of her topsails and topgallants with pale gold. He heard Stockton, a young man of promise and a romantic bent, mutter, 'Magnificent!'

Then, her entire windward side belched fire as the starboard batteries responded to the English broadsides. 'Very well, gentlemen, stand-to and take your posts.'

The order was a formality; they had been at their posts for hours, but the words reminded them, tightened their muscles, sharpened their attention. It was just as well, for events seemed to speed up, the closing rate of the two fleets suddenly increased by the tacking of the Dutch. As De With's division merged with Blake's, the ships were enveloped in their own gunsmoke so that, while the tops of their masts with their pennants and standards stood clear, the dark mass of their hulls seemed only vaguely perceptible, picked out by the sparks of gunfire that penetrated the thick obscurity.

But to the east of De With's division, parallel with him but now passing him as his ships hauled up their courses for the bloody struggle with Blake, came De Ruyter's squadron.

'They're intent on Bourne,' Faulkner muttered to himself, taking a quick look around the horizon. He had little idea what was happening to the north-west, though he briefly saw the massive bulk of the *Sovereign* far away and it crossed his mind that she was close to the tail of the Kentish Knock. But that was not his affair; his duty lay in keeping with Bourne and the *Basilisk* was the leeward-most ship of Bourne's division, which meant she would receive the full weight of shot of De Ruyter's van. This consisted, as far as he could see, of a ship of at least fifty guns with a consort on her larboard quarter. Both had crammed on sail, their yards braced sharp up as they made to cut off Bourne and get to windward of the English.

'Them squareheads have some lubberly ships for leeway, sir,' Clarkson remarked.

It was vaguely gratifying to know that Clarkson either did not know, or had forgotten, that Faulkner had been intimate with the Dutch. 'I know, Mr Clarkson, I know.' But his mind was on the opportunity he saw developing.

'Hands to the braces! Square away! Larboard your helm!' he called sharply. *Basilisk* began to turn to starboard, heading to cross the advancing line of the enemy.

'Sir . . .?' Clarkson queried, jolted out of his ruminations on Dutch ship design.

'I intend you to throw in raking shots. Tell Mr Stockton! Larboard battery when he is ready and at his discretion!' It did not do to hold the reins too close.

A messenger ran below, bringing back the news that Stockton was all ready. Across the deck, close by the helmsmen, Clarkson was praying out loud and unashamedly. This was, Faulkner had heard, how the Parliamentarians had gone into action at Marston Moor and Naseby. Despite his misgivings he was caught up in the fervour such a bold conviction carried; this was superb! Sublime! Elevating!

He suddenly found himself thinking of Judith, and then in a godless moment recalled the movements of her body beneath his as they roused themselves to the passion that had produced Nathaniel. What fools we men are, he chid himself silently, to think of such things as we stand on the edge of eternity!

He focused his attention on the enemy's leading ship. Their courses were converging and Clarkson swung their head another two points to starboard in order to carry out Faulkner's manoeuvre. These were good men, who used their initiative. He peered again at the enemy, watching her bury her bows into the sea as she heeled to the wind. That would make life difficult, throwing her shot high while the *Basilisk*, more nearly running before the wind, would – at least for the next few moments – present her gunners with a steadier platform. Moreover, with every second that passed, the *Basilisk* drew further ahead of her quarry. While the enemy's broadside could not be brought round to confront her with other Dutch ships coming up astern of her on her larboard quarter, all of the *Basilisk*'s larboard guns could fire the length of the enemy ship.

A puff of smoke surrounded a sharp flame from the enemy's bow, and then the deck beneath his feet shook and the thunderously rolling concussion of a ragged broadside from the *Basilisk*'s batteries hurled its iron projectiles at the enemy. Then all was for a moment obscured as the acrid white smoke rolled away towards the enemy, gradually thinning to show a tottering fore-mast following the descent of her sprit topmast and half her bowsprit into the sea under her onrushing bow. A cheer came up from below and Faulkner heard Stockton bawling for silence and for his men to reload.

Faulkner was aware that Clarkson had moved closer in anticipation of new orders.

'Hold on, Mr Clarkson. She's got a sister ship coming up her larboard side. Once we've given her a like dose of iron, we'll haul our wind and run ahead, before doubling round to support Bourne's rear. Is that clear?'

'Aye, sir. Perfectly'

The *Basilisk* shuddered as three or four shot from their enemy thudded into her quarter as the wounded ship attempted to hit her tormentor. But now Faulkner was looking at the next Dutch man-of-war, which was coming up hand over fist. Their next broadside did not seem to be as effective, but Clarkson had his helmsmen put over the helm and the yards came up hard against the catharpings as *Basilisk* swung on to a parallel course with the enemy, running just ahead and throwing shot off on her starboard quarter.

'Rise tacks and sheets!'

As the courses rose in their gear, the leading two Dutch ships appeared to overtake her until they too began to shorten sail and the nearer, the least affected by the *Basilisk*'s gunfire, began to turn on the impudent English frigate.

'Back the sprit topsail and the foreyards!' Faulkner roared. 'Up helm! Make ready the larboard broadside!' He waited a moment as the *Basilisk* turned on her heel. 'Mainsail haul!' Again he waited, his heart thumping in his chest, watching more Dutchmen approaching from the starboard side, the whole of De Ruyter's division bar his two leading men-of-war. The frigate completed her swing and he bellowed, 'Haul all!'

If he was lucky he could drive across the sterns of the two leading ships before the other came up, but he would run the gauntlet of the two he had struck at as they came round to fire their own broadsides.

'God's wounds!' he swore, seeing the next ships coming up also swing to starboard so that he had the enemy on either side parallel to him and *Basilisk* was exposed to the broadsides of four hostile men-of-war. 'Both batteries,' he roared even as the guns fired and the smoke and noise enveloped them. For two long minutes it seemed as if the entire Dutch fleet were firing into the *Basilisk* as she lay among the rushing van of De Ruyter's division but as the smoke shredded and cleared, just before the guns fired again and while the men serving them toiled at swabbing, reloading and ramming home their charges, Faulkner was aware of two facts. The first was that their main topmast was shattered and the spars, sails and gear above the main top were tottering before they crashed to the deck; the second was that ahead of them and coming towards them on the opposite tack, just as he had conned the *Basilisk* across the grain of De Ruyter's two leading fifty-gun ships, came the entire squadron of Rear-Admiral Nehemiah Bourne.

He heard Clarkson bellow, 'Stand from under!' Then the wreckage from aloft came crashing down, some falling on deck and catching men beneath it but most, thanks to the strength of the wind, falling over the starboard side. The *Basilisk's* rapid run was over, she slewed to starboard like a drunken horse, exposing the length of her hull to the last shots of her tormentors. Perhaps a dozen raking shots tore through her doing God knew what execution and then De Ruyter's ships had passed them, leaving the battered frigate wallowing in their wake as the engagement with Bourne's ships became general.

Faulkner felt unsteady on his feet and staggered towards the rail. What was the matter with him? He felt a childish urge to weep as his eyes filled with unbidden tears; he tried to stiffen his legs but found he could not breathe, nor could he hear other than a loud ringing in his ears. What the devil? And yet it seemed this had all happened a long time ago. He felt his knees buckle. One of the helmsmen, thrown on to the deck by the falling gear was picking himself up, apparently unhurt and Faulkner all but fell on top of him. The two bumped into each other in the confusion.

'Begging your pardon. Sir, you are hurt!' Faulkner felt the man's arms support him. The feeling was an immense relief, like surrendering to the inevitability of death. Was he dying? Surely not; not now . . .

He was aware of others and let his body fall. Expecting to strike the deck he was borne upwards and then, with a vast shuddering intake of breath his head began to clear and he could feel his heart pounding as a seizure of pure involuntary panic caused him to pant in great drafts of breath.

'A cannon shot,' Clarkson said, matter-of-factly. 'Passed him so close it took the wind from him.'

They propped him against the fife rail at the foot of the mizzen mast and he slowly recovered his senses. Stockton was there, paying him scant attention as he and Clarkson passed orders to get the wreckage of the main topmast cleared away and the ship under command again. From time to time he turned and gave Faulkner a reassuring look. Then the surgeon was alongside him with his box but Faulkner's wits had returned and he waved the man away.

'Nothing . . . for . . . you . . . here, Bones,' he said between greedy gasps of air. 'You'll . . . have . . . worse . . . cases . . . than . . . mine . . . to . . . attend to, I . . . don't . . . doubt.'

'That I have, sir.'

'Then . . . attend . . . them . . . if . . . you . . . please.'

He began to be aware of the battle raging about them as they drifted to leeward. Out of the smoke a huge ship loomed and for a moment they thought their end had come, for Dutch standards streamed out from her mastheads. But the great man-of-war was in the act of tacking in order to bear down upon Bourne's flagship, the *Andrew*, and none among the English fleet were aware of the confusion and near-mutinous condition of the men in the Dutch ships. An occasional shot struck them, ricocheting out of the advancing gloom as the onset of night stole over the battling ships. Somewhere to the north-west, both the *Sovereign* and Penn's flagship, the *James*, had touched on the Knock and had required the efforts of several boats to get them off, but by twilight the *Sovereign* had engaged a score of Dutch men-of-war and the field was left to the English as the Dutch withdrew.

The *Basilisk* drifted out of the action until she was able to make sail again and stood in under the lee of the North Foreland and anchored for the remainder of the night.

Dungeness to Portland

September 1652 – February 1653

Once brought up to their anchor, Faulkner pressed his men to further exertions. In the darkness, lit by three or four large lanterns, the officers drove the exhausted crew to prepare for re-rigging the *Basilisk* the following morning. The wreckage was cleared away, a survey of the damage taken, and some of the materials required for the repair were assembled. Faulkner left the matter largely to his officers. Clarkson, the master, with considerable experience, was ably seconded by another veteran, Whadcoat, the second lieutenant who, unlike Stockton and so many officers in the fleet, including Blake, had not begun his military career as a soldier. A bluff, stocky seaman who nevertheless wore his hair as short as any cavalry trooper in Cromwell's horse, he seemed possessed of reserves of energy that goaded the men to ever greater efforts. Faulkner was impressed with this quality of inspiriting inspiring leadership that was almost entirely absent from his experience among the Royalists. Certainly Prince Rupert was capable of rousing his men, but not in the same, intimate manner as Whadcoat, who toiled among the seamen, giving them no opportunity to complain. He had been as active during the action, Stockton told Faulkner when the latter remarked upon Whadcoat's industry, commanding the larboard battery.

At ten o'clock a boat arrived alongside. It was a hired Deal punt and bore an officer from the flagship who came up the ship's side, his face still bearing the stains of gunsmoke, his hair lank and matted with dried sweat. A young man of perhaps twenty summers, he introduced himself as Humphrey Hodson as he drew a sealed paper from his gauntlet and handed it to Faulkner.

'Come below, sir, where I have better light and can refresh you. Mr Stockton, see the Deal boatmen get a nip of rum for their trouble, they are like to have a long night.'

'That is thoughtful of you, Captain Faulkner,' Hodson said as they entered the cabin and the servant was summoned to reinforce the night-glim that would otherwise have served to illuminate the space. Once he had seen his visitor settled with a full glass, Faulkner gave a brief glance at the superscription to *Captain Faulkner, the BASILISK, frigate, Margate Roads*, opened the letter and perused its contents. It bore no date, only the time of *Seven O'Clock*, and *Triumph, The Downs*. He read on.

> *Sir,*
>
> *Having seen you gallantly carry your vessel into action this day and noticed that thou hast received some knocks, I have you appraise the bearer, Lieutenant H. Hodson, of your ability to command your ship further to the Service of the State and the sooner the better to my desire.*
>
> *Should you consider the possibility of rendering me due assistance by sunset tomorrow, pray without further reference to myself pass over to the coast of Holland and determine the location of our enemy. I am not persuaded that he is yet sufficiently beaten and would have early warning of his intentions.*
>
> *Knowing you to have knowledge of the Holland coast I place this important Service in your charge the better to have it executed to my wishes.*
>
> $\qquad\qquad$ *I am, Sir, your faithful servant,*
> $\qquad\qquad\qquad\qquad$ *R^{obt} Blake,*
> $\qquad\qquad\qquad\qquad$ *Genl-@-Sea*

Faulkner folded the letter and looked up at Hodson. He was fast asleep. A trickle of wine had run from his glass and stained his breeches and the glass would have fallen from his hand, if Faulkner had not rescued it. The sudden movement startled Hodson and he woke with a jerk.

He shook his head and ran his fingers through his filthy hair. 'I am so sorry, sir, I . . .' he flushed with embarrassment.

'Think nothing of it,' Faulkner said, smiling kindly. 'It has been a busy day.'

Hodson managed a wan grin. 'You have read the General's letter, sir?'

Faulkner nodded. 'Yes. You are to inform the General that I shall do my utmost to be away before sunset tomorrow and would consider myself remiss if I was not under command sooner.'

Hodson repeated the sentence and then picked his hat from the deck. Standing, he bowed to Faulkner and made to withdraw. After he had gone, Faulkner re-read the letter, then followed Hodson on deck.

'Mr Clarkson?' he called and a moment later the master appeared.

'Sir?'

'When convenient stand the men down and set an anchor watch. Do you think you can have the ship re-rigged by sunset tomorrow?'

'I'd be damned sorry if she weren't ready by noon, Cap'n Faulkner. The second lieutenant has worked a modest miracle with God's help.'

'Very well. That being so, we shall proceed to seek out the enemy as soon as we may.'

They had no trouble locating the Dutch fleet, which, as Faulkner had guessed, had made for Helvoetsluys. They raised the familiar low coastline, spiked with its church spires and windmills, and he felt a sudden pang for Katherine, wondering where she was and how she lived. But the size of the Dutch fleet swept all personal thoughts away as he gave orders to clew up the courses, back the main yards and heave to. His charge from Blake was specific and, he realized, the General was perceptive, even perhaps prescient. Whether Blake had received intelligence of Dutch intentions was impossible to say, but it was clear that something was afoot, for a frigate let fall her topsails and was soon under way, hauling round to intercept the *Basilisk* and chase her offshore and out of sight.

'Those are Indiamen,' Clarkson said standing beside him, his own glass levelled on the outer road.

'Aye, 'tis a convoy all right.'

'And a damn big one. D'you think they are going to try and force the Strait, sir?'

'I think that is what the General thinks.'

'Then we didn't drub them t'other day. At least not as hard as we thought we had.'

'No,' Faulkner ruminated, shifting his telescope on to the approaching frigate. 'I think they were merely swatting us aside.' It would certainly explain a good deal and although Faulkner was incorrect in his assumption, he was not wrong in his conclusion. He shut his glass with a decisive snap. 'Be so good as to haul the main yards, Mr Clarkson. We must run from this fellow and take the tidings to General Blake.'

The *Basilisk* reached The Downs three days later, after battling a strong headwind which seemed particularly contrary as it swung within four points of south-west and seemed diabolical in its intent to head them every time they tacked. Fortunately, the Dutch frigate did not pursue them far from the coast and they had lost her by the time that darkness fell that same evening. It was an uncomfortable season to be campaigning at sea but the situation was so uncertain that Faulkner perfectly understood Blake's reluctance to take his fleet into winter quarters. On boarding the *Triumph*, Faulkner could see evidence of the damage in the late action off the Kentish Knock. Ushered into the great cabin, Faulkner found Blake at his desk, his secretary, Francis Harvey, scribbling industriously at his elbow while he studied a chart of the Channel.

'Sit down, Captain Faulkner.' Blake rolled up the chart and stared at his guest. 'Well? What have you to tell me, sir?'

'It was difficult to determine exactly what ships the Dutch have at the present moment, General Blake, but besides their fleet they appear to be assembling a large convoy of Indiamen. All vessels have their yards hoisted and there was little sign of them passing into winter quarters. Besides, I do not think they would over-winter at Helvoetsluys; certainly I have never observed that to be their practice.'

'Which is why they tolerated Rupert's ships there and ours off-shore,' Blake put in.

Faulkner nodded. 'Indeed.'

Blake drummed his fingers on the desk in front of him. 'So, who is in command, d'you think? Eh?'

'I am afraid I have no idea, sir.' Faulkner felt uneasy under Blake's scrutiny. He had heard the General could prove merciless towards his commanders that failed his expectations. 'I thought it more important to acquaint you of the general situation immediately . . .' he said uncertainly.

Blake nodded appreciatively. 'Quite right, but I should like you to take your frigate back and keep watch and ward and glean what intelligence that you can. Take no risk, however. Is there anything you require? If so, acquaint my clerk here and we will see what we can muster for you. I have heard disturbing rumours that there have been mutinies in the Dutch fleet but that would not explain their present activity.' Blake rubbed his clean-shaven chin. 'I am wondering whether they have changed their commander, for it was De With we met off the Knock, not Tromp.'

For the whole of October, Faulkner dodged off the Goree Gat, withdrawing over the horizon for most of the day, but occasionally working close inshore under cover of darkness so that as the sun came up he could reconnoitre the anchorage. He flew Dutch colours and did this at irregular intervals, so that he could not be ambushed. Nevertheless, he had three close encounters with Dutch men-of-war, though none developed into more than an exchange of distant shot. He did, however, succeed in suborning the skipper of a small Dutch *schuyt* who for two sovereigns let it be known that the Dutch fleet was in a poor state of morale and that the hard-swearing and unpopular Van Tromp had replaced De With, having with him Jan Evertsen and De Ruyter as his subordinate flag officers.

'Zat, *Kapitein*, iss bad for you, I tink,' he said in his thick English, pocketing the money with a grin and polishing off the large glass of rum Faulkner had given him. Reporting all this to Blake, he was sent back to his cruising station and, for a further three tiring weeks, the *Basilisk* maintained her watch. Finally, on 20th November, short of water and with his crew grumbling, Faulkner decided to return to The Downs. He discovered Blake to be awaiting the appearance of refitted ships to relieve his own fleet and act as the Winter Guard. Discontent was rife throughout the fleet and the word among those senior officers, with whom Faulkner briefly rubbed shoulders aboard the *Triumph*, was a common eagerness to return to port and the comforts of a winter fireside.

On the morning of the 24th a mass of sail was observed to be off the North Foreland. Eighty ships were counted, a number that soon afterwards soared to several hundred. Blake sent word round his fleet to make ready to unmoor and sent officers to the *Triumph's* mastheads to observe the enemy. For two days the reports came down from aloft and on Monday 28th Blake summoned his captains aboard his flagship for a council-of-war.

It was clear that with some ninety men-of-war, the enemy was vastly superior to Blake, who had forty-two, and were demonstrably covering a huge convoy which lay closer to the French coast as they all tacked hither and thither against the strong south-westerly wind that had blown intermittently at gale force and held the Dutch from passing rapidly through the Strait of Dover.

The slow but seemingly inexorable windward progress of this vast fleet provoked Blake into giving the order to weigh anchor and his captains dispersed to their ships, shaking their heads at the odds stacked against them. For the whole of the following day the wind raged from the south-west, forcing both fleets to anchor. Blake's ships had got no further than Dover, with Van Tromp's some six miles to seaward.

The following morning, however, the wind had veered into the west-north-west and came off the land, allowing the Dutch to head westwards and attempt to get to windward of the English fleet. If this occurred they could then double round and, with an overwhelming force, run down on Blake's ships and destroy them piecemeal. Blake hoisted the signal to weigh and for some hours the English ran down the coastline, their van abreast of the Dutch rear as the enemy men-of-war covered the convoy farther offshore.

This was not a game that could be played indefinitely. As every English captain knew, the trend of the coast was to swing to seaward in the great shingle promontory of Dungeness and, while deep water ran close inshore, the headland would compel Blake's fleet to alter course to converge with Van Tromp.

It was Whadcoat who reported the large, red battle flag run up to the fore-masthead of the *Brederode* as the Dutch admiral crammed on sail to head off Blake's *Triumph*, but Captain

Robert Batten of the *Garland* gallantly interposed his forty-gun third-rate. The unequal battle that ensued between the two was somewhat levelled by a second intervention by Captain Walter Hoxton, commanding the armed merchantman *Anthony Bonaventure*, who opened fire on the *Brederode*'s unengaged side, drawing some of her men from concentrating on the hapless *Garland*. The *Anthony Bonaventure* was herself now attacked by Evertsen's flagship, the *Hollandia*, grappled and boarded. Hoxton and many of his men were killed and as Batten ordered his men to repel boarders, he, too, fell and despite the exploding of mines along the *Garland*'s deck to deter the Dutch from jumping across, the third-rate was taken by the enemy.

As the battle opened in the already fading daylight, the *Basilisk* had been keeping station on the *Triumph*. Seeing the remainder of the English fleet strung out astern of Blake, Faulkner ordered his ship's head round to engage the enemy now coming down upon them in a mass until he lost sight of Blake. In fact, Blake had run too far ahead and was obliged to haul round to come to the aid of his already stricken ships, only to have the *Triumph*'s main- and fore-masts damaged and partially shot away. Faulkner was never certain what happened; he was in action for about twenty minutes against three Dutch ships all of which passed him, as though heading for some more worthy objective, surrounded by dense smoke that came not merely from the great guns and small arms, but from fires aboard several ships. One Dutch man-of-war exploded with such a terrible concussion that, for a few moments, all action ceased and a strange but short-lived silence fell upon the tossing vessels. Then the English were all hauling their yards and standing away for Dover.

'God forgive them!' Whadcoat said, when he came on deck and saw Blake's fleet in full retreat, 'but they are very like to cowards.'

There was no denying it, and during the following day the entire English fleet ran north, past Dover, through The Downs, past the North Foreland and the Kentish Knock. Pursued by Van Tromp, who had seen the Indiamen clear of any danger, the English fleet doubled the Long Sand Head where the

Dutch were dissuaded from following them, now having an inbound convoy to protect. As the English ships came to their anchors it was clear that they had suffered a humiliating defeat. As an angry Faulkner afterwards wrote to Mainwaring:

> *It was a disgrace. Not twenty – half our strength – came to the general's assistance, the remainder pretending want of men to ply their tackle, and of them that stood to the engagement not eight did so to any purpose. We lost W^{alt} Hoxton and the good R^{obt} Batten, both sometime of our Fraternity . . .*

But Faulkner's anger was as nothing to Blake's. Known for the ferocity of his temper, he dismissed his own brother and flag captain, Benjamin, Anthony Young, who had attacked the *Antelope* in Helvoetsluys and Harvey, his secretary, and several other senior captains, offering the Council of State his own resignation. Though several of these, including Benjamin Blake, were afterwards quietly reinstated, Blake was in no doubt of the lack of support of his commanders. Among those who had fallen back were almost all the frigates, making Faulkner's own part in the action the more commendable, even though the Dutch had failed to engage the *Basilisk* with the vigour that would easily have overcome what resistance she might have offered. That he had been stupendously lucky did not escape the thoughtful Faulkner, though he sensed his men swaggered amid the recriminations that flew about the fleet.

'I hear the Council of State has appointed Sir Henry Vane to an Admiralty Commission,' Mainwaring informed Faulkner when he arrived at Camberwell for Christmas.

'Aye, he has already drawn up Articles of War to better regulate conduct in battle and made a decision not to include hired merchantmen under their own masters in the line of battle, though God knows Walter Hoxton did his utmost as God and those of us close-to observed.'

'It sounds like a bloody shambles for some.'

'But not for all. Still,' Faulkner went on reflectively, 'besides Vane, Bourne is appointed a Commissioner and it is to the General's credit that he did all he could for the men. He now petitions the Admiralty Commissioners for a rise in pay and a betterance of their allowances, which Heaven knows most deserve.'

'You sound to be privy to Blake's intentions,' Mainwaring said.

Faulkner smiled at his old friend who looked shockingly old and infirm. He shrugged. 'Perhaps. He did me the honour of consulting me upon one or two matters after he had struck his flag and come on shore.' Faulkner seemed to hesitate.

'And what more? I have seen that look upon your face before.'

Faulkner shrugged. ''Twould be immodest,' he began as Mainwaring insisted. 'It is nothing. But the General did mention that, if the Council of State do not accept his resignation and he was reappointed – bearing in mind, Sir Henry, that both Sir Richard Deane and General George Monck are now appointed Generals-at-Sea – he was minded to appoint me to at least a middling ship . . .'

'A third-rate! But that is good news, Kit, splendid news. Why, you shall be a General-at-Sea yourself before I am cold in my grave, you see if you aren't! Come, that calls for a drink!'

'A drink? Ha! Sir Henry, think of the slip that may come betwixt cup and lip.'

'Oh, fiddlesticks!' Mainwaring exclaimed as he fossicked over a bottle and two glasses.

'We lost five ships, Sir Henry. This thing may be a poisoned chalice, we have suffered badly.'

'Oh, damn your puns. My instinct tells me that you shall yet do great things.'

'Ah, yes, great things,' Faulkner smilingly murmured, half to himself.

'Your health and fortune.' Mainwaring handed a full glass to Faulkner and raised his own.

'And to your long life,' Faulkner responded.

'Fie, sir. I am as damn near to the end as I may be without falling into the eternal pit.'

Early in the New Year of 1653 Faulkner received a new commission. He was to repair immediately to Portsmouth and take command of the forty-gun *Union*. He was to be allowed his officers from the *Basilisk* and judged, correctly, that this was evidence of a mood of urgency. On arriving at Portsmouth he was sought out and presented with a letter from a now familiar hand. The tone of the language pleased him, for Blake had written that he 'confided in you and desire that you comport yourself with all the energy of which I know you capable . . .' It was a compliment, as was command of the *Union* herself, for although not a new ship, she was one of the so-called Middling Class and had been laid down as the *Union Royal*. The unaffected, anti-monarchical Commonwealth Commissioners had felt the name inappropriate and had selected a more elevating cognomen, and so as the *Union* she went to war.

It was clear to Faulkner as he made arrangements to board the *Union* that great exertions had been made by the Admiralty Commissioners and their various officers. Not only had a new pay-scale induced men to come forward, but drafts of soldiers would help make up the establishment of the fleet and quantities of stores were flowing into Portsmouth under armed guard. To his utter astonishment Faulkner discovered this energetic spirit of reform was to be found aboard individual ships and who but Clarkson and the indefatigable Whadcoat greeted his arrival, apologising that Stockton was just gone ashore to secure further supplies of powder and shot plus a replacement longboat and spare spars, for rot had been discovered in those aboard the ship.

'Mr Stockton was most particular that should you arrive in his absence,' Whadcoat said with an uncommon awkwardness that made Faulkner wonder what was coming next, 'but he has been using your name by way of requisition.'

'One thing the Parliamentary army seems to breed,' he responded, referring to Stockton's past, 'is a commendable initiative.'

'Even a fool can see when a horse needs a shoe, Captain Faulkner,' Whadcoat replied enigmatically.

The following morning a boat arrived alongside from the flagship demanding to know when Faulkner's ship would be readied for sea and two days later the fully manned *Union* warped out and, letting fall her topsails, edged out of the harbour against a young flood tide.

'I am not certain, sir,' Whadcoat said, lowering his glass as Faulkner came on deck at the summons of the second lieutenant who had the watch, 'but the army's initiative may have unravelled us in the face of the enemy. We are mightily extended.'

'We are indeed, Mr Whadcoat,' Faulkner replied, looking around the horizon at the scattered English men-of-war. 'Where away do you make the enemy? Oh, God's wounds! I beg your pardon, Mr Whadcoat, but . . .'

Faulkner regretted the oath, much used by the Royalists but anathema to the sturdy Puritan soul who stood beside him. It was a February morning of sparkling visibility and in the far distance to the north-west they could see the horizon dotted with the grey-white topgallant sails of an enemy fleet. In common with every other commander in the English fleet, Faulkner knew the rapid mobilization of Blake's fleet of eighty men-of-war had been undertaken in the full knowledge that Van Tromp was coming up Channel with his fleet of a similar number – as they had learned to their cost off Dungeness – covering a large homeward convoy. Information from France, where the convoy had been sheltering and awaiting its escort, indicated that it consisted of around one hundred and fifty deeply laden merchantmen.

The clear air came on the wings of a north-westerly, that same wind that had ruined Blake at Dungeness, allowing Van Tromp to sail up Channel ahead of the convoy, the flanks of his fleet of three divisions spread out to cover it. Still, with De Ruyter and Evertsen in support and with a winter largely of keeping the sea, Van Tromp had commendable control of his fleet, in contrast to Blake whose qualities, and those of many of his captains and one fellow General-at-Sea, George Monck, were better adapted to the cavalry charge than wind-governed manoeuvre.

While Faulkner and Whadcoat could almost see the entire dispositions of the Dutch fleet, or at least gauge from its concentration where its main strength lay, he had no idea where

Blake's *Triumph* then was. True, the *Union* was part of the White squadron led by Monck, a man Faulkner had only met but briefly aboard the *Triumph* before their departure from Spithead. But even Monck's whereabouts were uncertain, though they had tacked in company when off Alderney the previous day. Both Faulkner and Whadcoat, being experienced sea officers, were close to despair at the ease with which the English fleet lost cohesion.

'Cavalry tactics are all very well,' Faulkner murmured, voicing both their thoughts aloud. 'May be all very well at times like the action off the Kentish Knock, but they are to be neither relied upon nor advocated.'

'Indeed not, sir. I had hoped the new Articles of War . . . Well, there is nothing for it now, for we cannot stand alone between Van Tromp and the Strait.'

'No.' Faulkner was thinking furiously. He did not doubt either Blake's courage or his desire to grapple with the enemy. He had a force equal to his opponent and would be eager to avenge himself for the humiliation Van Tromp had inflicted. He had heard a rumour in London that the Dutch admiral had hoisted a broom to his main masthead as a symbol of having swept Blake aside and although Faulkner did not believe a word of it, he knew the power of such imagery in the popular mind. Blake's trouble was that he lacked frigate captains of sufficient experience to carry out a proper reconnaissance and had failed to send any to windward of the fleet to watch for Van Tromp. Well, he thought to himself, the *Union* is not as fast as the *Basilisk* but she was as able as any Dutch man-of-war and, in the lack of a visible flag officer, he had better play the part of a frigate and cling on to the enemy's flanks and maybe pick off a Dutch merchantman. The thought, though silly, lifted his spirits.

'I think, Mr Whadcoat, we will have the men sent to their battle stations. My guess is that Van Tromp will not spare his ships from covering his convoy. We will take station on them and, if we cannot harry them a little, at least mark them.'

'Very well, sir.' And a moment later the pipes were twittering at the hatchways.

In the hours that followed, Faulkner came in sight of several other scattered members of Monck's squadron and later, towards the middle of the forenoon, the flagship of Monck himself. Then, to the north, they spotted more ships. These they soon identified as the sails of Blake's and Penn's squadrons, which appeared to be falling back ahead of Van Tromp until Whadcoat, having volunteered to climb to the masthead with a long glass, returned to the deck, convinced that Blake had hove to ahead of the Dutch.

'I can see Penn clearly,' Whadcoat said as Stockton and Clarkson gathered round Faulkner on the quarterdeck. 'His division is spread out and beyond him I can make out the *Triumph*. My guess is that Penn is closing up before making for Blake . . .' He looked round at his fellows.

Faulkner looked round, watching Monck's flag as a faint and distant concussion rolled over the dancing waves and declared an engagement had begun. 'The General is making a signal.'

All swung round to watch Monck's flagship. 'The division is to form on the larboard tack,' someone said.

'Very well, let us brace the yards a little and haul the tacks hard a-weather.'

The officers went about their business and the *Union* leaned to the breeze. She already lay on the larboard tack but she needed to recover her station towards the van of Monck's squadron. As the group of men-of-war closed up and headed north, the sound of gunfire increased and clouds of smoke were conspicuous before the wind shredded them to leeward in long, attenuated streamers.

Two hours later Monck made the signal to tack again. Away to the north they could make out the blue lump of land that was Portland Bill and, as they turned their sterns towards it, ahead of them, almost in the eye of the sun, lay the contending fleets, with the convoy strung out astern of the embattled men-of-war.

'Not bad for a soldier,' Faulkner murmured to himself as they bore down on the gap that was opening up between the smoke and fire of action and the immense gaggle of merchantmen.

'They're turning away!' snapped Clarkson excitedly as it became increasingly clear that as Monck's ships bore down onto them, the convoy was turning to the west.

Faulkner turned his attention to the action that was growing closer, perhaps five miles from them now.

'Dutch man-of-war detaching . . . and another, and another,' Clarkson called.

Faulkner could see first one, and then several Dutch vessels, hauling their wind to head north and attempt to interpose themselves between the convoy and Monck's as-yet-unengaged vessels.

'Watch the General,' Faulkner ordered as Monck, unable to get closer to the convoy accepted the challenge of engaging Van Tromp. 'Steer one point to leeward,' he ordered, 'ease the braces.'

Twenty minutes later the *Union* opened fire.

Night found the two fleets licking their wounds. The *Union* had suffered some damage aloft and had received some thirty shot between wind and water. She had lost twelve men and a further fifteen lay wounded in the surgeon's charge. The wind had dropped and boats rowed round the fleet as Blake sent several badly damaged ships into Portsmouth along with a number of prizes. The following day the English fleet clung on the wings of the Dutch, much as their ancestors had done sixty-four years earlier when harrying the Spanish Armada. A number of Dutch merchantmen were taken and then three of Evertsen's squadron were captured. The *Union* was in action for extended periods as both fleets sailed slowly eastwards. It was hot and bloody work, a giving and taking of punishment and though no enemy warship struck to the *Union*, she had the satisfaction of taking a large merchantman and dismasting a man-of-war that was supported by a large Dutchman that emerged out of the smoke. Faulkner withdrew under a sudden gust of wind, engaging another enemy shortly thereafter.

By darkness, Faulkner and his men were tired and frustrated, having been in action for the entire day they yet had failed to engage decisively with any enemy man-of-war. In later years, Faulkner, when asked about the three-day battle off Portland, was apt to say that Providence cheated them of the laurels on the 18th and 19th of February in order to reward their patience on the 20th. Up until this time, Van Tromp's ships had maintained their defence of the bulk of the convoy that had thus far evaded capture by allowing it to work ahead of his main fleet. But the constant harrying of the English had weakened the resolve of the Dutch and time and again broken their cohesion. In a freshening wind, on the third and final morning of the running battle, Faulkner woke from an uneasy doze on deck wrapped in his cloak to find an excited Stockton pointing out two ships a mere two miles away, their shapes etched against the first grey streak of dawn.

'I give you good day, Captain Faulkner,' Stockton said in a low voice, as though speaking normally might alert the unwary Dutch of their presence. 'I think we have two of the birds at our mercy before they escape us.'

Faulkner took a look through Stockton's glass. His mouth tasted sour, his eyes gritty with fatigue, his brain sluggish. He took a deep breath to clear his head.

'Pass word for the men to break their fasts by messes. We must keep sufficient men available to man one broadside and haul the yards, just in case. Get Clarkson up here.'

'Here sir.'

'Very well, Mr Clarkson. We'll run after these fellows for half an hour while the men break their fasts but I want you to lay me alongside the nearer shortly thereafter. Do you get some burgoo inside you then relieve me for a few minutes.'

Faulkner watched the master hurry below, his full-skirted coat whipped about his spindly legs with their wrinkled stockings, but for all his rickety appearance he was a sound and reliable officer. 'Quartermaster!'

'Sir?'

'Have Dutch colours hoisted and stand by to strike them and haul up our own upon the word.'

'Hoist Dutch colours and stand by. Aye, aye, sir.'

The following twenty minutes were an agony of expectant waiting. When Clarkson reappeared Faulkner dashed below to change his shirt for fear of a wound, and haul on half-armour over his doublet. With his sword on he returned to the deck to find the men, having been fed, were all gathered at their stations. Ahead, the Dutch men-of-war loomed against the growing light and he could see more stretched out to the south as Van Tromp's line drew in a defensive crescent about the convoy laying ahead of it to the eastwards. He could see the concentration of vague silhouettes as they crept up on the northern flank of the mass of enemy vessels.

He walked forward and toured the upper deck, nodding to the petty officers and speaking in a quietly confident voice as he passed along the lines of guns, each with their crouching crews and, in passing, also addressing the men at the braces.

'One final effort, my lads, and let's seize a prize and turn this whole affair to the advantage of our country and those who love us.'

He was rather pleased with this last, a direct appeal to the men's avarice not being consonant with a sea officer in the service of the Commonwealth, but the allusion to subterfuge and a prize at the end of it nevertheless reminded them of his earlier successes. When he had toured the upper deck he went below and repeated the process on the lower gun deck and, among the denizens of the orlop where, amid his gleaming saws, catlings and scalpels, the surgeon waited with his loblollies. Faulkner was gratified by the nods and grins his words elicited from some of the men. A few stared at him with indifference, but many, he sensed, were invigorated by his taking the trouble to walk among them.

As he returned to his post on the quarterdeck it occurred to him that where his last sentence applied to himself, it rang hollow. The thought of Katherine caused a violent twist in his gut and set his jaw so that Clarkson, watching him approach, saw a look of such steely determination cross his captain's face that he never afterwards forgot it.

'We're coming up on them, sir,' he almost whispered. 'They'll be smelling a rat.'

Clarkson got no further for the wary Dutch were undeceived by the barely visible tricolour flying from the peak of the mizzen and two stern chasers barked from the transom of the nearer and larger of the Dutchmen. A second later he felt the *thud thud* of the shots going home in the *Union*'s solid timber sides and saw the pale ovals of faces looking aft, awaiting an order to respond.

There was nothing that could be done as yet, for only one

bow chaser could be brought to bear. Faulkner ran forward to the knightheads and shouted a torrent of Dutch oaths that he had picked up in Helvoetsluys. A query was shouted back at him but he was already running aft, calling for the starboard batteries to make ready.

Back alongside Clarkson he heard the query repeated and turned to the master. 'Ease her to larboard, Mr Clarkson, two points, I think. Quartermaster, strike those false colours and hoist our own.'

The Dutch bunting was already on deck and he spun round and called out, 'Fire when you bear!'

There was what seemed like a long moment of silence. Then the Dutch vessel began to slew to larboard an instant before Stockton and Whadcoat unleashed the *Union*'s gunfire. The action developed rapidly, the Dutchman clewing up his courses and accepting battle. She was a sixty- or seventy-gun ship, but, like most of her fellows, less heavily armed than the English whose greater weight of metal had been a surprise to their enemy in every action fought since hostilities had begun.

Smoke and thunder filled the air and dinned the senses as the two vessels closed. Fortunately for Faulkner, by engaging the larboard side of the enemy's northernmost ship it would prove some time before any of her consorts could come to her aid and, in the event, with a fair wind and the English astern, none turned back, so that the *Union* and her victim lay locked in combat as the Dutch moved steadily away and the English came up astern and passed them. Those English vessels passing close enough to the Dutchman's unengaged side poured in a broadside in passing, work that greatly aided the task of Faulkner and his men so that, within twenty minutes, the *Union*'s gunfire had so battered the enemy's side that hardly a gun was firing in response.

Faulkner called for boarders and men ran to pick up cutlasses and boarding pikes. Stockton was up on the breech of an upper-deck gun, his sword drawn, his powder-blackened face adding a manic look to his eyes as he hollered for the men to follow him. A moment later the two hulls came together with a jarring crash and grappling irons whipped out on the ends of their lines from both ships and they were bound together in a mutual acceptance of what must now follow.

Faulkner watched as the first wave went over the gap between the upper gunwhales of the two vessels occasioned by the tumblehome of each. Men were now coming up from below with Whadcoat at their head. Most were former soldiers, men more familiar with hand-to-hand combat than working artillery and they went to their savage work with a grim and terrible purpose. Whooping uncharacteristically, Whadcoat led them over the gap and, turning to Clarkson, Faulkner said, 'Watch her, Mr Clarkson, watch her!' And then he too followed, caught up in the madness of the moment.

He all but lost his life as well as his dignity in the scramble to get from the *Union* to the enemy's deck and only an open gun-port lid saved him from becoming stuck ignominiously between the two ships. But he quickly recovered, hauled himself upwards and was over the side, dropping down on to a scene from hell as he slithered in the gore running across the once-immaculate planking of the scrubbed deck.

There was barely any resistance amidships, though a violent contest was in train for possession of the Dutchman's afterdeck. The desperate defenders fought with demonic courage and were in the act of throwing the Englishmen back. Faulkner saw Stockton fall and the sight galvanized him. He ran forward, almost lost his footing in the blood and viscera, and threw himself into the fight. Slashing left and right, he bellowed for his men to move forward as he fought his way to stand over Stockton. Their captain's presence in their midst seemed to rally the boarders as the shouts of fury, pain and exertion filled the air, punctuated by the clash and scrape of steel on steel, the thump and bang of body or cuirass in collision, and the occasional pop of a wheellock pistol. Faulkner felled a large Dutchman to his knees, then ran him through. The man had already been wounded and he stepped clear of Stockton's body, thrust the tottering Dutchman aside and saw, towards the stern of the ship, a group of armoured and sashed gentlemen regroup, panting, several bearing wounds, and all streaming in sweat. They were obviously what remained of the enemy's officers.

'Come on!' Faulkner shouted as on either side of him a

group of his own men took post in a ragged line. There was a moment's hesitation.

'*Meneer!*' Faulkner called out. 'Capitulate . . .'

One of the Dutchmen, short of breath, shook his head. Beside him one of the men from the *Union*, who Faulkner afterwards learned had served as a dragoon, held a wheellock that he had quickly loaded. Raising it, he levelled it and fired. The spurt of the priming and snap of the discharge took Faulkner by surprise, but he was relieved when the panting Dutchman fell, a neat hole in his cuirass. Outnumbered, his officers dropped their swords and turned their hands up in gestures of abject helplessness. One of them turned to a cleat and began slipping the flag halliards. Then, as the huge Dutch ensign fluttered to the deck like a dying bird, Whadcoat appeared, saying that resistance below had crumpled. The ship was theirs.

'She's the *Alkmaar*, sir,' someone said. 'Her third lieutenant speaks a little English.'

'Find out the number of men she carries and from what Admiralty she is. Mr Whadcoat, pick thirty men for your prize crew. Let me know when you have the enemy below hatches.'

It was victory, and a vindication of sorts, but Faulkner felt nothing, only the necessity to return to the *Union*, make sail and continue the pursuit.

A Reconciliation

March – April 1653

'It was a missed opportunity, whatever may be said about an English victory,' Faulkner said as he sat and regarded his patron. Mainwaring, sitting huddled by a fire of sea-coal despite both the cost of the fuel and the warmth of the early spring day, looked like a man close to death. His heavy features had collapsed, his jowls hung like those of an old bloodhound and his hair was lank, sparse and entirely missing from the crown of his head.

Only his eyes burned, eager for information about the encounters with the Dutch, and Faulkner, unable to find any consolation in the circumstances in which he found his old benefactor, took refuge in a diatribe against the mismanagement of recent events.

'What,' asked Mainwaring, in a voice wheezy with infection, 'happened to allow Van Tromp to escape?'

'In a word – complacency. We had them to loo'ard, pinned hard against the French coast under the Grey Cape, the fleet and the convoy all together when the General threw out the signal to anchor. I suppose General Blake assumed we could finish the business in the morning. True, we were worn out with three days of posturing and fighting, besides being low on ammunition, but so were the Dutch and in no like case to ourselves, having lost about eight of their men-of-war and above two dozen of the convoy with the loss of only one of our own.'

'And Tromp escaped?' Mainwaring asked, his bristling eyebrows raised in incredulity.

Faulkner nodded. 'Alas, yes. He weighed and carried the tide round the headland, past Calais and into Gravelines, running through the banks he knew so well.'

'Did we not know them equally?'

'There were those amongst us who thought so but not until the Dutch had escaped and the deed had been done.'

They fell silent, each man enveloped in his own thoughts. Then Mainwaring said, 'So they came up the Channel in the old way and you fought them in the old way but when Tromp anchored as Medina-Sidonia did, there was no Drake to send in fire ships.'

Faulkner shook his head but, detecting Mainwaring's generally censorious tone, he responded. 'No, and no gale to blow them to the devil either, though they did form a crescent, just as the Spanish in eighty-eight. Had they not done so,' he added to remind Mainwaring of his own modest achievement in the general action, 'I should not have had the opportunity to peck at its northernmost limb.'

Mainwaring smiled, a wry grin stretching his purple lips. 'No, you did your best, Kit. I did not mean to impugn your spirit. A superior ship, you say?'

'Aye, sixty guns. The *Alkmaar.*'

'Well, I suppose that when you are a General-at-Sea, you will benefit from Blake's error.'

Faulkner smiled back. 'I should not think that circumstance is very likely, Sir Henry.'

Faulkner spent a week in Camberwell, leaving Mainwaring with a sum of money to see him through until the warmer weather of summer eased his rheumatics and his rasping breathing. His own finances were increasingly straightened thanks to the war, and although his prospects of credit were enhanced by the capture of the *Alkmaar*, it would yet be months before this would be translated into ready money. Returning to London, Faulkner took lodgings in the City, finding a room in The Ship by St Olave's, Hart Street, whose bells he had – not so long ago – heard from his room in the Tower. He had hardly settled in his room when he received a summons to wait upon Monck, himself lodged in Westminster. With Blake wounded, Monck and his fellow General-at-Sea, Sir Richard Deane, were co-ordinating another rapid reconstruction of the battle-battered fleet in anticipation of renewed action with the energetic Dutch. Faulkner's *Union* was herself in Chatham, having her wounds dressed and her damages repaired under the supervision of Commissioner Pett who, if Faulkner had his way, would be hounded daily by Whadcoat.

If Blake was stern, bluff and bad tempered, George Monck was an even more stolid man. Of medium height, powerfully built with a stern expression and a penetrating eye that flashed with a quick intelligence gleaned in a hundred fights, on land as well as on sea, Monck was an imposing character. Faulkner had hardly presented himself before Monck came to the point.

'General Deane and I,' he began, 'have been considering the lessons learned in our late action and Sir Richard suggested that, knowing your experience and energy in these matters, you should be charged with drafting Fighting Instructions for the fleet. I can arrange for you to have the services of two clerks at the Navy Office and one week in which to present us with your conclusions.' He handed Faulkner a paper. 'Here are some rough conclusions Sir Richard and I have come to regarding the deficiencies in the conduct of the fleet lately in action. These need addressing and rectifying. We thought it wise to request a commander to draft them in the first instance, on the basis of not asking for the impossible. Do you take my point, Captain Faulkner?'

He nodded, glancing at the document and getting to his feet. 'Perfectly, General Monck.' It was clear that Monck was dismissing him, yet he hesitated.

'Is there something troubling you, Captain?'

'Only, sir, that there are other captains in the fleet of greater seniority and longer service than my own.'

He thought he saw a smile flicker across Monck's face. If so, it was no more than a fleeting expression. 'You are concerned about jealousy?'

'Not personally, General, only in that I should not like to be thought forward . . .'

'There is no fear of that. You are being charged with this task in secret. The two clerks assigned to you are sworn-confidence men. Your name will not be associated with the final outcome. Are you content?'

Faulkner nodded and murmured his thanks.

'Very well. I shall expect your return in a week's time.'

Faulkner found he had been allocated a small room in the Navy Office in Water Lane and two clerks who rejoiced in the names of Black and White. Having long worked in tandem, the two men were wearily aware of the curiosity and seemed gratified when Faulkner put them to work without any comment beyond a raising of his eyebrows as he confirmed their identities. Black, the senior, would take dictation from Faulkner and White would copy the final regulations as he and Black roughed them out.

Having read Monck's paper, Faulkner was left in no doubt that his was a responsible task, but his crisp intellect soon isolated the requirements of cohesive and disciplined action, insofar as such could be maintained under the conditions of battle, with its smoke, noise, confusion and disruption. Captains should not be permitted wide latitude of action but form a line upon the signal for action being shown by their chief, each forming on his divisional flag officer. If to windward, they should sail in line ahead until in position to attack and then bear down in line abreast, each upon an opponent. No ship was to get upwind of his admiral and should a flagship be disabled, his squadron was to form on the next to be seen to exploit what had become obvious in the ships captured from the Dutch – their superiority in gun-power. It had been this revelation that had led, as Monck and Deane had concluded, to Blake's fatal overconfidence at the end of the battle that had begun off Portland and terminated with the enemy escaping off Calais.

Three days into his work he had returned to The Ship, a stone's throw from the Navy Office, and was tucking into a beef pie when the pot-boy announced someone to see him. 'Who the devil . . .' Faulkner queried as the pot-boy dodged outside. He had not informed anyone other than Mainwaring of his whereabouts, for there was no one with whom he wished to communicate. Nor did he immediately recognize the newcomer, though there was something about his sober garb that was familiar.

'Captain Faulkner?' The voice was hesitant but instantly recognizable with its west-country burr.

'Nathan! But you have lost your hair!' His brother-in-law,

Nathan Gooding, stood twirling his hat between his hands, his cloak over his arm and a look of excruciating embarrassment on his honest face. Without a second thought Faulkner impulsively thrust out his hand but Gooding, flushing crimson, seemed reluctant to take it.

'Ah, yes, I had momentarily forgot – Judith.'

Gooding sighed. 'I am sorry, Captain.'

'Captain? What is the matter, Nathan, why not plain Kit?'

An expression of utter confusion crossed Gooding's face and he swallowed so hard that it was almost painfully obvious, ruffling the lace at his throat.

'Is there something dire that you have to tell me . . . about Judith or the children? What of Nathaniel? Has his ship been seized by the Dutch?'

'Would you care?' Gooding asked, clearly finding it difficult to articulate so bald a question.

Faulkner was about to reply but then stopped himself; he recalled the pot-boy, ordered wine and bid Gooding sit down. When he had offered a portion of beef pie to his guest and been refused, he set his own dinner aside, filled two tankards and stared at Gooding.

'I do not know what you have sought me out for, Nathan, but I would make some things clear. My abandonment of Judith was, as you know, a painful business, mostly for her and the children. I am not a saint and I have – at least in part – paid for my sins. You will doubtless know that Judith came to me when I was imprisoned in the Tower. I see you knew of that. As did Nathaniel, but you knew that too. Events have sundered us and I have not thought it proper to attempt a reconciliation because I did not think it possible and you know well that I made generous provision—'

'I am not here for this, Kit,' Gooding suddenly broke in with such a change of mood that Faulkner would have thought him pot-valiant had he taken more than a sip of his wine. 'True, this encounter is charged by past events and true you have walked with the Malignants and lain with . . . with . . .'

'Katherine was *not* a whore, if that is what you are about to say,' Faulkner said in a low voice.

'*Was* not?'

'I know little or nothing about her present circumstances.'

'That is all?'

'That is all there is to tell. My life has been one of incessant turmoil. I did not think it possible or wise to attempt to turn back.'

'And now you are an established officer in the service of the Commonwealth's State Navy.'

'Do you say that as a jealous man, or – as a good Puritan – my moral judge?'

'Actually, Captain Faulkner,' Gooding said, recovering the wits that had made him a shrewd ship owner, 'I say it as a bald statement of fact.' His face and tone softened. 'And I say it from pleasure, too.' He smiled and drank deeply.

Faulkner smiled back. 'Ahh, that I have come to my senses at last.'

'Perhaps. But I would not wish you to think that I come here without a motive that is free from family trammels.'

'Oh? Now you intrigue me.'

'I imagine that you require a prize agent,' Gooding said.

Faulkner almost spluttered into his drink. 'My God, Nathan, you do not miss a trick, do you!'

Faulkner stared at his visitor whose slightly pained expression was a reaction to a blasphemy he must have heard a thousand times on the lips of the ship masters with whom he dealt daily. 'So, you are not averse to re-associating your name with mine, by way of business, of course?'

'Not in the least.'

'And what does Judith think of this proposal?'

Gooding cleared his throat and seemed to resume his cavilling air. Watching him, Faulkner was quick to seize on his discomfiture. 'This is her idea, is it not?'

Gooding nodded. 'In part, yes.'

'In part? What part is there other than the possibility that the house of Gooding profits from my actions in this war against the Dutch?'

'Do you despise us for that?'

'What if I do?'

Gooding shrugged, recovering some of his poise. 'It would be of no matter; where you despise us for what? Cupidity, perhaps, we could despise you for, er, turning your coat.' Faulkner was aware that Gooding watched for a furious reaction and so he merely smiled.

'Is that so very unusual in times of civil strife? There are others – General Monck, for example – that began the war in the King's service, were imprisoned and later released to assume far higher commands than Captain Faulkner. As for you and your cupidity, I should expect nothing less from a man charged with seeing that my estranged wife and her children do not starve. I understand that you have executed that commission to the very letter and, if only for that and forgetting all previous and past associations, would have you again as my friend.' Faulkner paused, to see what effect his words were having on Gooding. Clearly the man was touched, if embarrassed.

'I am grown too old for such feelings,' he muttered.

'Then accept an appointment as my prize agent and God bless you for it, for I have other matters on my hands.'

Gooding appeared transformed. His face lightened but he asked, 'You are sure?'

'I am certain. I can think of no one I would rather have. We were as one in the past and may be so again. But what of Judith? Where does she play in all this?'

'Ahh.' Gooding's mood shifted again and he fished in a pocket, taking out a letter and handing it to Faulkner. 'She asked me to give this to you.'

'Would you have me read it now?'

Gooding shook his head. 'I think not. Study it at your leisure and return an answer in due course.'

'You know its contents then.'

'I have some inkling.'

'Will you dine with me, say two days' hence? They do good beef pie.'

Gooding agreed and took his leave. After he had gone, Faulkner sat staring at Judith's letter, almost in fear of its contents. His memory of her visit to him in the Tower was muddled, yet it had left so profound a distaste that he wished for nothing from her and could not understand why she had written. In the light of that last meeting, he could only guess at the extent to which she was behind her brother's visit to him and, while prey to a torrent of misgivings, he remained reluctant to open the letter with its possibility of answering his questions. In the end he left it and went to bed, only to wake in the middle of the night, determined to read it. Striking a light he finally cracked the seal, crouched over the guttering candle flame, and began to read.

When he had finished he blew out the glim and sat staring for a long time into the darkness.

Faulkner waited on General Monck as he had been bidden, handing over the completed draft meticulously entitled in by Mr White's elegant script, *Fighting Instructions for the Fleet*. Waving him to a seat, Monck read the entire paper before nodding his approval.

'My thanks, Captain Faulkner. I am sure Sir Richard will agree that this is most competently executed.' Faulkner muttered his thanks and rose to take his leave. 'A moment if you please, Captain. I had word from Chatham that your own, among a number of other men-of-war, are all but ready and warrants have been issued for impressments. You will receive orders shortly to rejoin and have your ship at The Nore by early April.'

'I shall remain at my present lodging until I hear from the Commissioners or you, General.'

'Good.' Monck gave him a brief smile as he withdrew.

'You have read the letter?' Gooding asked as they each tucked into a substantial slice of mutton.

'I have.'

'And what conclusion have you come to?'

'I am touched. You had not said that Hannah was betrothed.'

'You did not ask after her,' Gooding responded coolly. 'Besides, I can only assume responsibility for your business affairs, even when they touch your family,' he added pointedly.

Faulkner sighed. 'I deserve your censure, Nathan,' he admitted, then asked, 'and have you never thought of marrying yourself?'

Gooding looked up, busily chewing his meat. When he had swallowed it he cleared his throat and observed, 'Oh, a man

thinks of little else until the realities of life confront him. I
seem never to have had the time nor met the person with
whom I thought it possible to share my life.'

'That is a pity. You are not ill favoured, even without your
hair.'

Gooding bridled. 'Come, come, I have not lost it all!'

'True. But speaking as a poor example of either condition,
you would have made a good husband and father.'

'And now Judith offers you a path to redemption.' Gooding
looked up, studying Faulkner's face. 'Have you nothing to say?
I must tell her something.'

'I could not read her letter when first you left it with me,
for I feared its contents. What lay between us has been washed
away by time and other matters have come between us. I
understand that your views of Katherine Villiers are coloured
not only by your perception of the scarlet woman insinuating
herself between your sister and me, but by her name and all
that that recalls, besides her association with the Royalist
cause . . .'

'She is a Malignant,' Gooding said with uncompromising
and quiet certainty.

'True, and these are intolerant times, I might add . . .'

'Not intolerant, merely honest and God-fearing.'

'Well most assuredly God-fearing,' Faulkner said drily, 'but
there is a shadow left by her.'

'There is a hollow in a mattress where a whore has been
but that can be removed and I think that Judith's intentions
towards you are extraordinarily generous.'

'Is not forgiveness a cardinal point of the Christian faith,
Nathan?'

'If you are worried about abasing yourself, there will be
nothing public about any reconciliation.'

'God forbid it! I should not accept on any such terms.'
Faulkner's imagination shied away from any public confession
before some sanctimonious Puritan congregation. 'But she
mentions only a quiet reconciliation. What am I to understand
her as meaning?'

'A return to our home . . . a place in her bed. She is lonely,
Kit.'

'All human souls are lonely. I would have thought her reconciled to the fact by now. She has adult children, grand-children and doubtless more in prospect. What does she want with a husband who abandoned her for a woman she conceives a whore and was himself for a while condemned as a pirate?'

'That is why she wants you quietly, Kit.'

'But why she wants me in the first place?'

'She is of an age . . . an itch . . .' Gooding said vaguely and Faulkner stared at him at first with an air of incredulity until the penny dropped.

'An itch. Why, my good Nathan, you are not so innocent as you would have me believe, eh? Behind that God-fearing mask you have eschewed marriage in favour of, well, other favours.'

'Well, I . . .' Gooding protested.

'Dost find them among your pious congregation, or root them out from behind a barrow in Cheapside?' Faulkner was almost laughing now. He held his hand up. 'No, no, pray do not tell me, I should not like to hear but oh, how good it is to find you have feet of clay!' Gooding was spluttering with embarrassment. 'An itch, by God . . . We all have that affliction!'

'Confound you, Kit, you have still a quick and perceptive wit.'

'So I am told,' Faulkner replied drily. 'But tell me,' he said, affecting a serious expression, 'what would Judith say were she to know that I am ordered to my ship? Would she scratch her itch for a few more months?'

'Why can you not scratch it for her before you depart? Surely you might spend an evening with her and Hannah, even perhaps Henry might be induced to attend, though he holds you in little esteem.'

'What manner of man is he?'

'Clever and diligent, Puritan in his religion and devoted to his mother.'

'And does he have the itch?' Faulkner asked, smiling.

'He has a young woman in mind so I suppose he has.'

'And she has your blessing?'

'Indeed. She is both accomplished and beautiful. As for

money, she has that too. With his present portion of our business, marriage would make Henry a wealthy man.'

'Then he should proceed without further ado.'

'Perhaps you would wish to tell him yourself.'

'Where do you suggest?'

'You should come home. That is the proper place for such
things to be discussed.'

Faulkner's meeting with his estranged family was as awkward
as it could have been and he returned to The Ship inwardly
cursing Gooding for having mooted the idea. Henry had been
chillingly cold and though Faulkner could not blame him, he
deeply resented the young man's sense of overwhelming
propriety. Hannah was sweet and conciliatory, obviously
delighted at her betrothal and apt to forgive all mankind its
sins as she enjoyed her time of happiness. But it was Judith
who troubled him most, both during the evening and afterwards. They had had no time together and their conversation,
overseen by others, had been stilted and forced. She had
expressed her pleasure at seeing him in so much better condition than he had appeared in the Tower, and he had paid her
a few compliments as to her health and complexion as he
presented her with a bunch of violets he had, almost as an
afterthought, purchased from a comely wench on Tower Hill.

'Violets are for faithfulness, husband,' she said in a low voice,
her tone full of irony.

He regretted his ignorance over such subliminal folk messages
but managed to murmur, 'Perhaps, madam, you might accept
them as a compliment to your own steadfastness.'

It was the closest they came to any intimate exchange and,
in retrospect, he rued the expression, thinking it went further
than he meant to over this painful matter of reconciliation.
His pride came like a lump between them and although he
found himself looking at her enviously, remembering her
passionate nature, it was always with the whisper of Katherine's
name in his inner ear.

Perhaps nothing would have come of the matter had not
Brenton called upon him one evening. It was a few days before
Faulkner was due to depart for Chatham and he was assembling

a few personal effects, his thoughts occupied with the composition of the letter he had agreed to send Judith before his departure. Brenton, also on his way to Chatham, insisted they dined together, and dined well. Although not drunk, Faulkner saw Brenton off in a mellow mood. They had enjoyed a convivially pleasant evening, righted most of the world's wrongs and discussed the new *Fighting Instructions*, a copy of which Brenton had brought with him. It was clear Brenton had no idea Faulkner was already privy to the contents, though not to the minor modifications Deane and Monck had made to his draft. Nor was he indiscreet enough to tell even a close friend such as Brenton, so the two pored over the document assiduously, discussing the effect it would have on the fighting ability of the fleet.

'I think,' said Brenton somewhat thickly as they drew the evening to a close, 'that the proof of the pudding will be in the eating when we next take on the *meneers*.'

Faulkner nodded gravely. 'They will, of course, fail in their intentions if individual commanders do not fall in with them. I conceive overwhelming and mass concentration to be the objective; to make a single striking force out of the whole fleet.'

'My word, Kit,' Brenton said, draining his tankard, 'you sound like Sir Henry or a General-at-Sea.'

After Brenton had gone, Faulkner sat in thought for a while and then, impulsively, drew a blank sheet of paper towards him, found a quill and ink, re-cut the nib and began to write. It was only a short letter and he had almost forgotten he had written it the following morning. As for despatching it last thing the previous evening, the realization of that only occurred to him after he had ordered two horses from a neighbouring livery stable and was asking for the reckoning from the landlord of The Ship.

'Will there be anything else, sir?' the man had asked when Faulkner recalled that he had invited Judith to dine with him that last evening in his room. When he had given his order, he sat in his room and wondered if she would come. Surrounded by his dunnage, most of which was packed in two portmanteaux, the room already looked bare and inhospitable, and he half hoped that Judith would find her feet too cold to venture forth. He did not recall her as adventurous, but remembered a wild streak that not even the severest Puritanism could properly curb.

'What have I done?' he asked himself, looking over his effects, pulling out a folio of newly purchased charts and pretending to study them, all the while denying the fact that he had an itch to match hers – or at least hoped he had. He was not long left in doubt. Before six had struck she was at the door and came in flushed and guilty.

'Judith,' he began, but she came forward, her finger pressed against his lips, her eyes full of fire and tears. Nor did she leave until the morning when, in the first glimmer of dawn, they descended the creaking stairs and Faulkner escorted her home before her own servants were about. Returning to his own bed, his head giddy with a contrary mixture of hope and despair, he fell asleep to be woken much later to the thunder of the guns of the Tower of London.

By the time he reached Chatham, Faulkner had caught up with the events of the day from which he had unconsciously been running. Preoccupied by his own affairs and untouched by the tumultuous political events which had been taking place only a few miles further up the River Thames, he had been aware of the Parliamentary row that had been brewing without troubling himself as to its likely outcome. Apart from the purely personal, he had other matters more closely touching his reappointment to the *Union*, and in determining the condition of the ship in a series of letters to and from both Whadcoat and Clarkson. Clarkson had paid him a visit from which he had returned to the ship with a purse of money and the wherewithal to raise some extra men by way of bribes, while he left Faulkner with a request for the new charts with which Faulkner had diverted himself the previous evening.

Having long passed out of the sound of the cannon at the Tower, he was greeted by street revels in Rochester that evening. Toasts were being drunk by those disposed to consider the political upheaval that had taken place that day in Westminster as beneficial. There were some souls who wore expressions of disapproval, but they were careful not to articulate their misgivings. Only the landlord of The Griffin, with whom Faulkner intended to lodge for the night and whither he had summoned Whadcoat and Clarkson to dine, expressed an opinion contrary to that finding public expression in the street outside.

'Oh, they'd all drink to a monkey if he sat on a cart and threw pennies at their feet!' the man said, showing Faulkner to his room. 'Lord Protector, indeed! More like King Oliver, by God! Well, damn the Parliament and good riddance to them! We'll just have to see what a muck of it King Oliver makes of things.'

And with that Faulkner had to be content as to the mood of the country upon the elevation of Oliver Cromwell, late general in the Parliamentary army and sitting Member for Huntingdon, to the office of Lord Protector.

Later that evening, the conversation between Faulkner and his officers turned from the preoccupations of the ship to that of the news of the day.

'They say it was like a coronation, the ceremony,' said Whadcoat. 'I'd never have thought that Cromwell would have thrown over the Parliament! He of all people!'

'It will make little difference to us, Mr Whadcoat,' Clarkson said. 'It don't change our task one whit.'

'No indeed.'

And so they went again to war.

The Battle of the Gabbard

June 1653

'Katherine!'

Faulkner woke in a lather of sweat. He was sodden, feverish and terrified that he had shouted aloud. The small hour of his awakening was such that even so foolish a thing as calling out Kate's name could frighten him. He lay back, realizing that he had only shouted in his dream, for the ship lay quiet, gently rising and falling to the seas, silent but for the creaking of her fabric as she worked in the seaway. But she was not quiet; it was just that he was insulated here, in his cabin, from the piteous groans of the wounded below in the orlop. He calmed himself with an effort and felt the burn of the wound in his upper arm and shoulder. Although the surgeon had extracted the splinter hours earlier, he felt the inflammation. Was it the first onset of blood poisoning? He made to touch his right shoulder with his left hand, then recalled Mr Surgeon Whitaker had left a hog's bristle in the wound that it might drain properly.

Katherine . . . The memory of her tormented him, so that in his feverish state she seemed like a succubus, real rather than imagined. Or did she? Was it not his own conscience that tortured him? He was no better, for he had betrayed her by lying with Judith. Filled with self-loathing, he was caught between two twin fires of passion, drawn inexorably towards Judith when Katherine had scorned him. That is what he told himself, until he recovered his wits, along with his integrity and realized that in effect he had himself abandoned Katherine after his capture. It was no good protesting to his inner self that he had been swept up by events beyond his control. Now she lay in the King's arms, until he tired of her – which was a certainty, for she was older than him by some measure and only her beauty and proximity could possibly recommend her to so young and vigorous a prince as was His Majesty King Charles II.

Faulkner threw off the blanket and tentatively set his feet on the deck, bracing himself by the deck beams above him. For a moment his head spun and then he slowly came to himself. What was he mooning over these women for? He had other, more pressing matters to attend to, for God's sake. He groped his way to the chair behind the table that served as both desk and dining board. Swivelling the chair round he stared astern through the windows at the wake, shivering and burning at the same time, wretched in the isolation of his situation.

The ship was barely moving, the wind no stronger now than it had been for the last two days of action, a coil of water trailing astern as the rudder bit at the flow coming under the transom.

Heavens, but it had been hard work after weeks of beating about in response to reports. Tromp had gone north with a convoy said to be two hundred strong; Tromp was back in Helvoetsluys, or was it the Texel, or the Zuider Zee, or Enkhuizen? Now he was reported at sea again and with a fleet the like of which had never been seen before. And they had gone to meet him, sweeping up from Portsmouth under Monck and Deane, two Generals-at-Sea both in command in equal measure with eighty-eight men-of-war and over one hundred armed merchantmen. Tromp was nowhere to be found off the Dutch coast, so they sailed back across the North Sea to Great Yarmouth where they anchored, only to hear that Tromp had slipped past them and had bombarded Dover. It was incredible!

Little fly-boats were sent off with messages. Blake, still unwell after his wounding in February, was said to be mustering more ships in the outer estuary of the Thames, summoning them to join him under the lee of the Gunfleet Sand, a few miles from the Naze of Essex. Meanwhile, Monck and Deane, having held a council of war aboard their joint flagship, the *Resolution*, slipped south to Sole Bay off Southwold with a fleet of over one hundred ships. They were supported by Penn in the *James* and Lawson in the *George*, both leading their respective divisions. The English fleet stood out to sea and early on the

morning of the 1st June the scouting frigates, off the Gabbard
Shoal, had briefly let fly their topsail sheets, the distant signal
for an enemy fleet in sight, but there had followed a day of
fruitless manoeuvring at the end of which the signal to anchor
had been hoisted. The Dutch followed suit some miles away
and when the misty morning of the 2nd dawned, they weighed
and, following the orders of the two Generals, formed up in
line, each division closed on its admiral with Lawson in the
van, Monck and Deane the centre and Penn the rear. There
was barely sufficient of the north-westerly wind to allow them
to get into their proper stations, but the attentiveness of the
commanders and their sailing masters enabled the English to
work to windward of the Dutch who obligingly formed a
similar ragged line with Ruyter in their vanguard, Tromp in
the centre, and De With the rear.

The two fleets drew closer, the hours of the forenoon ticking
past until, at about an hour before noon, the action opened.
Within half an hour it had become general, the ships locked
in a bloody battle in which the English stood off, under strict
orders not to board until their guns had done their savage
work. No one aboard the *Union* knew it until later, but Sir
Richard Deane had been killed in the first exchange of fire
and De Ruyter, it later transpired, had tried to work ahead of
Lawson, double his line and rake as he crossed it, but the fickle
wind frustrated this bold manoeuvre and – despite launching
boats to have his ships' heads pulled round – frustrated the
Dutch admiral's audacity. Instead, a bloody mêlée ensued, each
ship seeking out an opponent and battering her until their
sides were shattered, their decks strewn with the dead and
dying and blood ran red from their scuppers, staining the sea
alongside the lumbering hulls. The noise and smoke were
tremendous, the air seemed hellish hot from the fiery breath
of the cannon, thick with smoke, shot and splinters, one of
which struck Faulkner at the height of the fight. He did not
notice it at first, thinking his head reeled and his ears sang
from the deafening concussion of the guns, but at last he realized he had been wounded and was losing blood. He got
himself below and had the splinter drawn, a savage, searing
pain that tore at the muscles of his upper arm and shoulder,

leaving him sick and weak. A draught of strong wine fortified him and, roughly bandaged and with Whitaker's admonition that 'something would have to be done about that wound later, Captain,' Faulkner returned to the quarterdeck.

Here he found Clarkson had been wounded in his right hand and was sitting at the base of the mizen mast, his face the colour of cartridge linen, contemplating the bloody wreckage of three fingers.

Faulkner relieved the indomitable and doughty Whadcoat of his temporary command, sending his lieutenant back to exhort those serving the guns to exert themselves to their utmost. Faulkner was dizzy with the fury of the battle, only vaguely aware of what he did, of ordering the helm put over and the ragged sails re-trimmed as they hauled round and avoided close contact with their enemy. They had a Dutchman on both sides at one time, the *Union* belching fire and iron in a relentless thunder that seemed to Faulkner to have been going on for such an immensity of time that there was neither past nor future, only this dreadful, cacophonous present, this roaring in his ears, this thumping, throbbing heartbeat that seemed to have migrated up into his shoulder.

It ended at last, though Faulkner had no clear notion of when exactly that was. The sun seemed still high in the heavens, but Whadcoat afterwards told him that it was six hours past noon that the Dutch stood off towards their home coast under a freshening wind. This, held Whadcoat, was the clear and unequivocal judgement of God, for normally in such circumstances, the concussion of the guns killed a light wind and generated a calm. Instead, the Lord God of Hosts had sent a wind which had by this time veered into the north-east quarter, enabling the Dutch to make sail.

The English fleet followed and that evening, as the sun set and the men were busy cutting away the damaged fore topmast and main topgallant, knotting and splicing the damaged rigging, sending down the ragged fore topsails and making some fist of a jury rig, Whitaker dressed Faulkner's wound, inserting the bristle to allow the pus to drain from it. When at last Faulkner and Whadcoat expressed themselves satisfied with the running repairs, the watches were set, station was taken up on the lanterns hoisted in the rigging of the *Resolution*, the *James* and the *George* and the fleet settled down for the night as it shadowed the Dutch down the coast of Holland. The *Union's* men were exhausted but Faulkner saw that they were fed and issued with beer. To a groaning acceptance of the inevitable, he passed word that they should rest from their labours which, he felt certain, would not be over for some hours yet.

By dawn the tide and wind had carried both fleets south until they lay not far from Dunkirk. Just as Faulkner had thought, Tromp renewed the action the following morning, turning on his pursuers for a few more hours of fighting but the Dutch had lost the taste for English iron, their shallower-draughted ships outgunned by their heavier opponents as they retreated into the estuary of the Schelde. Making the best of his way into the heart of the action, Faulkner took the *Union* inshore, engaging two Dutch men-of-war. His gunners warmed to their work and had compelled both of the enemy's ships to strike their ensigns to the hoarse cheers of the *Union's* people.

It was now that the Dutch suffered their heaviest losses, some twenty ships, eleven captured, six sunk and three destroyed by exploding magazines. With Blake arriving on the scene, Tromp's fleet was blockaded between Flushing and Breskens, the action ending in a decisive victory for the English.

By the evening of the 3rd June, Monck had ordered the worst-damaged ships back into home waters. Among them lumbered the crippled *Union*, under what sail that could be set upon her shattered masts, her captain retreating to his cabin with a note from Monck ordering him home, but bearing the compliment that 'no captain has done more this day than you'.

Faulkner stiffly rose from his contemplation of the sea astern. Somewhere over the horizon, Monck and Blake were anchored, bottling up the flower of the Dutch fleet. A pale square caught his eye, lying upon the dark planking. He picked it up and, in the faint light, recognized it as the order to withdraw.

Weak and feverish, Faulkner submitted to further ministrations from Whitaker once they had anchored in the Medway, off Blackstakes. The surgeon shook his head over the wound, drew out the bristle and sniffed at it with a grunt.

'Lie down, sir, this will not take a moment. Have you some

fortified wine?' The servant Jackson brought a bottle and Whitaker decanted half a pint into a dish, dipped his scalpel in the wine then began his excoriating curetting of the wound. Faulkner writhed with the painful intrusion, unable to stifle the cry of agony it produced, but Whitaker was skilled in his butchery, quick and sure. Having withdrawn the knife, he poured the remainder of the wine into the wound and drew the flesh together with adeptly made sutures.

'Consider yourself fortunate, Captain Faulkner, to have wine to hand. I believe it maketh all the difference.'

'Why so?' asked Faulkner through gritted teeth as Whitaker applied a pledget and bound up his shoulder.

'I have observed it deters putrefaction, sir. One cannot guarantee it, of course, but the advantage lies with you for submitting to it.'

'I think,' Faulkner gasped as he recovered himself, 'I should rather drink the stuff . . . Steward, two glasses, if you please.'

One was passed to Whitaker who acknowledged his commander's generosity with an appreciative nod. 'One glass will do you no harm, sir, but more will, I have observed, stimulate bleeding.'

'I shall heed your advice, Mr Whitaker.'

The following morning Faulkner felt much better but the ascent of his spirits was short-lived. At noon he received some papers from the dockyard, brought downstream from the Commissioner at Chatham. As the dockyard officer accepted the list of requirements to put the *Union* back into fighting order, Faulkner noticed a personal letter to himself among those dropped on his desk. He did not at first recognize the hand, though he afterwards found out it was from his son, Henry, but the news, already some weeks old, was all too clear: in May Sir Henry Mainwaring had died.

For a moment Faulkner felt nothing. It took him time to realize what this meant: that Sir Henry, who had, as it were, brought him forth into the world in which he now functioned with such confidence, no longer existed. Death was commonplace, but specific deaths such as so closely touched his very being, emptied him of life. He sat, carefully, lowering himself like a man prematurely aged as the import of this news sank in and it struck him that, for all the swaggering self-conceit, for all the ready wit and the smooth phrase, the grasp of his profession and his ability to handle a ship and command the respect of his fellow men, his future was somehow imperilled by the lack of Sir Henry. Sir Henry had been more than a father to him, for fathers have a habit of casting out their young to fend for themselves, if they do not bind them in to some family enterprise. He himself had done it rather differently by abandoning his sons, but the result had been the same, as young Nathaniel had demonstrated. But Sir Henry had been so much more, so very much more than a mere paternal figure, more than a mentor. He had been an intellectual companion, a sounding board, a man against whom Faulkner could measure himself. He had once heard Brenton describe the man who taught him sword play: 'He made me fight as if I, too, was as brilliant at the feint, the deception, the lunge and parry as was he.' And he remembered thinking, in one of those quick, intuitive flashes of knowledge that fix in the brain as certainties, that that was exactly what Sir Henry was then to him. And now he was no more, already laid to rest alongside the body of his short-lived wife whom Faulkner had seen but twice before she died.

He sighed deeply, re-read the letter and then put it away. It had been good of Henry, who had himself been named after his father's patron, to let him know. Faulkner rose. Sir Henry would have not approved of moping when there was work to do and a ship to refit.

It was only as he passed out on deck that Faulkner had the odd fancy that, in that recollection, Sir Henry still walked with him. It also occurred to him that his wound ached much less this morning.

As a man may do in the privacy of his own thoughts, Faulkner conceived a curious notion that the rapid healing of his wound owed more to the intercession of the dead Mainwaring than the skill of his surgeon. He chid himself for so Popish a notion, but nevertheless the conviction grew so that he always thereafter held it to be Mainwaring's last beneficent act towards the wretched, starveling boy he had lifted from the gutter.

Scheveningen and After

Some weeks later, as Faulkner readied the *Union* for sea, he received an order by fly-boat from General Monck. 'My dear Captain,' he read, flattered by the cordiality of the mode of address,

> *I intend to withdraw the main part of the fleet shortly and am earnest that you should as soon as may be convenient, but at all costs before the end of the present week, station yourself off the Texel whither De With withdrew after the late action. I understand from intelligencers at Den Helder that the Dutch squadron under him is ready for sea and anxious to rejoin Tromp here off Flushing. Pray, therefore, bring me notice of any such move that De With might make. This is properly work for a frigate, but I would have a ship of force there, for fear of a lesser vessel being overwhelmed.*

It was a concise brief in which Faulkner knew likely as much as his commander-in-chief and this sense of personal inclusion seemed to be embodied in the simple signature: 'Monck'. Faulkner was gratified by the confidence the General clearly felt in him, for the task was a post of honour, and particularly so, given Faulkner's past. He passed word for Clarkson and his charts.

Two weeks later, in mid-July, having been on station off Den Helder with the Haak Sand under his lee and a few nights of anxiety under his belt, Faulkner received a second note from Monck which simply informed him that he was back on his station in the mouth of the Schelde but would come north and show himself off the Texel. 'The enemy having made no move, this is the period of greatest danger,' Monck had concluded.

A few days later Monck's fleet, or the greater part of it, some eighty sail of men-of-war, came up from the south and, for a week, cruised off the Texel. Then, suspecting his absence from the Schelde would have tempted Van Tromp to move, he brought the *Resolution* close up under the *Union*'s stern and hailed her.

'I shall be gone from here after nightfall, Captain Faulkner,' he shouted in his harsh voice. 'Maintain your station and keep me informed. Do you hoist an admiral's lanterns tonight.'

Jumping up on the carriage of a gun, Faulkner waved his acknowledgement of the instruction. The *Union* bearing Monck's lanterns would maintain the pretence at least until tomorrow's dawn, beyond which it would be impossible to conceal the truth from any watcher on the dunes at Kirkduin, but it might prove sufficient. Thus, shortly after nightfall, he was aware of Monck's ships slipping away like predatory owls, dark and sinister shapes, half seen, yet pregnant with menace.

The deception failed, however. The following forenoon a sail was seen heading towards them from the south, beating up against the wind. As she got closer she fired a gun to leeward and hoisted a signal that, owing to her aspect, no one aboard *Union* could make out until one of the junior officers with better sight than his seniors expressed the opinion that it signified an urgent despatch. Although none of his seniors could agree, the outcome proved him right. Heaving to under the *Union*'s lee and hoisting out a boat, her commander had himself pulled across to the larger vessel, and almost ran up the *Union*'s side.

Faulkner had hardly read the note, seen the captain of the fly-boat over the side of the *Union* with a glass of wine inside him and returned to his cabin to consult his charts in the light that Van Tromp was at sea, than Whadcoat sent down for him.

'They're coming out,' he said shortly, by way of explanation, when Faulkner reached the deck and took the proffered tele-scope. It was a bright summer day with masses of white, fleecy cloud building over the land as Whadcoat pointed to the low line of sandy coast which gleamed yellow in the sunlight. Where the yellow line broke, indicating the gap between the mainland of Holland and the island of Texel, he could clearly see the mass of shipping, the dark, beetle-like hulls each with its heap of white sails as the squadron of De With emerged for battle.

Faulkner looked aloft. The *Union* was hove to under easy canvas on the starboard tack, dipping to the low swell and leaning slightly to the wind from the west-north-west. The enemy would be hard on the wind coming out, but the moment they were clear and could head south, the wind would be fair.

'Very well, let us fill the main tops'l and make for the General.'

'Head south. Aye, aye, sir.'

Whadcoat turned away to bellow orders and a moment later the pipes twittered, the main braces made the block-sheaves rattle and the main yards came round. Suddenly the *Union* was under way, finished with dipping and curtseying to the enemy's shoreline, filled with a sense of urgent purpose that no amount of assurance that lying off an enemy's coast keeping watch could match. Faulkner could almost feel the mood of the men lift. He summoned all his officers to his cabin, and told them what he knew.

'Van Tromp is at sea, gentlemen,' he said, looking round at their faces. He picked up a pair of dividers and referred to the chart that showed the gentle curve of the coast of the province of Holland, with the Frisian island of Texel to the north and the archipelago of large islands in the estuary of the Schelde that formed the province of Zealand in the south. As for their own cruising ground, it occupied that swathe of the sea known as the Broad Fourteens, owing to the uniformity of its fourteen-fathom depth. 'There has been an inconclusive engagement off Katwijk.' He indicated the little town to the south with his dividers. 'De With is clearly seeking a junction with Tromp. The General is pursuing Tromp and we lie betwixt the two fleets.' He paused to let the gravity of their situation sink in. 'We must, of course, maintain contact with De With, but keep out of trouble ourselves.' A murmur of assent ran through the assembled officers. 'My guess is that the two fleets will engage here. He laid the points of the dividers on a coastal town. They leaned forward, several trying to pronounce it with its harsh guttural sound. 'I think I have the advantage of you,'

Faulkner said with a hint of irony, referring to his period of
exile among the Dutch. 'Schveningen,' he articulated, scraping
the name, so odd to English ears, from the back of his throat.
Some of them sniggered like schoolboys; there was no
explaining the strange ways of foreigners, no wonder they had
to be fought. Conscious of their thoughts, Faulkner smiled to
himself. If it helped them risk their lives in battle, he would
not deny them their xenophobia. 'That is all for now,' he said.
'When the time comes I have no doubt but that I may rely
upon you all.'

They shuffled out, only Whadcoat remaining. 'Skayven . . .
what-do-you-call it?' he said and Faulkner stared at him, unsure
whether Whadcoat was manifesting a hitherto hidden sense of
humour, or exhibiting a serious sense of curiosity. Faulkner
pointed again to the location on the chart and repeated the
name in a manner more phonetically comprehensible to an
Englishman of Whadcoat's background.

'Skay-ven-ing-gen.'

'A fit place for an enemy,' Whadcoat pronounced solemnly.

'I suppose so,' Faulkner said with a smile. 'And now I suppose
we had better observe the enemy's motions.'

Matters moved swiftly that day. De With sent three of his
fastest frigates to cut off the *Union*, so Faulkner was obliged
to stand to the south-west to avoid being caught between the
two Dutch fleets, knowing that De With would not pursue
him far off his native coast. It was therefore the following
morning, once he was certain that the enemy frigates had
thrown up the chase, before Faulkner dared turn east and
within an hour they could see from the *Union*'s quarterdeck a
pall of grey smoke lying like a fog bank along the horizon.
Shortly afterwards they could hear the thunder of guns.

Her yards braced up and every stitch of sail drawing, the
Union drove down into the battle which, as they approached,
seemed to stretch from north to south. Each fleet was over
one hundred strong, an immensity of sea power contesting for
the advantage. As Faulkner, flanked by Whadcoat and Clarkson,
whose hand now bore only a thumb and two fingers, studied
the action, they could form no real appreciation of the disposition of the contending squadrons. Much was obscured by dense

smoke, but occasionally they could see a man-of-war tack, so that Whadcoat, remarking that these seemed to be wearing the English ensign, observed that, 'They're passing back and forth through the enemy formations.'

'Just like a troop of horse,' added Clarkson with some little contempt for the cavalrymen sent to command seamen, but with more prescience than he then knew.

'We had better follow their lead,' Faulkner said, closing his glass with a resolute snap. 'We'll haul up the courses the moment we get into the smoke, so I'd be obliged if you would take your posts. Good fortune . . .'

'And may the Lord of Hosts favour our just cause,' said Whadcoat with that solemnity that Faulkner had grown accustomed to.

'Amen to that,' added Clarkson as he moved away to pick up his speaking-trumpet and stand beside the helmsmen.

'Cripple 'em before we hull 'em, sir?' asked Whadcoat. 'It renders them better to our purpose.'

'Double-shots aloft and then knock out your quoins, if you think you can do it without losing time.'

On the point of walking off to command his guns, Whadcoat swung round. 'Rest assured of that, Captain Faulkner,' he said with reassuring warmth. Faulkner stared after him for a moment, listening to him roar encouragement to his gun crews as, in passing, he relayed Faulkner's intentions to the junior officers at their batteries.

Twenty minutes later the *Union* and her people were in the very thick of what proved the fiercest battle of the war.

Although the action had begun at seven that morning and the *Union* did not engage an enemy ship until about eleven, there nevertheless followed hours of fighting in which, like all the other ships of both sides, no man knew clearly what was afoot. Brooding upon the fight in the days that followed, Faulkner was apt to think the common seaman, working at his gun with monotonous servitude, had the better bargain. He had, of course, to keep what the terrifying experience left of his wits about him to maintain the religious sequence of sponge, load, ram and fire for fear that, as sometimes happened when men were exhausted or drugged by the smoke, smell, noise and horror of it all, the drill got out of kilter and a charge was rammed home before a gun had been sponged. The hot chamber would ignite the charge and the rammer might be killed stone dead, speared by his own ramrod while the gun, going off prematurely, would recoil unexpectedly, its entire weight driving its loaded carriage over the bare feet of the rammer's mates who might be clearing the touchhole. Such accidents occurred from time to time and were the chief concern of Whadcoat's fellow lieutenants as they held their men back from such follies, while at the same time driving them to ceaseless exertion.

But at least these men, down in the lower gun deck, were generally better protected than their fellows on the upper deck where the darting splinters, or wreckage shot down from aloft, could maim and wound. Perhaps the most vulnerable of the seamen were those directed to tend the braces as the ship was manoeuvred under Faulkner's direction and Clarkson's detailed supervision. They had to expose themselves in handling the braces, the clew and buntlines and, where necessary, in dousing or making sail. In an action such as was fought of Scheveningen that last day of July 1653, there was a constant trimming of the yards as the warring ships passed each other, wheeled and re-passed, all the while pouring a withering fire at and into each other as they sought not the advantage over their opponents, but their destruction.

In the terrible hours that followed the *Union*'s opening broadside, discharged into a Dutch frigate on the fringe of the main battle as Faulkner carried her into the mêlée under a press of canvas, the superior weight of shot combined with the brutal speed with which the English gunners plied their weapons told against the Dutch. For all their gallantry and Tromp's brilliant manoeuvring, the work of attrition could but have one outcome. As the day died and the sun set against the flaming glory of the western sky, the Dutch began to fall out of the action. One by one they deserted their flagship, the battered *Brederode,* where Admiral Marteen van Tromp's body lay as it had done since before noon, when an arquebusier in the English ship *Tulip* had shot him. Some twenty Dutch ships either were sunk or surrendered as their fellows drifted away, followed by the English who chased them back into the Texelstroom, the anchorage off Den Helder.

Just before the daylight faded, Monck threw out the signal to anchor off the English coast and the fleet to withdraw.

It was past four bells in the first watch, ten of the clock that evening, before Faulkner left the deck. Clarkson had been killed and Whadcoat wounded. Faulkner himself was, mercifully, relatively unscathed. He had suffered a terrific thump in the breast, but his cuirass had saved him, though its smoothly curved plate was dented and the impacted depression pressed painfully upon his body when he drew a deep breath in exerting himself. He had − somehow, though he never recollected how or quite when − also suffered the entire destruction of the right sleeve of his broadcloth coat. The presence of wooden slivers indicated the passing of a larger splinter, perhaps a shower of the deadly things, for the upperworks of the *Union* were found to be badly knocked up at daylight next morning.

Nor was he ever quite clear how many enemy ships they had engaged, or how many times they had engaged the same enemy man-of-war, though he had clear and distinct impressions of fleeting moments − of Clarkson's hideous death when a Dutch round shot passed through his lower body so that his loins were shot out and his trunk was blown clean off his legs and seemed to dump him, limbless on the planking. He and Faulkner had been addressing one another, shouting to make themselves heard and the sudden descent of Clarkson's face transfixed with a look of stark incredulity had been almost comic. Blood poured from him, spattering Faulkner's breeches and boots as it slowly fell over, the face wearing the same astonished look. The passing of the ball spun Faulkner so that he slithered in the gore and all but fell, recovering himself as the horror of what he had witnessed coalesced into the realization that Clarkson was dead.

From that moment he had to handle the ship directly himself. The twin tasks of looking for any move the enemy might make, the descent on their unengaged side − when they *were* unengaged − and of giving the precise orders to handle the ship, fell upon him with the removal of Clarkson. However,

their rig was so maimed that the requirement for smart manoeuvring petered out as the afternoon drew on and by the end
of the battle he was grateful that they had the stumps of three
masts, a bowsprit and its short topmast to spread some sail
upon.

He remembered, too, a lengthy engagement with a Dutch
man-of-war of larger size than the *Union*. Although he could
not recall her name, his mind's eye carried the recollection of
her guns spitting fire into the *Union* and the stout ship shuddering to the multiple impact of their shot. He also recollected
her captain, a large man with a florid face exhorting his men
who, catching sight of Faulkner, doffed his hat. The action,
so unexpected, so oddly civil among the parody of the civiliz-
ation of which the two commanders were representative,
prompted a reciprocal action on Faulkner's part.

As he sank on to the deck under the shattered windows of
his cabin, there being no furniture to hand, he summoned
Whadcoat to join him. Staring at his first lieutenant who, apart
from a face blackened by powder smoke, looked little different
from the officer who had left him hours earlier, Faulkner
offered him a glass of wine.

'My God, Mr Whadcoat, but the Lord looketh after his
own.'

'Indeed, I am blessed, sir, though we have a butcher's bill
of near thirty men.' Whadcoat eased himself down, his back
to a gun carriage so that, in a different setting, they might
have been taken for a couple of farm labourers taking a spell
from their work.

Faulkner blew air from his lips in a low whistle. 'All dead?'

'Nineteen, with six bearing mortal wounds, so Whitaker
tells me.'

'And the wounded?'

'Forty-six likely to survive, if the surgeon and his boys do
not kill 'em with their ministrationing.'

Faulkner nodded at the curious turn of phrase. 'And you,
you are unhurt, or are you deceiving me?'

'A few passing balls winded me, a small bore ball shot off
my baldric, damn it, but I am otherwise unscathed.'

'Remarkable.'

'Poor Clarkson. I saw what was left of him before they tipped him to the fishes.'

Faulkner nodded as the horror of the memory flooded back and made his blood run cold. 'We were speaking together when he was hit . . .' Whadcoat remained silent, then drained his glass. 'Have another,' Faulkner suggested. Whadcoat thanked him and they refilled their glasses.

'We lost Lieutenant Black, a promising young man, and two of Clarkson's mates were wounded, one of them is among those not expected to live.'

'Which one?'

'I forget his name,' Whadcoat said casually, adding, 'the one with the curly hair.'

'John Gooch,' said Faulkner.

'That's him.'

'What was the large Dutchman we engaged? Did you get her name?'

Whadcoat smiled. 'I might have done if they called their ships sensible names but she was eighty guns and we passed her four times and . . .'

'Four times? I had no idea and would not have put money on it being more than twice.'

'Four times, for the truth of it, and we had her alongside for at least twenty minutes at one stage.'

'God's wounds but the din of battle leaves one confused.'

'Aye, you are exposed to the hot hell of it all on deck. One gets a respite down below and can take a peek through a gun port from time to time. I saw her name across her transom, all red and gold and as long as a horse's tail but I could make not a head nor a tail of it.' Whadcoat drew greedily on the wine, then added, 'I think she must have been a flagship by her size.'

'We shall never know,' Faulkner mused, 'whose deaths we caused or what ship they manned.'

''Tis no matter, sir. 'Tis not our business but the Lord's. He is our sure shield and will gather the Godly to his bosom and leave the rest to the devil.'

'You take a sanguine view, Mr Whadcoat.'

'I live in bloody times, Captain Faulkner, and get little liberty to worry. My time will come one day and while I am thankful it came not today, I am ready to answer for my sins before the throne of the Lord of Hosts.'

'As we all must surely do but I too am glad that it was not today.'

'Who has the deck?' Faulkner asked.

'Lieutenant Jefferies.'

'He is unhurt?'

'A scratch enough to impress his lady, but nothing to worry about.'

'Good. He is a competent young man.'

A silence fell and Faulkner had almost fallen asleep when Whadcoat asked, 'What do you think the General will do, sir?'

Faulkner shrugged. He could barely see Whadcoat now in the gloom of night. His face was a pale oval that seemed to swim in his tired vision. 'Oh, we will anchor in Hollesley Bay under Orfordness, or Sole Bay off Southwold, depending upon the tide and then recruit and re-rig. Then, I wouldn't wonder, we shall be back off the Texel and the Schelde until the Dutch realize they are beaten.'

'I think they took drubbing enough today. I do not think they will look for another fight for a while.'

'I hope that you are right.'

But Whadcoat's head had fallen forward upon his knees and a gentle snore drifted through the cabin so that Faulkner, too, let go of the day and drifted into oblivion.

'Well, Kit, you are well regarded, I believe. Indeed, I heard the Lord Protector noticed you.'

'You speak as though I had secured the regard of a King, Nathan.'

'Well, your name was among those mentioned in Parliament.'

Faulkner made a gesture of deprecation. He found his brother-in-law's adulation strangely at odds with his usual sober view of the world. There were rumours of peace, it was true, and Gooding's business would better prosper if shipping could proceed upon its lawful occasions without the intervention of hostile Dutchmen, but this was all too much. He had not yet laid up the *Union* and had only a few days in London before he must return to Chatham and await events. 'That was entirely due to General Monck's kindness,' he said by way of explanation. 'I rendered some service to him but I was not the only one to have done so.'

'And peace must surely follow after so signal a victory. They say the Dutch fleet is shattered and Tromp dead.'

'So I have heard but how is it that you know . . .' Faulkner paused, then, grasping the reason for Gooding's euphoria, remarked, 'I see, you have been in touch with Helvoetsluys, or Amsterdam.'

'Meneer Goudschmidt, to be precise, Kit, and your money is safe.'

'I was never in any doubt but that it would be. States make war while merchants make money and you, my dear Nathan, are a merchant.' A cloud crossed Faulkner's face and Gooding noticed it.

'I am unable to glean news of . . .' He did not finish the sentence, but both men knew of whom he spoke.

'Did you try?' asked Faulkner, his mouth suddenly dry.

'I made some enquiries.'

Faulkner gave Gooding a long, hard look. 'And?'

Gooding shrugged. 'No words of comfort,' he said hesitantly, judging Faulkner's mood. 'Either way, Kit. She is gone, lost to you and it would be better for us all, not least Hannah, Henry and . . . well, my sister who is your wife.'

Faulkner felt a constriction in his throat and his voice rasped when he spoke. 'Is there news of Charles Stuart?'

'Oh, there is much of that. God knows we are spared much by the intervention of the Lord.'

'Never mind the Lord, Nathan, what of the King?'

Gooding caught at Faulkner's unfortunate expression. 'Is that how you think of him still?'

'What the devil does it matter what I think of him?' he snapped, anger directed at Nathan that better applied to his own slip of the tongue. 'And what does it matter for me if I cannot speak freely in . . . in this house.' He gestured round the room that had once been his own.

'Please, Kit, this is unnecessary,' Gooding temporized. 'This is as difficult for me as for you but life . . .'

'Must go on, I suppose you were about to say.' Gooding nodded. 'Well,' Faulkner went on, 'we used to run a sound enterprise between us. I suppose that we must do so again. Have we any investments to make?'

'Are you willing to come back in?'

'I have my pay and such prize money as you have been able to secure.'

'And money in Amsterdam.'

'And money in Amsterdam.'

'You should make reparation for those ships of ours that you damaged at The Nore.'

'You are a wry dog and as close a negotiator as any Israelite,' Faulkner said with a half smile. 'And you are right; I should make reparation.'

'And,' Gooding dropped his voice, embarrassed, 'what about Judith?'

Faulkner laughed. 'Has she not told you? We have slept together. It is only natural, Nathan, she is my wife and the mother of three of my children.'

'Are there others?' Gooding asked quickly before he perceived Faulkner was having fun with him. 'Oh . . . I see, yes of course.'

'And how does Judith feel about all this consideration which, if I divine matters correctly, has more to do with how much Nathan Gooding can make out of the fortunate and well-regarded Captain Faulkner?'

'Come, Kit, that is not fair!' Gooding protested.

'Life is seldom fair, Nathan, as Judith will testify.'

Gooding threw up his hands. 'Oh, I cannot play this with you, you must make your own peace with my sister.'

'I never had any intention of doing otherwise, Brother-in-law. Now, perhaps a wealthy man like yourself could offer some hospitality. A glass of wine, perhaps, even a bite if the house possesses anything other than the meal pie and dried beef which maketh thee a dull fellow.'

'Wine, yes, but tobacco, no. As for victuals, my good Captain, I believe that your wife has something prepared in anticipation.'

'Then you may cease your prattle, call for some wine and tell me where I shall find this paragon of the vestal virtues.'

'She waits upstairs.'

'Ahh. Then I think we should take wine first.'

They dined together that first night, Nathan and the two children, Hannah and Henry. Nathaniel was absent at sea, unfortunately, otherwise the appearance would have been one of complete and happy reconciliation. It was, Faulkner was aware, not quite what it seemed, though Puritan manners and constraint made it seem so to the servants, who prattled late into the evening about 'how the master had come home after his heroic adventures'. That, of course, resulted from the accounts of the late fights that were circulating in pamphlets in which Faulkner, among others, was singled out for praise.

For Faulkner, the regard was an embarrassment, for he kept seeing the astonished look upon Clarkson's face as his life leached out of his entrails upon the *Union*'s white deck and covered the boots of his commander. It was not an easy thing to forget, an epitome of all the horrors of the late and savage sea war.

'You know,' he said, breaking an awkward silence as the servants cleared the first course and brought in the second, 'in the heat of the late action of Scheveningen,' and here he said the word with the most accurate Dutch intonation he could muster, so much so that Judith, sitting quietly opposite, winced at this reminder of his time in Holland, and Hannah winced at the guttural sound, 'in the very heat of the battle, a Dutch captain raised his hat to me in salute.'

No one knew quite what to say. Henry thought his father to be attempting some crude claim on their admiration, Hannah was still wondering over the strange Dutch name, and Gooding considered the scene was far beyond his imagination. But Faulkner was looking at Judith as he spoke and his steady stare seemed to demand some response.

She returned his gaze and he felt her whole character struggling with the task of responding. She had fine eyes and full lips, he thought to himself, and while he could never love her as he had loved Katherine, they had three children and had survived civil war and separation. As for Katherine, there was no news of her other than that her name was no longer associated with – and here, in the privacy of his thoughts, he considered the matter carefully – the King. Whatever power ruled in London was England's business, but there was a legitimate King over the water, a King in waiting, perhaps, for who would follow Oliver?

Unable to find the words her husband expected, Judith had flushed at his over-long scrutiny.

'Who will follow Cromwell as Protector, d'you think, Henry?' he asked his son by way of stimulating conversation.

The young man shrugged. 'Perhaps we shall have a Parliament again,' he said.

'Hannah?' She coloured up and Faulkner flicked a look from her to her mother and bit off a remark that they flushed much the same when caught for something to say.

'Nathan?'

'Perhaps one of your Generals-at-Sea, for even with a Parliament we shall need a head of state and the House does not much like the Army. What would you say to Blake . . . or Monck?'

'Both are soldiers at heart,' Faulkner remarked, 'and either would be competent enough, but surely Parliament's mood might change if it were a new Parliament.'

'True, but I think perhaps the Lord Protector has his own plans.'

'For what?'

'His son, Richard, I hear.'

'Is that not very like kingly succession?'

'Not if it required the ratification of Parliament.'

'That is not what I understand Oliver submitted to.'

'No, perhaps, but it was then different.'

'I suppose you want the King back,' said Judith, breaking into the conversation monopolized by the older men.

Faulkner suppressed a smile and shook his head. 'I do not have any preference. I would, however, see this country Godly and quietly governed.'

'Amen to that,' said Gooding.

'My anxiety arises from the uncertainty that would follow the death of Oliver Cromwell.'

'Do you intend to kill him?' asked Henry with such asperity that they all turned to stare at him so that he too flushed.

'Henry!' exclaimed his mother at the impropriety of the remark.

My, my, thought Faulkner sardonically, we are fast becoming a table full of beetroots.

'Are you suggesting that I might?' Faulkner asked, his mouth in a lop-sided smile.

'I am not certain, sir,' Henry replied coldly, recovering himself.

Faulkner smiled at the boy. 'Do you know, Henry, I was not certain about *my* father. Indeed I have no recollection of him at all, for he was lost at sea when I was small. But I think you may rest assured that it is not my intention to end my days on the gallows, or enjoy the evisceration that precedes it.'

'Oh, Father!' Hannah protested disgustedly at the reference to disembowelling.

'I know, my dear,' Faulkner said, still smiling, 'but Henry needs to consider the import of his remarks. One would have expected something a little less tactless on our first night together again.'

With a raw scraping of his chair on the boards and the flash of his napkin as he threw it down on the table, Henry rose, glaring at his father. Now he was the perfect beetroot, Faulkner thought before commanding him to sit. Henry remained on his feet but did not leave the room and Judith quietly said, 'Be seated, Henry, please.'

The young man subsided into his chair.

'I think,' Judith said slowly in her measured tone, 'that that was the point of your father telling us of the Dutch captain who saluted him.'

Faulkner looked the length of the table and smiled broadly at his wife. 'Quite right, Goodwife Faulkner. And as for you, Henry, do not flare up so fast; a man must turn many things in his mind as your uncle here will testify, before he comes to a decision, whatever he does in life.'

Henry was staring into his lap. Faulkner would have to make amends there, for Henry resented his homecoming. But if the Lord willed the war at an end, there would be time enough for that.

'You were hard on Henry,' Judith said later as they prepared for bed.

'Yes, I know, but the lad must understand . . .'

'You cannot expect obedience immediately. They have their own memories.'

'Of course they have and I would not demand obedience, but I shall have respect.'

He heard her sigh and turned to her, drawing her face up so that she looked directly at him. 'I know the sense of the reprehensible he has towards me and I understand if he hates me, but I shall not have a lack of respect between us. Did I not ask him his opinion first, before I consulted you or Nathan? Whatever he may think of me as a father and a husband, I have some small claim on his respect for it was not entirely without my help that he has been able to grow to manhood in some comfort.'

Judith sighed again. 'Very well. In justice I could not claim that you left us paupers and I always knew that your heart lay elsewhere.'

'Did you? How so when you had lived so constrained a life when we met?'

'Something told me that you had encountered a passion before me. I did not know she would reappear.'

'And yet you . . .'

'I loved you,' she said simply. 'I could not help that any more than I now know you could help yourself with . . . with her.'

'She has a name.'

'I know she has a name and that she lives still.'

'Then you know more than me, for I am uncertain of her whereabouts.'

'And what if she should reappear and make some claim upon you? I could not tolerate the humiliation again for we no longer live in so topsy-turvy a world.'

'I should not see her starve, Judith, that I must tell you in all honesty, but I would not desert you for her, nor subject my children to any further distress.'

'And what of me, Kit?'

'You are my wife. Let us lay the matter there and lie our bodies together as the Lord wills it.'

'You speak less like a Malignant, I must admit,' she responded